I0679346

A Puhaka Books Selection

puhakabooks.com

It Started in Manila

W.B. Martin

Also by W. B. Martin

The Jack Wesley Series
> Trouble Leaves Too Slow
> Shoving Back the Shadows
> Only Pretty Lies
> Forever Now
> Chasing the Black Bird
> Just Empty Every Pocket
> Shaking Off Futility
> Pleasure Smiles
> Be Prepared to Bleed
> Too Stupid To Survive

Other W. B. Martin Novels
> German Golfers Who Changed the World
> Sweetness in the Dark
> Endangered Species
> Task Force Bismarck

Young Adult Novels
> Cubo Zoan
> Vincent van Gogh Likes Cats

Memoir
> Urbiztondo
> NPA - No Permanent Address

To Dominador and Lolita

Notice

This is a work of memory as the author recalls events. Any inaccuracies as to the true events are strictly an oversight due to time and recollection and is not intended to portray events in any but to the author's intent.

Printed by permission of
Puhaka Publishing

Printed in the United States of America

Cover Layout by Morwenna Rakestraw

Version 2.0

Print ISBN 978-1-940554-40-2

First Edition April 22, 2020

An Alternative History Novel

Historical Figures

Jose Rizal

National hero of the Philippines for his writings on independence. Eye doctor trained in Spain and Germany attended the Paris World's Fair. Exiled by Spain where he ran a hospital and school. Executed by Spain.

Andres Bonifacio

Founder of the Katipunan movement seeking independence for the Philippines. Inspired by Dr. Rizal's writings.

Paul von Hetrzoldt

German diplomat

Prince Henry

Younger brother of Kaiser Wilhelm II of Germany. Commander of the German East Asia Squadron at time of the Boxer Rebellion.

Otto von Diederichs

German Admiral commanding the East Asia Squadron at the time of the Spanish-American War. Had ships that were an equal match to the American squadron.

George Hoar

U.S. Senator form Massachusetts and leading anti-imperialists in debate over America gaining colonies in the world.

Rockwood Hoar

Son of George Hoar and U.S. Congressman from Massachusetts. Married to Christine Rice when he died.

Fredrick Gillett

Member of the U.S. House of Representatives for 32 years from Massachusetts. Speaker of the House during Washington Naval Conference. Married the widow of Rockwood Hoar.

Admiral George Dewey

Winner of the Battle of Manila Bay. U.S. Commodore of the U.S. Asiatic Squadron at the time.

Sir Edward Malet, 4th Baronet

British diplomat.

Queen Regent of Spain

Maria Christina of Austria married King Alfonso XII. Became Queen Regent when Alfonso died until her son become an adult.

Kaiser Wilhelm II

Last German Emperor and King of Prussia. Moved Imperial Germany into aggressive action in the world.

Gilbert Grosvenor

Editor of National Geographic magazine until 1954. Attended Worcester Academy in Massachusetts.

'Uncle Dan' Beard

Noted illustrator for Mark Twain and supporter of the Anti-Imperialist League's efforts.

Charles Even Hughes

Secretary of State in the Harding Administration. Main impetus for the Washington Naval Conference in 1922.

Calvin Coolidge

Governor of Massachusetts, Vice President of the United States. Became President upon the death of Warren G. Harding. Well known for his thrift and silence

Fictional Characters

Alexander Dull

Youngest Dull brother, famous photographer, related to George Hoar through mother's sister. Married to Donita Calvero of the Philippines, friend to Dr. Jose Rizal, professor of photo-journalism at the University of Hawaii

Cornelius Dull

Second Dull brother, graduate of Annapolis and U.S. Navy officer. Fought with Dewey at Manila Bay

Maximilian Dull

Oldest Dull brother, graduated Harvard University Law, Boston lawyer, chief of Staff to Calvin Coolidge as governor and vice president.

Zachariah Dull

Third oldest Dull brother, medical doctor

Captain Wilhelm von Mueller

German captain of light cruiser assigned to the German East Asia Squadron during the Spanish American war.

Donita Calvero

Nurse for Dr. Jose Rizal at his hospital on Mindanao, married Alexander Dull, had eight children

Felipe Calvero

Father to Donita, gun runner for Germans during American-Philippines War, lives on family compound in Lapu-Lapu, Mactan Island in Cebu Province

Max Dull

U.S. Navy officer, fourth son of Alex and Donita.

Chapter 1

Bolinao, Luzon Island, Philippines
Saturday, April 30, 1898

The South China Sea lay easy on a moonlight night. As a light ocean swell gently washed into the shore cliffs nearby, the white foam of the waves shown in the moonlight. Off to the south the golden beaches of Patar Beach sat illuminated in the night time light.

A lone fisherman bobbed gently in his dug-out craft, a homemade rope attached to a rock as an anchor holding him in place. With bamboo outrigger on each side he had the stability to stand and patiently wait for his catch. A thin bamboo pole attached to one of the cross members held an oil lamp high above his head.

Another bamboo pole with a metal hoop sat hooked below the lantern, the hoop end laying easy in the water. The fisherman stood motionless staring at the water beneath him as fish gathered in the artificial light. When a sufficient number had grouped under him, he swung the net stretched over the metal hoop, scooping up his catch.

Pulling the fishing net into his dugout, he grabbed the bottom of the net and tipped out its contents into a homemade basket in the bottom of his boat. He then replaced the bamboo pole onto its attachment and waited for more fish to gather.

Facing the nearby cliffs, he looked up at the stony escarpment and the trees arrayed along the top.

Large akasya trees lined the shore here with a high broad canopy that provided shade in the day time. But tonight the fisherman could smell the fragrance of its white flowers drifting down onto the sea.

His dugout canoe had been made by hand from a downed akasya tree. Using a bolo knife he chopped down and hollowed out the wood. Besides his dugout canoe, building materials for other needs had been provided. Along with the ubiquitous bamboo, the earth provided for his family almost everything they needed.

Sprinkling rice chaff on the water as chum, fish swam in quickly to nibble on the enticing treat. The fisherman swept his net and added another catch to his growing load. Although mostly small fish, he knew his wife would boil them and make a fish soup to be poured over rice. Meat was a luxury in this part of Luzon Island as animals needed feed. Rice had to be brought in from the paddies to the north and although a dirt cart track had been cut through the jungle from Bolinao proper, there was still no bridge over the Balingasay River. And the dirt track only run up to Cape Bolinao. To reach Patar Beach, a single dirt trail ran up and over the cape.

The Patar settlement was isolated except by the sea. Carabao loaded with rice sacks would make the trek over the cape. Otherwise, only the most important things were transported in or out of the village. Life was as simple here as life could be in the Philippines. Fish and rice were eaten everyday along with whatever wild fruits and vegetables grew in the jungle around them.

The fisherman had five mouths to feed each day besides he and his wife. He worked each night tending his area. He slept in the afternoon during the hottest part of the day after working on his household projects in the morning. And with his wife pregnant, he had been gathering bamboo to start construction on an addition to his house.

As he looked toward the beach where he would land his canoe, unload his catch and pull his boat out of the water, he could make out two other boats belonging to his neighbors high on the beach. Some preferred fishing in the daytime and only two other men ventured out at night like he did.

Staring at the glow of beach sand in the moonlight he felt something. He looked up at the cliff in front of him for a bird or maybe a bat flying by. The vibration he felt grew in intensity as he looked around as to what could be producing such a feeling.

He turned to look out on the open ocean, forgetting his job. Ignoring the gathered fish beneath him he tried to see out at sea, something could make this low pitched vibration. He saw nothing.

Realizing the overhead lantern was affecting his eyes, he lowered the lantern, turned the wick down, and extinguished the light. Now with just moonlight filtering through the tropical cloud cover, he strained his eyes attempting to see out to sea. As the vibration grew, a mechanical sound rose to meet him.

His eyes adjusted to the darkness and he saw more clearly as a shape loomed up to the north. While hard to tell, the object appeared to be about two miles off Cape Bolinao. As the noise increased in intensity more detail emerged of a ship bearing south toward Manila.

Ships routinely passed by his fishing spot as Cape Bolinao sat on the western edge of Luzon Island and any ship heading between Hong Kong or Japan and Manila would naturally pass this spot. Merchant ships of many nations made stops in Manila and the fisherman knew the capital city's reputation as the Pearl of the Orient. He had never been to the big city but knew people who had gone there.

But as he stared into the dark, the ship passing by out to sea was not shaped like the merchant ships he had seen over the years. This ship had two masts with two funnels placed between them. Freighters typically had one funnel. And this ship, as it grew abeam of the man, showed something merchant ships lacked.

Forward of the ship as well as aft the fisherman could just make out a box like protrusion sticking out of the deck. The man stared hard as the ship passed him and could make out a long pipe of some kind protruding from the box. The stars on the horizon disappeared and reappeared as the ship's outline was highlighted.

A similar box and pipe appeared on on the aft deck, which could only mean this was a warship passing by. As the man's eye's strained at the ship continuing south, another ship soon loomed out of the murk, engines throbbing. This ship appeared different with no distinguishing deck protrusions. The man stared as it passed, then it was followed by another, similar in shape to the second ship.

A fourth ship came along and this one was different. The part of the ship between the two masts was higher then the bow and stern but no protrusions showed like the first ship. Soon two more ships of smaller size came past. These ships had three masts but only one funnel.

Seeing six warships heading south made the man think what that meant. He had no idea which country the ships belonged to nor why they were passing him. As he pondered things that were strange to him, three more ships passed in line. He recognized that these had an outline familiar to him of merchant ships, although one was much smaller then the other two.

He stood in his boat debating what he should do. He wanted to paddle back to the beach to tell someone what he had seen. He had adequate fish for the day and started to pull on the homemade rope attached to his anchor. The steady rumble of coal fired boilers faded as the ships disappeared into the nighttime darkness. He grabbed the rock that served as his anchor and placed it in the bottom of his dugout. Moving to the stern of his boat, he picked up his hand carved paddle and took a stroke towards the beach.

Halfway to his landing spot he felt it again. He stopped, stood and looked out to sea. The vibration grew and then the noise caught up to him. Another ship loomed out of the dark and was outlined by the stars on the horizon. Having just seen six obvious warships, the first thing the man noticed was the chisel like bow. Merchant ships had bows that swept back where as this one swept forward as if to come to a point under water for ramming another ship.

There was not much else to see except the two masts and single funnel, its size smaller then first three other ships, but rather about the size of the second two. The man wondered why this ship was so far behind the others. If it had been part of the other ships it should should have been closer. But the man knew it just added to the mystery tonight. He pulled on his paddle to get home. He had exciting news for his village but no answers what it all meant.

* * *

"Lookouts, report," the order barked.

"We have the Americans in sight sir," came back the reply from the lookout on the forward mast.

"Very good," the first officer yelled. He turned to the captain and added, "Still on station sir."

Captain Wilhelm von Mueller said nothing. As captain of his majesty's unprotected cruiser *SMS Prinzess Sophia* he knew his crew. He had trained them since the ship's commissioning in 1883 and knew they were the best. But it did make him slightly nervous trailing along behind the American Asiatic Squadron as it appeared to be on its way to war with Spain.

His mission was to shadow the squadron and observe if and when the Americans went into action against the Spanish Empire. All the events that had been reported led up to this. The sinking of the American battleship *USS Maine* in Havana's harbor had been relayed to the German East Asia Squadron admiral with instructions to report any action taken by belligerents in the Pacific.

Captain von Mueller shifted his stance along the leeward side of the bridge. His binoculars hung around his neck as he knew in this darkness they would be useless. The lookout had been given a high powered spotting scope to make out the outline of the trailing Americna ship they were following.

His second in command walked across the open bridge and von Mueller turned as he approached.

"Are we sure the Americans are ready to go to war against Spain, sir?"

"Our sources in Hong Kong report that the American officers had dinner with their British counterparts three days ago. The British toasted the Yanks in salute of their pending death. Their commodore seems to be a hard charger so I'm certain he is about to go to battle."

"But can these Americans pull it off sir?"

"Doubtful lieutenant. Our reports list both sides having six warships, but we know the American ships are more capable," the captain said. "But the American have to get into Manila Bay to engage the Spaniards. If the Spanish shore batteries are on guard, that is a tall task. We've been in Manila and surveyed the coastal batteries. If they take the main channel, Boca Grande channel will place then between Corregidor Island and

El Fraile island. Both have strong guns ranged to ward off intruders.."

"And possibly mines sir," the second in command added.

"The Spaniards would be incompetent if they didn't have a mine field laid out."

"So we may get to witness the Americans fleeting grab at world power come crashing down," the lieutenant said.

"We shall see," von Mueller said and turned away, ending any more conversation. He held the safety of his ship and with the entire American fleet ahead of him, he had to be ready if they did anything to endanger his ship.

The SMS *Prinzess Sophia* had been named after the Kaiser's sister and it would not be good if he personally risked its safety. The Kaiser took great pride in his navy and as an avid yachtsman, the head of the German Empire would often sail his yacht among he fleet.

The eight four inch guns his ship carried were no match for the combined broadside of the six warships ahead of him. If the Americans took exception to his tailing the squadron, they could turn on him and blast him out of the water. Not that that was highly likely.

The east Asian waters were rich in warships as the competing nations of Europe all maneuvered for colonies and favors. Where they couldn't take over a country, each worked for trade concessions and dedicated trading ports.

The British were ahead of the game with Hong Kong and Singapore as naval bases for their ships. France was busy in Indochina while Spain had been in the Philippines since Ferdinand Magellan first claimed his initial islands in 1512. Over the years all the islands of the archipelago were brought under Spanish control.

Germany was a late comer to the Asian land grab and as it continued to gain colonies Germany still had to rely on the British for coal. As the Americans were discovering, modern ships needed coaling stations. That America had annexed the Hawaiian Islands four years earlier set the Americans on a path into the Pacific.

Japan had joined the Europeans in the hunt for the colonies sparking a war with with China. The Japanese had defeated the Chinese three years ago and had grabbed Taiwan and the Chinese Liaodong Peninsular. This had been added to their control of the Korean peninsular.

Germany had just this year fought the Chinese over the Shandong Peninsular and von Mueller knew that a treaty had just been signed giving Germany a base of operations on China's coast. Over the next several years a naval base would be constructed to serve the German East Asian squadron.

So in the scramble for bases and colonies, each of the world's naval powers was interested in each others action. From his visit to the Yokohama Naval Base on a good will visit, von Mueller had had dinner with his Japanese counterparts. Even through the translator he heard the grumble of Japan missing out on annexing the Hawaiian Islands. That the American's had organized a coup to overthrow the native queen didn't set well with the Japanese.

And now if the Americans were successful and defeated the Spaniards, the Yankees would be right in the middle of the western Pacific, a very hotly contested area. With the turn to the century right around the corner the 20th Century stood to be a highly contentious time in east Asia.

"Still on station," the cry from the topmast came, indicating they were still in sight of the trailing American ship.

"Very good," the second in command yelled in response.

Von Mueller took his mind back to the business at hand and stopped dwelling on world events. He might be mixed up in changing those world events, but his immediate task was critical if Germany would gain from it. And that's where he focused. Moving the fatherland up closer to where the British sat. The moon disappeared behind a bank of clouds arriving from Indochina as the world got darker.

* * *

"Still there captain," the American officer said.

"Very good," the ship's captain said.

The steamer *Zafiro* carried supplies for the American squadron and took up the final line of battle. Its lookouts had spotted a ship in the dark following them and had continued the watch aft. With its forward lookouts maintaining distance to the collier *Nanshan* in front of them, the captain was anxious as to who or what was tracking them.

With their war time operations underway, he couldn't pass his information forward with his signal light. All ships were on a strict black-out regime so as to not warn the Spaniards of their approach. The ships had all been painted dark gray from their peacetime white configuration to add to the disguise.

The captain of the small supply ship would trust that the combined strength of the warships ahead of him would keep any potential threat at bay. But if it was a Spanish ship, who knew what might happen. War had been declared but the captain didn't have any idea if that message had made it this far out in the Spanish Empire. He would trust in the squadron's strength and hope he could weather things. He didn't have much of any other option. But the captain knew by the course they were steering that they had another day in reaching Manila. A day where the mystery ship couldn't hide in the dark. And a day where he could signal the information up to the flagship.

Chapter 2

On Board the *USS Boston*
April 30, 1898

Fourth in line of battle, the *USS Boston* steamed behind the *USS Raleigh*. The *USS Concord* trailed the *Boston*. As a protected cruiser of 3,000 tons, the *Boston* carried two eight inch guns and six six inch guns. In charge of the starboard battery was Commander Cornelius Dull of Worcester, Massachusetts.

That he had been assigned to a ship named for the city 40 miles to the east of his home was special. But at age 36, he was overdue for a ship of his own. He hoped he would distinguish himself in the coming battle and come out alive. With the newly expanding U.S. Navy, there would be plenty of ships for capable young men.

And men with connections. Promotions always hinged on who you might be connected to. Just as Admiral Dewey, Commodore of the East Asian Squadron, and the man in charge today, had used connections to reach his posting. Scuttlebutt on the *Boston* was that senior men had been by-passed by Assistant Navy Secretary Theodore Roosevelt in order for Dewey to take command in Asia.

The Dull family certainly had their connections. Most importantly had been Cornelius' father, a Civil War hero. Cornelius didn't remember his father as he had been born during the war in 1862. In fact, his brother Alexander Dull was born after their father had been killed fighting with the Army of the Potomac early in the battle of Cold Harbor.

Paul Dull had joined the 15th Massachusetts Regiment made up of Worcester County men. Being a college graduate, he had been made a lieutenant. Surviving a long list of battles he had been promoted to colonel by the time of his death. And surviving wasn't easy as the 15th Massachusetts sustained the tenth highest number of men killed and wounded out of all Union regiments.

The II Corps under General Winfield Scott Hancock held the right flank of the Union line. When the Confederate Corps of A.P. Hill attempted to turn the flank, it was the 15th Massachusetts along with the entire II Corps that fought the move to a bloody standstill. In doing so, Colonel Paul Dull along with sixty seven of his men were casualties.

Dull had survived the Battles of Antietam and Gettysburg to be killed at Cold Harbor. His surviving the war until near the end meant that Cornelius and his two brother's had been born.

Colonel Dull was awarded the Medal of Honor posthumously for his gallantry added to his father's status. If having a war hero father wasn't sufficient, then having an uncle who was a U.S. Senator would help. George Hoar had been elected in 1877 and was the leading critic of America's move to imperialism.

But thoughts of advancement were far from the commander's mind. Cornelius Dull was on a ship headed into harm's way. Not a good place to be if one's thoughts were of a long life. That the British had made those remarks about their odds on beating the Spanish fleet added to his worries. He would focus on making sure his command would be ready and that was the task he bent to.

"Seaman, let's get this area squared away," Cornelius directed toward of his crew.

"Yes sir."

With four guns to command, his would be the broadside when the starboard side came into range. The *U.S.S. Boston* had its two large caliber guns on the forward deck and swiveled in a turret. As with the old style fighting ships the remaining guns were along the side of the ship, protruding from the superstructure. If the enemy was on the port side, his guns would be useless. The two large guns could swivel from side to side but were useless for any ships behind them.

It was the Captain's job as well as Commodore Dewey to plan their attack so the heaviest broadside could be used. It meant maneuvering the squadron so the maximum advantage could be found. But Corny, as he was called by his fellow officers, was concerned as the Boston was the slowest ship in the squadron. With a maximum speed of 13 knots, it lacked the speed of the three other cruisers. They could maneuver at twenty knots which the Boston would crippled if the squadron stayed together.

Around noon the *Boston* picked up speed slightly and Cornelius got word that the ship had been detached to scout Subic Bay. The Spanish had a naval base in Subic Bay and its waters were confining for a sea engagement. Along with the gunboat *Concord*, the *Boston* reached Subic Bay and found no Spanish ships. Cornelius watched out the gun ports as his ship reversed direction back to the main squadron. As the day droned on, the coal fired engines rumbled ahead as nighttime descended.

The crew took turns standing watch and when Corny came back on duty, he looked out one of the open gun ports and saw nothing but open water. He walked over to the port battery and greeted his fellow officer in charge of the guns. He looked out toward land and saw the dark shape of Luzon Island sliding by. All was darkness with the outline visible in the moonlight. As the clouds drifted the moonlight intensified and Cornelius could make out a few details on shore.

His counterpart in command was a younger man and the two looked over the port side gun crew. Orders for the crew to quarters came at nine-thirty-five p.m. and the men were lounging by their guns trying to relax. Manila Bay lay just ahead and an unknown welcome awaited.

"Are you ready?" Corny said to his fellow gun commander.

"Yes, and you? We are bringing up the rear now since our run to Subic Bay. Everyone else will have it wrapped up before our guns get into range."

"Oh, I think they'll be enough targets for everybody today," Corny said.

The two men smiled weakly as they both looked out at a large island looming up in the darkness

"Corregidor."

"Time for me to join my men. Good luck," Corny said.

"And you too."

Cornelius crossed over to the starboard gun battery and noticed his men all staring at his return. He picked up his handheld megaphone that was designed to project his voice over the battle noise.

"All right men, Corregidor Island is off our port side. We will be following the flagship into Manila bay. Look sharp now."

His men turned to their guns to wait. Soon El Fraile loomed up out of the night on their side of the ship. El Fraile was a much smaller island then Corregidor but held a Spanish gun emplacement.

Word came over from the port side battery that a warning rocket had flown off Corregidor, but nothing was happening. A faint bugle sound carried across the water into the throbbing ship. A passing rain squall cooled the ship but increased the humidity. It moved on, clearing the sky as the moon came back out. Sweat ran down the men's backs waiting for the order to fire.

As Cornelius stood by the speaker tube to the bridge awaiting orders, the night outside grew bright. One of Cornelius' men stuck his head out the port and reported. "Those fools on the *McCulloch* just flew sparks out its stack."

Cornelius knew that the squadron carried soft coal that would emit a shower of sparks. The Spanish finally reacted seeing the American ships clearly in the light provided by the mistake. A bugle sounded and a flash announced a single artillery piece firing. Soon two more shots were let loose from the Spanish toward the squadron.

"Starboard battery, open fire as you bear. Range 800 yards," the bridge ordered through the speaker tube.

"All right men, as you bear. Range 800 yards. Open fire," the Cornelius yelled.

The range finder topside on the *Boston* would be feeding the guns current information on the distance to targets. Each gun captain would set its elevation according to the range given. Firing then was up to each captain as he observed each target in his gun sight, not much advanced from the old sailing ship broadsides of the early part of the century.

But with breech loading guns versus muzzle loaders the frequency of firing was increased. With modern powder over black powder each shot went further with more accuracy. The ship rocked as each gun fired a salvo at the rocky island. As the men worked to reload and fire again the order came to cease fire. The Spanish had stopped firing and the ship's ammunition was limited. The real action lay just ahead.

Expecting mine explosions at any time, Corny held his breath as the squadron crept into Manila Bay. He estimated they were running at about eight knots, slow but necessary to keep all nine ships together. Manila itself lay thirty miles across the bay from the entrance and the gun crew settled down from their first engagement.

The Spanish Fleet had obviously been warned of their arrival and they could be in a full fleet action at any time. Nerves were on edge as the waiting grew longer. Soon Manila itself rose up on the port side with no Spanish ships anchored.

Cornelius felt the *Boston* shift slightly in its course as the squadron turned south toward the Cavite Naval Base. He knew the port side would be the first to engage the enemy ships if they were anchored at Cavite. The day break grew and more of Manila Bay became visible. Drums beating to quarters ran through the ship and a crew stuck his head out the port to announce he could see the Spanish ships ahead.

Just as he pulled his head back in gun fire erupted in the distance but no orders came down from the bridge. Not being able to see what was transpiring tore at Cornelius, but he waited with his men. Soon they heard cheering just as the voice pipe from the bridge announced, "Signal from the Commodore. Remember the Maine."

Cornelius repeated the message though his megaphone and his men joined the thousand cheers of the squadron. He checked his watch, five forty-two. Just as he closed the pocket gold watch the Olympia's guns let loose.

"Port side. Range 5,500 yards. Fire as you bear." the speaker tube announced.

"Steady men. Port side gets first licks," he yelled at his men.

There was a loud grumbling at the other side of the ship getting to fire first. But Corny knew it would be their turn soon enough.

The ship reverberated with guns firing. A second set of explosions announced that the port side gun crews got two salvos off before they moved out of range. Everyone felt the large cruiser pitch to one side as the squadron maneuvered to return to the Spanish.

"Look sir." One of the crew yelled.

Cornelius stepped over to the open gun port and looked out. The *USS Olympia* was passing on their starboard side. Right behind followed the *Baltimore, Petrel, Raleigh* and *Concord*. As soon as the *Boston* made the complete tack, orders came down.

"Starboard battrey. Range 4,000 yards. Fire as you bear."

The commander lifted his megaphone and yelled the range to his gun captains. "Fire as you bear. And look lively on those reloads men."

A cheer went up with the crew as guns were adjusted and captains took aim. The ship erupted in smoke and din as the broadside let loose. Cornelius watched each gun crew work at their reload and realign the aim for a second salvo. As the ship passed out of range the crews reloaded and awaited further action.

The voice pipe spoke as the *Boston* swung though another 180 degree turn. "Continue to concentrate fire on the *Reina Cristina*."

Each gun commander in the squadron had been instructed prior to the battle to concentrate on the

Spanish flagship. Cornelius yelled out instructions to his crews and added. "Men, let's see if we can get three broadsides in on tis pass. So look lively."

"Aye aye sir," a chorus of yells came back at their commander. The men were excited that they had survived so far and wanted to put the enemy out of action as soon as they could. Soon the port guns were letting loose and again after two salvos the ship was out of range and tacking to the opposite side.

"Range 3,000 yards. Fire as you bear." Cornelius yelled out the instructions from the bridge. His guns fired and his crews worked fast and another broadside let loose. A third followed as the ships drew away from the Spanish. It was now just past noon as Dewey took the squadron out into Manila Bay.

Realizing the squadron was disengaging, Cornelius walked among his crew congratulating them on their good work. Soon word came down that a white flag had gone up on Cavite and that the Spanish fleet, all twelve ships, were destroyed and beached in the shallow water. One of the gun captains, upon hearing the news led the men in a rousing cheer for their victory.

Later in the day Cornelius passed on that only one man had died in the battle, from heat stroke, with six slightly wounded. Truly a stunning victory for America's first fleet action in its history. While the U.S. Navy had won individual ship actions in the Revolutionary War, the War of 1812 and the Civil War, it had never beat an enemy fleet on the sea before.

Cornelius sat relaxing and pondered the meaning of what had just taken place. He had graduated from Annapolis and had read and discussed Alfred Mahan's *The Influence of Sea Power upon History*. The book had shaped all the great powers of the world and had driven the search for colonies to support the fleets each was building.

Spain had just been handed a defeat that might lead her to loose her empire. While much would be decided in the next few months, Cornelius knew enough to conclude that America was stepping out into the world while Spain was leaving. Almost four hundred years in the Philippines was coming to an end, and he had played a part in it.

Soon the Americans would invade Cuba and in another fleet action, destroy the remaining Spanish ships. The Spanish Empire ended as an American one gave birth. A peace conference to end the war and determine the spoils would finalize everything.

* * *

Just off the mouth to Manila Bay a German cruiser slowly turned to starboard and swung around for another pass near Corregidor Island. It had been circling just off the mouth to Manila Bay observing the events taking place inside the bay. Captain von Mueller had even climbed the mast with his telescope for a better view. He would be racing back to Hong Kong to report the results of the fleet action and he wanted to be able to report first hand. As he observed the American squadron break off and steam into the middle of the bay, he could see the smoldering results of the battle. Seeing the white flag raised over Cavite he knew the Americans had won a great victory. He scampered down to the bridge and gave orders to make full steam, setting a course back to Hong Kong and a wireless station. He would write his report and then convert it into the Imperial Naval Code for dispatching. Events were about to transpire that would further shock the world.

Chapter 2

Manila, Philippines
April, 1882

Sixteen years prior to Dewey's Battle of Manila Bay and the eventual collapse of Spain in Asia, a young twenty-one year old man walked slowly along the Manila waterfront. A slightly older man walked beside him. Unknown to cither, the younger man held the end of the Spanish hold over his native Philippines in his head. Not realizing it at the time but needing to leave the islands, the older brother consoled his younger brother that leaving home was the best option for him.

Ahead of them sat a ocean liner at the main Manila pier. Sailing in three hours for Barcelona, Spain, the ship would make port calls for coal in Singapore, Colombo, Ceylon, and Port Said, Egypt on its. The two brothers were quiet as they strolled the waterfront, not wanting to part. That Jose Rizal was leaving the Philippines was not known to his parents. It had been his brothers idea to go to Europe to further the younger brother's education.

A law student at the University of Santo Tomas, Jose had been recognized as an exceptional student. Switching to the university's medical school, Jose studied ophthalmology.

"Are you really sure about this brother?" Jose said.

"It is best," his brother Paciano said. "You are too talented for the schools here. You need to study with the best. And I can afford to support you in that effort."

"But our parents. They should know."

"I'll tell them after you leave. It will be easier this way."

The younger brother made no argument as they reached the dockside and the gathering crowd of travelers. People were saying their goodbyes as the two brothers embraced. Tears flowed as Jose knew it would be a long time until he returned to his homeland. The Philippines meant everything to him and already in his writings he expressed his vision of a free Philippines. Free from Spanish rule.

Which was part of the reason Paciano wanted his brother out of the country. Speaking of a free Philippines was treason against the Spanish rulers in the islands, a serious offense leading to imprisonment. Sending Jose to Europe would get him to relative safety.

The Filipino reached Spain and soon completed his studies in Madrid earning his medial degree. He traveled to Paris for medical lectures before landing in Heidelberg, Germany where he resumed his study of the human eye. But Jose continued his search for Philippine freedom with a lecture in Berlin on the Tagolog language while continuing his writing.

Conversant in twenty-two languages, Rizal completed his specialization in ophthalmology in Heidelberg while studying the German language.

Along with his writings Rizal painted and sculptured. A polymath, Rizal exceled in both the sciences and the arts.

But it was his writings on the Spanish colonization of the Philippines that brought him the most attention. Peaceful reformers as well as armed revolutionaries took his writings as their own in the struggle for changes in the Philippines. Truly a renaissance man, Rizal had many interests as he cared for his eye patients but freedom for the Philippines was his first interest.

* * *

"Will the Graduating Class of 1887 please rise," the President of Holy Cross College said.

Forty two students rose as one as the front row turned to their right. The graduate on the far right led the first row around to the stairs leading onto the stage where the president stood next to the school chancellor. A table holding the assorted degrees was carried forward to the lectern. The president nodded to the first student and he climbed the four steps and walked across the stage as his name was read out to the crowd. His degree major was called as the young man took his diploma and accepted the president's handshake.

The first twelve graduates ran through receiving their degrees and as the last student reached the bottom of the stairs, the second row turned and moved in behind. One student in particular stepped in behind the last row. As he stepped onto the first steep his name was called.

"Alexander Dull. Philosophy Degree."

Alexander walked briskly across the stage, shook hands with his right as his degree was placed in his left. He smiled as he walked off the stage, turning to look up to where his mother was sitting in the audience. He refocused as the descended back to the auditorium floor and walked back to his seat. As the rest of the class was called, he stared at his diploma and then turned to the classmate next to him. They smiled at each other at their accomplishment.

The diploma ceremony finished, the Catholic college priest stood up and gave the closing benediction. Alexander bowed his head along with his class. As the priest sat down, the president stood and thanked everyone for attending, officially ending graduation. As one, Alexander's class took off their mitre boards and threw them into the air. The audience all stood and clapped its approval at their college graduates.

Walking to the reception in the college's Great Hall, Alexander spotted one of his brothers. The brother was hard to miss in his U.S. Navy uniform. Standing besides his brother Cornelius was his two other brothers, Maximilian and Zachariah. His mother stood proudly between them. Alex, as he liked to be called, gritted his teeth. He knew what was coming before he even reached his family.

"Congratulations," all four of them said in unison. There was the customary handshakes and backslapping and of course a long hug from his mother. Not lost in the moment was the missing father, dead before Alex was even born, and unknown to even his older brothers.

"I'm so proud of you, son," his mother said, tears forming. Alex fought for control. "Your father would be so proud of you. Of all of you," she added looking at her four boys. "Cornelius, a graduate of Annapolis three years before and already a lieutenant."

"Junior grade mother," Corny added.

"Zachariah a medical doctor," his mother added, ignoring her son's qualifier.

"Mom, I just graduated. I still have to pass my boards," Zach said.

"And my oldest, Maximilian. Harvard Law and already working for Worcester's top firm.

Max, as he preferred, offered no qualifiers to his mother's praise.

"And now my baby. All grown up," the mother said. She lowered her eyes and pulled a lace handkerchief out of her purse to dab her eyes.

It was the oldest, Max, that broke the somber mood. "So, what now little brother. You taking that philosophy degree and doing what?"

Alexander bristled at his brother. This had been an ongoing dig every time he saw his brothers. Each of the three had sought out a high powered career and they threw it in the younger brothers face each time. That he had chosen a liberal arts education with emphasis on languages had been his choice, not theirs. He was fluent in French and German. The German

41

coming form his mother speaking it at home due to their German heritage. French from his Holy Cross studies. That he knew some Japanese as well made him content in his mind. That he loved photography and wanted to pursue that course certainly confused his brothers.

Photography was undergoing a tremendous transformation in the late 1800's as smaller, more portable cameras were being developed. The large contraptions that took a horse and wagon to move around were fading. Along with the large glass plates required for development. Newer technologies were coming out and Alexander was excited about the possibilities.

"I've been accepted to the Sorbonne. I start in the Fall," Alex said.

He witnessed three sets of eyeballs all roll in unison as the brothers each looked at the other. His studying photography at the Sorbonne had been raised the year before when he had decided what he wanted to do. Their reaction then matched theirs now.

It was his naval officer brother that spoke next. "And you can earn a living at his picture taking?"

"Yes I can. Photography will change the world. I've read that a man named George Eastman is working on a handheld camera with film that is on a roll inside. When cameras are small and compact, images will be captured that have been impossible with the large tripod, cameras and glass plates."

"I think Alexander can be anything he wants to be,' his mother said.."He has his father in him like all you boys. Champions all."

That ended any criticism of the younger brother. Their mother had spoken and the three sons would acquiesce to their mother's wishes. She controlled the finances that the younger brother would need to study abroad. Wealth from her family's industrial empire and the money it brought them. It had made Worcester one of the hot beds of the Industrial Revolution in the United States. Many comparable fortunes had been made after the Civil War as America switched from an agricultural country to the preeminent industrial powerhouse in the world.

"Well, there he is. Congratulations cousin. Well done," Rockwood Hoar announced in a booming voice as he walked up to the Dull family gathering. Rockwood was the son of George Hoar and cousin to the Dull brothers. They were related through their mothers, which were sisters.

"Oh, my favorite nephew. I'm so glad you attended today," the mother said.

"Wouldn't have missed it. My father sends his regrets. Busy in Washington you know," Rockwood said.

George Hoar, Rockwood's father, was a U.S. Senator from Massachusetts and one of the leaders in Congress. George had been a surrogate father in many ways to the four Dull brothers and they had spent many days growing up with Rockwood.

Rockwood turned to Maximilian and said, "Good to see you here Max. Our meeting this week was certainly exciting."

Rockwood Hoar had graduated from Harvard Law eight years prior to Max and worked for the other top Worcester law firm. Between the two firms, they represented the accumulated wealth of the industrial firms in central New England. Known as the "Heart of New England", Worcester sat on rail, canal and road networks spiderwebbing across the six state region.

Max acknowledged his cousins comment when Rockwood asked Alexander what his future plans were. The three bothers all protested at the question and Rockwood turned to his aunt for a answer.

"Alexander has chosen a different path then his brothers. He will studying at the Sorbonne in Paris."

"Well, don't let those foreign ways go to your head," Rockwood said. He chuckled at the implication. Paris' reputation as a libertine city of many pleasures was well know to everyone present. That reputation was decidedly the opposite of staid Yankee views of how life should be led. Worcester's attitude was hard work and few pleasures made the man. Paris had a bit different attitude.

"I'm sure he will behave himself," Alexander's mother said.

Rockwood turned slightly away from his aunt and gave the three bothers a knowing wink. He knew what a city like Paris could do to a young twenty two year old male. But he would keep an further comment to himself.

"So, let's get some drinks. There's some good looking food over there. I know I'm staring," Rockwood said.

* * *

Before Alexander could unpack his bags in Paris, he had family to visit in Germany. Both his maternal and fraternal families had emigrated from Germany. More specifically, Baden-Wuttemberg for his mother and Bavaria for his father's family. Both families had left Germany before Chancellor Bismarck had officially merged Prussia with the other German States to from modern Germany in 1871.

His steamship landed in Wilhelmshaven and Alex boarded a train for Heidelberg. Arriving at the station, he hired a carriage and handed the teamster his uncle's address. His first time away from America, Alex marveled at the city as the horse trotted through the streets of Heidelberg. They crossed the Neckar River and Alex noted the famous university off to his left. The carriage took a right and was soon at a large stone house. He paid the driver and grabbed his one suitcase. His aunt and uncle opened the door to greet him.

For the American the next two weeks were a whirlwind of relatives and visits. It was also an awakening in Alexander of his Germaness as his language skills grew exponentially. He realized the German that he had spoken in his home was basic German. Now immersed in German with no English being spoken, his vocabulary grew.

"Come on cousin. It is a beautiful Sunday in May. We Germans love to go outdoors on such a day. Which would you like to do today, tramping or football?" one cousin asked.

Alexander was realizing his German cousins were very active. The two weeks had been one outing after another; hiking here, cycling there, swimming, rowing and playing football. He knew it as soccer, not well known in America. He'd had enough hiking by the complaints in his calf muscles. Being a student with his studies, exercising at Holy Cross had been a hit and miss thing. And mostly miss as he finished his studies and prepared for his studies at the Sorbonne.

"I'll try football I guess," he finally said.

"Wonderful choice. Karl has a league he plays in. I'm sure they'd love a new player."

Suddenly Alexander regretted his choice. His cousin Karl playing in a league meant serious football. He was a new comer to the sport and didn't want to hurt the team through his inexperience.

"I don't know about playing on a league team," Alexander said.

"Nonsense, they'll love to have you."

They gathered their sports wear and were soon at the football field near the university. Introductions were made by Karl of his American cousin. The smiles on the other players faces belied what Alex was feeling. He knew enough of German attitudes that the other players were all looking at this moment as a competition against America. He would be shown superior German skills to the hapless American. He

46

knew he might be about to become an example of the superiority of German culture over American culture.

The game went about as Alex expected. Karl's team placed him as a half back, deemed not as critical as the defensive or offensive positions to the front and back of him. Alexander did his best running back and forth trying to kick the ball to a teammate but it was rather hopeless. And the elbows from the opposing players let him knew the German aggression factor was on full display.

After halftime Alexander made his case that maybe someone else should be inserted in his place. Karl and his teammates would have none of it. They were ahead by two goals so it appeared his play didn't hurt their chances of winning. Karl did confide that they had played this team the previous week and had won by six goals. Alex took that information as his cousin's encouragement to play through.

At about the seventy-fifth minute of the ninety minute game the opposing team got a break away. The goalie did an excellent high kick right toward Alexander's side of the field. Their striker met the ball as it hit the field, controlled it and then reared back with his right leg to boom a hit toward the streaking main striker in center field. Unfortunately, Alexander's face moved into the balls path and from a short six feet away took the full force of the ball to his right eye. He immediately collapsed onto the grass screaming, holding the right side of his face.

Karl, who had witnessed the hit, ran to his cousin. Both teams gathered around as Karl pried

Alexander's hands off his face. Making a quick examination of the damage, he announced they needed a doctor right away. Someone offered that there was an eye clinic near the university and that he would lead the two men there.

"But its Sunday," someone offered.

"That's right. We better go right to the hospital then.," Karl said.

Karl and the other man helped Alexander to his feet and supporting him on both sides, walked briskly toward the university hospital. Entering the front doors, they were met by a staffer that directed them to the proper area. Sitting down in an examination room, the three men waited. Soon the door opened and a short dark man walked in.

"I'm Doctor Rizal. What seems to be the problem. They said you needed an eye specialist." The man's German was fluent but his accent let the men knew he was not a native German speaker. By his stature and skin color, it made it doubly obvious.

Karl explained what had happened and Dr. Rizal sat on a chair and leaned into Alexander. He moved Alex's hand off his face and carefully pulled the swollen eye open. Alex grimaced in pain but held his composure. The doctor swing his reflective mirror off his head and directed the light into Alex's eye. He brought a hand held magnifying device up and looked closely into the injured eye.

"I don't see any detachment of the retina. There is some blood vessels broken so you are going to have an ugly eye for a few days. Do you have any dates planned with a pretty girl?"

Alexander laughed a bit and said no, there were no dates planned. But he did ask if this would affect his vision as he was heading off to university to study art and his eyes were critical. Out of his good eye he noticed the doctor perk up at that news. When Alex related that he would be at the Sorbonne studying photography the doctor became very interested.

"Your accent, you are not German, are you?" Dr. Rizal asked.

"No, I'm American of German heritage. I was raised speaking German at home This is my first time seeing my German relatives."

"Well, we will be extra cautious then with this eye. I'll have you wear an eye patch for five days. Come back and see me in my clinic after that and I'll make sure that the healing has happened properly." Dr. Rizal pulled a business card out of his breast pocket and handed it to Alex.

The next five days were torment for Alexander for the good natured ribbing he received from the relatives on the American pirate they had visiting. Friday arrived and Alex made his way by himself to the eye clinic. After a short wait Dr. Rizal walked in and sat down in front of his patent. He removed the eye patch and flipped his head mounted mirror down. He carefully examined the eye and pronounced it healing nicely. Flipping the mirror up onto his head he shoved his chair back and relaxed a bit.

"So you are from America. I've never actually met an American before. And an artist at that."

"I hope to be an artist someday, Dr. Rizal," Alex said.

"Jose please. And if I may call you Alexander, you are an artist already. If you are heading to the Sorbonne for graduate studies they certainly consider you an artist. Not just anyone gets to attend there."

"Alex please. So, may I ask you. You are not German. Where are you from?"

"The Philippine Islands," Jose said. "I've been studying and practicing here in Europe for, let me think. Ah yes, five years now. Time has a way of moving quickly."

At the mention of the Philippines Alex brought up his recollection of his college class in geography. About all he could remember was that the Philippines sat off the coast of China and was part of the Spanish Empire.

"So, you are Spanish then."

"Only for now. And certainly a second class citizen of Spain by the way my fellow countrymen are treated."

Alex felt the fire in the man when he spoke of his homeland. There was an anger there that he imagined existed in all colonized people. It was the age of imperialism and Alex was bright enough to realize that many peoples of the world felt subjugated by their European rulers. His country had been in the same position not that many yearn ago and had fought a revolution to gain their freedom.

"I have an idea," Jose said. "I myself do a little art work. Sculpture and painting but I've seen this photography and can see its artistic potential. Would you like to join me. I could show you my work."

The smile out of Alex indicated that would be splendid. While he certainly loved his German relatives, he needed a break, and with an artist made it even better. He agreed heartily.

"Perhaps tomorrow, if that wouldn't be too soon. And I have to admit I have an ulterior motive. I know many languages but English is one I wish to gain experience with. And if we can talk about what freedom means in America, I want to learn more about your American Revolution."

"If we can do a trade then. I studied languages in college and would like to learn more. What do they speak in the Philippines?"

Jose laughed at the question and Alex gave him a quizzical look. Jose raised his hands to apologize and that he wasn't laughing at Alex.

"I'm sorry, that isn't directed at you. It's just my country has over one hundred languages spoken on its various islands. No one knows for sure. I speak many of them but my main language is Tagalog. That is the language spoken by the people who live around Manila which is also the most numerous spoken. And I would be happy to teach you."

The two men stood and shook hands. The next two months they were together each time the could. Alex was impressed by the artistic abilities of the medial doctor and his desire to understand how a people could gain their freedom. Jose seemed intrigued by the American and his confident attitude toward all things. No arrogance like Germans could display, just knowledge that the world was there and anyone could accomplish what they set their mind to. They didn't know it at the time, it would be a friendship that would be short lived but it would change the world.

Chapter 4

Het Oude Loo Castle
Apeldoorn, Netherlands
July 1887

The world continued to change over the five years since Alexander Dull first reached Europe. In a rural part of the Netherlands a carriage ride from the train station took its passenger past the Het Loo Palace where the Dutch royal family lived. Het Oude Loo was the original castle on the vast grounds near the palace. Originally built in the 15th Century, the castle now served the interests of the ruling family in the Netherlands.

And this weekend special guests had been invited by the Dutch Foreign Minister to a gathering of import. Announced as a hunting weekend in the forest, the real purpose was a bit more intriguing. The ruling elite were always conspiring amongst themselves to assure that the royal families of Europe remained on top. The common people might benefit from laws and policies passed by the government but the elite always benefited.

Sir Edward Mahet, 4th Baronet, part of the ruling class of Great Britain sat stiff in his carriage. He had served his queen well first with the Ottoman Empire and then as Minister to Belgium. Currently he was ambassador to the German Empire and as such was critical to this meeting. Sir Edward looked over the immaculate grounds surrounding the Het Loo Palace before the carriage plunged into the forest surrounding the castle. Here were the pheasants they soon would be hunting tomorrow.

Crossing the drawbridge laying over the water moat, the horses hoofs clattered on the cobblestones in the courtyard. The sound reverberated off the walls as the carriage stopped in front of the grand entrance. Sir Edward was met by the castle staff which hustled his three suitcases off to his room deep in the halls of the castle.

Standing at the giant double doors of the Great Hall stood Paul von Hatzfeldt. Edward and Paul were old friends from their time serving their respective governments in Constantinople. Now Germany's ambassador to London, Paul walked down the steps to greet Sir Edward.

"So glad you could make it Sir Edward," Paul said.

"Good to see you Paul. Who else are you expecting? Your invitation made things seem very urgent."

As they shook hands, their attention was distracted by the hollow clump sound of hoofs on wood. They both turned as a second carriage entered the keep and pulled to a stop in front of the stairs.

"Count Merry, thank you for coming," Paul walked over to greet the Spanish ambassador to Germany. Merry y Colom, 1st Count of Benomar, was one more part of the ruling class of Europe.

The three men walked up the steps into the Great Hall as Paul guided them to bottles set out. He lifted and poured drinks as he already knew what each man's favorite beverage was. Holding high his glass to salute, he said nothing. The implied toast was to the ruling class of Europe, and to each of their sovereigns. Sovereigns that were all related to each other.

The men took seats in the Great Hall and chatted, nothing of import. Art work purchased. Maybe changes in their villas. Complaints about workmen. If it had been just Sir Edward and Paul present, mistresses would be discussed. But they didn't know the Spanish Count well enough to go into such things.

Soon dinner was called and they retired to a smaller more intimate dining room. More drinks along with cigars after dinner keep them entertained until it was time to retire, an early call for hunting on the agenda.

Breakfast and an early walk to a clearing in the forest yielded hunting stands where servants provided a tent and chairs. The three men would take up their shotguns and wait for the beaters to drive the birds to them from across the field.

When enough pheasants were shot, lunch in the tent was prepared and served. The men sat and ate heartily on fresh fish and local vegetables. Sir Edward knew that this was probably the time when Paul would raise the real issue of this gathering. The servants disappeared leaving the three alone.

"Gentlemen, I do have a reason that I've invited you here" Paul said. "I was hoping the Dutch ambassador would be here by now. You all know Philipp van der Hoeven. He informed me this week that something might come up to delay him."

Sir Edward had been wondering why the Germans were using a Dutch castle to hold a meeting. But such was the interworking of European politics that it didn't surprise him. He had worked with van der Hoeven before and liked the man.

"What do you have in mind Paul?" Sir Edwaed said. The Spanish Count sat quiet.

"We all worked well on the Madrid Protocol. I thought we could see if any further developments could be worked out."

Germany, Great Britain and Spain had agreed to the Madrid Protocol of 1885 to settle conflicting claims on lands in the Sulu Archipelago which lay in the southern islands of the Philippines. In the treaty Spain had relinquished any designs on the island of Borneo. This protocol was in conjunction with the Protocol of Sulu of 1885 which recognized Spain's sovereignty over the Sulu Archipelago.

Germany was a new imperialist in the area having become the protectorate of the northeastern portion of New Guinea. The area included the Bismarck Islands, named after the German Chancellor.

Count Merry finally asked, "What type of arrangement are we talking here. My government has just agreed to the transfer of the Marshall Islands to Germany."

The Hispano-German Protocol of Rome had Germany paying $4.5 million to Spain for the island group. Talk was swirling of the island of Nauru being transferred to Germany to join the Marshall Islands.

Such shuffling of territory was part of the great game the European powers played in the world. While the British Empire had been essentially set for decades, even the British were part of the game. Most recently the British were making moves into South East Asia. While the Philippines had part of Spain since the 1500's, much of the rest of East Asia didn't get divided up until the 19th century.

The English and the Dutch had established their areas of influence in 1824 with the Dutch East Indies taking up the islands surrounding Sumatra. While Spain held the northern islands, the islands around Borneo sat in between the two empires and Britain had made inroads into the area.

The strangest inroad saw the White Raj of Sarawak, James Brooke, an Englishman, establish his personal monarchy in 1842 with land granted to him by the Sultan of Brunei. Sarawak took up the northwest corner of the island of Borneo and gave the British a hold in the area. This was added to their hold on the Malay Peninsular and their trading port of Singapore.

But the Germans were the up and coming power in Europe, arriving late in the imperial game. The Franco-Prussian War of 1870 had settled Germany's dominate position in Europe. Germany had then grabbed their few colonies in Africa.

Currently Germany, Britain and the United States were each supporting competing rival factions in a civil war over the Samoan Islands. With its growing industrial strength, like its European counterparts, Germany searched the world for raw materials, colonies to market their goods and ports to support their ships

Paul said, "Well, Count Merry, as you know, Germany is late. Our Chancellor didn't think colonies were necessary as he focused on putting the various parts of the German Empire together. Pulling Bavaria, Baden Mecklenburg and all the other realms together into one nation was enough at the time."

"And now you play catch-up," Sir Edward said.

"Exactly. But Germany is willing pay for its acquisitions. Unlike some that use force to get what they want."

Each of them knew he referred to the French action in Indochina of late. The French had been muscling their way into ever more land since the they had signed the Treaty of Saigon in 1862. They had forced their way into more Vietnamese territory before absorbing Cambodia and parts of Siam

"What did you have in mind? Our Empire has been reduced by revolution in the Americas. What's left?" Count Merry asked.

"Germany needs better access to China. Britain has Hong Kong, Spain Manila, Portugal has Macao, even Japan has been pushing for a trading port. With its control of the Korean Peninsular Japan moves closer each year to China."

"And Germany would like what?" the Count asked.

"I know that Her Majesty the Queen Regent is in a difficult position," Paul carefully spoke.

Queen Marie Christina of Spain was the regent as her young son, King Alfonso XIII was only a year old. Marie Christina would be the ruling figure until he reached the age of attainment. And everyone knew in European circles that the Spanish Empire was on hard times.

Lasting from about 1812 to 1836, a series of wars were fought throughout the Spanish New World leading to independence in Central and South America. Only the islands of Cuba and Puerto Rico remained of the once vast Spanish control in the new world.

"And Germany would like to buy more of our territory?"

"And pay a generous price."

Sir Edward sat and watched his friend carefully maneuver around Spanish pride. While he knew Spain's time was waining, Spanish pride would have a difficult time relinquishing their shrinking empire.

Count Merry continued, "From the mention of access to China, the only land near there that is Spanish would be in the Philippines. You wish to purchase the Philippines?"

The counts blood pressure grew from the tone of his voice and the redness of his face.

"My dear Count. we would never be so bold to suggest such a purchase. But you have thousands of islands there. What is one, more or less matter. We just need a port for our ships. A simple small island that can handle ships. Nothing more."

"And what do you consider a generous price?"

"I would leave that to your government to decide. You decide how much one small island is worth. We would then decide if it was a fair price."

The Spanish Count sat for a bit and let the offer settle. Finally he answered, "An interesting proposal. And I assume their would be a small fee for the agent that could make this happen."

"Of course, we would be most generous to the person who could arrange such an agreement."

Sir Edward knew that this was the way the ruling class worked. Gratuities for the handling of royal business kept the elite in the lifestyle to which they were accustomed. Vilas. mistresses, wardrobes and horses certainly didn't come cheap. SIde payments for sovereign work kept the ruling elite happy.

* * *

The Exposition Universelle of 1889 was the hottest item of the year in Europe. A world's fair in Paris brought hordes of people from around the world. The second half of the 1800's had seen an explosion in World's Fairs. It started with twenty two fairs in the 18960's. That was followed by thirty five in the 1870's soon to be eclipsed by thirty seven in the 1880's. Australian itself accounted for five world fairs in separate cities.

Only three had been scheduled for 1889, Dunedin, New Zealand and Buffalo, New York. But it was the fair in Paris that had attracted the well to do from around the world. Topping off all of the pavilions and exhibits in Paris stood the edifice built by the engineer Gustave Eiffel. Dubbed the Eiffel Tower, guests paid five French francs to ride to its peak. Considering that the forty cent fair admission was four times the cost of a typical economy lunch in Paris at the time, the cost to ascend the tower was considerable.

Soaring an amazing 1,063 feet over the nearby Seine River, fair attendees gained an incredible view of the City of Lights. Even standing beneath the steel latticework drew amazement as people strolled beneath the four massive outstretched legs.

The best view of the giant steel structure was from the Trocadero. Built as part of the exposition, the promenade high on the hill overlooked the gardens beneath that stretched to the river. The tower loomed across the Seine.

Two men with a tripod worked attaching a wooden box camera. Maneuvering to obtain his desired view of the Eiffel Tower, Alex Dull held his hands to his face to make a rudimentary picture frame. With no viewfinder on his "76 Camera" he aligned his photo image in his mind.

Having finished his studies at the Sorbonne University, Alexander had decided to stay in Paris, at least through the run of the fair. He had been a regular attendee and today he had a new helper. His camera was the newest model of the Americana Optical Company, built by Scovile Manufacturing in New York , and clearly printed on the back of the four by five inch camera's wooden body. His was the latest model with a real shutter and a rod and piston bellows for focusing. It still used glass plates but of the dry method. The dry method had pushed aside the wet plates that required immediate development.

The famous photographers of the American Civil War carried wet plates that required all the equipment to develop the plates immediately. At least Alex could forgo the horse and wagon those photographers required. But between the camera, a tripod to hold the camera steady and the glass plates, having a second abled body person to carry things made life easier.

"What do you think Jose?" Alex asked his filipino friend.

"You are the photographer. Why ask me?"

"You're the artist. I respect your eye on these things."

Dr. Jose Rizal had arrived from Germany two days before. After their summer together two years prior in Heidelberg, Alex had left for Paris and his studies. Dr. Rizal had left Germany to return to his native Philippines.

Alex knew of Jose love interest there and how lonely he had been. Rivera Mercado had moved back to Dagupan in Pangasinan Province north of Manila. But her father forbid the two from seeing each other for fear that already Dr. Rizal was considered a subversive by the authorities.

"So you never got to see Rivera, Jose?" Alex asked. They had not fully talked of his trip home and he carefully opened the subject.

"No, her father would not have it. I finally received a letter from her after no word for a year. She told me her mother contrived a marriage for her to an English railway engineer."

"I'm sorry, Jose," Alex said. He felt the pain his friend showed at the loss of a woman he had loved. "But my friend, we are in Paris. Look around you."

The two men looked up at the milling crowds admiring the view. Young women with parasols and fine dresses easily moved past them, some staring at the camera.

Alex had learned in his young photographic career one of the easiest ways to met eligible women was to offer to take their picture. Photography outdoors was still a novel thing as most would have had to hire in studio to have a portrait done. But at the cost of each dry plate, Alex went easy on impressing the girls.

"Yes, its good to be here. It is so gay and exciting. I'm looking forward to all the exhibits," Jose said.

"Lets set this shot up first and then we can walk over to the American pavilion."

Alex adjusted his angle and judged the light. Taking a glass plate out of the box on the ground, he slipped it into the back of the camera. He removed the protective sheets that kept the emulsion from the sunlight and took the shutter in his hand. He waited for the clouds to cover the sun partially and clicked his image.

Placing the sheets back over the exposed plate, he withdrew the photo and placed it in the carrying box. The two men dismantled the camera from the tripod and as Jose took up the tripod, Alex placed the camera in its carrying case and grabbed the case with the plates. They walked down the steps and along the fountain pool that led to the river. Crossing the Seine they walked under the Eiffel Tower and took the route Alex knew gained the American Pavilion.

Walking through the displays on America, Jose asked questions of Alex. He had always been interested in the revolution the United States won that had set them free from British colonial rule. That the Paris World's Fair was being held on the one hundred year anniversary of the storming of the Bastille in the French Revolution added to Jose interest.

None of the monarchies, such as Germany, Britain and Spain, were participating in the the fair out of protest to the anti-royal spirit of the event. Jose thought it wonderful, as he told Alex his hopes that one day his Philippine would also be free.

Alex announced he needed a picture of his friend in front of the American pavilion. They found a setting where Jose could stand and Alex walked away to where his friend and the pavilion made a good scene. He set out his tripod before pulling his camera out. He made a frame with his hands and moved his outfit slightly. As he did, he bumped into a woman busy looking forward.

"Excuse me," he said. He turned to see a beautiful woman in a large feather hat turning her focus from where she was looking.

"I hope you didn't step on my dress."

"I'm sorry. I don't think so," Alex said. "I am sorry. It's this camera tripod, its heavy."

"Well, maybe you should just be more careful."

Alex noticed how beautiful this woman was and realized he needed to be polite. "Excuse my manners. I'm Alexander Dull. Lately of Massachusetts."

"Ann Garner, from Ohio."

"Well, Miss Garner. I am very pleased to make you acquaintance. And it is Miss Garner?" Alex asked.

"Yes, and with a chaperone I should add. She's standing right over there with my sister."

But Alex's eyes remained staring at the enchanting woman before him. Knowing he needed to be on his best behavior, Alex offered to take her picture. As he discussed where he wished to have her stand, Jose yelled across the walkway.

"Are we going to take this picture or not?"

"Oh, I forgot. Excuse me Miss Garner, my friend wanted his picture in front of the pavilion."

"That's fine. I'll join him."

Before Alex could protest she confidently walked over to the short brown man standing in the sun.

"As she walked up she asked, "You don't mind do you. My name is Ann Garner, from Ohio. That's in the United States."

"Nice to meet you Miss Garner from Ohio. And no, please join me," Jose said.

The two turned to look at Alex framing their photo with his hands. He picked up the camera and moved closer before he had the two move in under the shade of the pavilion roof. Out of the sun, Alex knew their would be no shadows or sun to over expose his photo. And at this distance it would be more a portrait of the two since he was too close to take in the pavalion. Which was just what he wanted as he held up his arm as his other hand gripped the shutter. The couple froze in place and put their best expression on their faces.

"Nice. Thank you both," Alex said.

He packed up his camera and strapped his tripod legs together. He walked over under the shade and placed his equipment down. Ann's sister strolled over finally.

"Do I get introductions?"

"Yes, my sister Mary Garner. This is Alexander Dull of Massachusetts. And I haven't met my photo companion yet."

Alex jumped to introduce his friend. "Let me introduce my good friend, Dr. Jose Rizal, lately of Germany but originally from the Philippines Islands."

The four people all completed their formal introductions before Ann asked. "What type of doctor are you, Dr. Rizal?"

"He is an ophthalmoligists in Heidelberg. He saved my eye after I got hit in the face playing football," Alex said.

"Well, I'm very glad to meet you," Ann said, her sister smiling.

"Please call my Jose. Dr. Rizal is so formal."

"Well, are we heading to the tower now," a booming voice broke up the conversation.

All four young people turned to a large woman with a man walking up to them. Ann rolled her eyes at the intrusion before turning to Alex and Jose.

"Mr. Dull and Dr. Rizal, I'd like to introduce my chaperone, Miss Bors. And her brother Mr. Bors." Ann said it load enough so the doctor reference was clearly announced.

Both men spoke politely to the pair. Alex noted a certain chill in the air at their presence but noticed Ann didn't shrink at the intrusion.

"Gentlemen, we are due to go up the tower now, have you been?"

Alex feigned ignorance although he had been up twice since the fair opened. Being a resident of Paris, he had taken every opportunity to visit the exhibits, usually without his camera. Today he had hoped to get a few shots of the fair and its crowds. And now he had something more interesting.

"No mam'. But we've been looking forward to it," Alex lied.

"Well, would you care to accompany us. If you can handle that load of yours," Ann said. She looked at her two chaperones as she said it and Alex noticed her defiance. *There would be no protest by Miss Bors today* he thought.

Jose and Mary smiled as everyone headed toward the northwest leg of the tower and the first elevator. Alex offered to pay for everyone but Ann would not hear of it. Relieved at dodging a big hit on his monthly allowance from his mother, he stepped into line with the others to await the next car.

Soon all six were walking around the first level, the chaperones a few paces behind the others.Alex knew there was a second level so waited to take picture from higher up. The next elevator took them up and they strolled over to the handrail to take in Paris. It was a grand view and they waked around the deck till Alex stopped. He began setting up his camera outfit as he weighed the correct angle he wanted. Ann stood beside him and watched.

Alex had chosen the side with the Arc de Triomphe visible over the rooftops. The sun shown over his shoulder so their would be no glare on the lens. As he grabbed the shutter and clicked. Placing the glass plate back in his carrying box he took a second glass plate out and slipped into the back of his camera. Having just taken a scenic shot of the city, Alex wanted a more personal shot. He slid his tripod back from the handrail and motioned Jose into the picture.

"We need a group shot. Come on Ann and Mary," Alex said.

"Whose going to click the shutter?" Ann asked.

Alex motioned to Mr. Bors to move over to where he stood. He provided a quick instruction in clicking the shutter and when confident that the man could do one thing, Alex joined the others by the edge.

"Everybody ready?" he asked the group. Everyone took a pose and smiled. "Anytime Mr. Bors. Just like I showed you."

The chaperone hit the shutter and stood back. Alex walked over and switched out the glass plate. The others gathered around while he packed up his gear.

Knowing from his previous visits that the top level was very confined. Taking the camera gear up with him would be a nuisance and impede the other guests.

"I hear it is a very small room at the top," he lied. "Jose and I will have to take turns watching my camera gear while the other goes up for the view. I hear it is stupendous."

Mary spoke right up, "I'll go up with Dr. Rizal then. If you don't mind doctor?"

Alex noticed Ann's sister also emphasizes Jose's doctor status. He had been in the world enough to know that non-white people could be discriminated against. And that places like Ohio could be more discriminatory then cities like Paris. He had seen the unfair treatment of Irish emigrants in his native Massachusetts so even white people often bore the brunt of hostility. Both chaperones raised an eyebrow at Mary's invitation.

Before they could say anything, Mary took Jose's arm and led him toward the next elevator. Miss Bors looked back and forth quickly and decided to follow Mary. Her brother stood watch over the older sister.

"So Miss Garner, how long are you in Europe?" Alex asked.

"Father gave us a six month grand tour. We started in the British Isles. After Paris we head to the Alps and then to Italy."

They chatted about Paris and Alex asked what Ann thought of the city. She asked how he had ended up in Paris and was excited that Alex had been living in Paris for the past two years.

"Are you fluent in French then?" she asked. "I thought about staying here and learning French myself."

"French, and German. And it would be wonderful if you stayed.?"

"I heard that Buffalo Bill's Wild West Show was here at the fair but tickets were very hard to obtain. I thought you knowing the local language could help us get tickets."

"Well, the show isn't here at the fair. They are set up over by Neuilly. That's about there, just beyond that big park you can see." Alex leaned close to Ann and out stretched his arm, pointing to a park off to the northwest. "That's Boise de Boulogane. See the Seine where it takes a big turn and comes back around?"

Ann leaned in so she could aim down Alex's arm to where he pointed. He gathered her powdered aroma into his nostrils at the closeness. A throat clearing behind him reminded them of the chaperone standing near. He leaned away from Ann.

"Thank you Mr. Dull. So do you know of any tickets available?"

"Jose and I are attending tomorrow, perhaps I can find some for you. How long are you in Paris?"

"Tomorrow would be marvelous. We are staying in the 4th arrondissement. The Hotel Place des Vosges. On the south side of the park. Did I pronounce that right?"

"Yes, arrondissement," Alex repeated the pronunciation. "I live in the 5th arrondissement, so I'm close by. It's the Latin Quarter near the university. So we are close. Jose and I can get the tickets and rent a carriage tomorrow."

"And if its not too much bother, I need four tickets," Ann said as she looked over her shoulder at the chaperone.

They were enjoying their time together when Jose and Mary returned. Ann once again took Alex's arm and led him to the elevator, Mr. Bors following. Three separate elevators took them to the third level. In one of the exchanges Mr. Bors got separated from the couple.

Reaching the small observation room alone, the two young people moved close, Ann remarking that it was a small tight space as Alex made room at one of the windows so she could see from this elevation. They were packed in the crowd holding their spot when Mr. Bors finally arrived, forcing them to add a respectable distance between them

Chapter 5

Paris, France
August, 1889

The next day Alex rose early, ate breakfast and then began his walk to Ann's hotel. He crossed the Seine on the Pont de Sully. Upon reaching Quai Des Celestins he had to divert his walk around the massive construction project that had the street blocked. The new Metro underground railroad was being constructed and a large trench ran up the length of Quai des Celestins.

When completed next year the first Metro line would run from Port Vincennes to Port Mailot, thus connecting the center of Paris to neighborhoods to the east and west. Paralleling the Seine River, the underground railroad drew excitement from the city residents.

As he reached Place des Vosges he located Ann's hotel and then looked around for a carriage. There seemed to be plenty so he would wait to call one until they were all set to go see Buffalo Bill. He walked into the lobby and announced his name to the desk clerk and whom he was there to see. A message was sent to the room and a short time later Ann and Mary arrived with the two chaperones close behind.

"Where's Dr. Rizal?" Ann asked.

"His hotel is on the other side of the city so will meet us at the entrance."

"And I'm assuming you were able to obtain four additional tickets, Alex."

Alex pulled them from his dress coat pocket and held them aloft. Ann thanked him for his effort and made an offer to pay for them which Alex would not accept.

"If we are ready, we can catch a carriage just outside," Alex said.

The five stepped out onto the sidewalk and Alex raised his hand and spoke in French to one of the teamsters waiting. He snapped his reins slightly and the single horse trotted over to the waiting riders. Announcing they were headed to the Wild West show the driver got animated.

"Oh oui. Le Roi des Hommes de la Frontiere Cody," the driver said.

"What did he say?" Ann asked.

"Mr. Cody seems to be the rage of Paris. That long bit is the name they have given him."

Alex and the driver carried on in French as the carriage made its way along Rue Danielle Casanova. He turned his attention to Ann.

"We are on Casanova Street. Are you familiar with ..." Alex was cut off by Miss Bors clearing her throat loudly. Ann siting across from him gave him a slight smile in recognition of the famous Italian adventurer and noted woman seducer.

The carriage gained the show grounds in Neuilly and Alex reached for his wallet to pay the driver. Ann immediately stopped him, arguing that he had purchased the tickets and she would at least pay for the carriage. A small discussion took place before Alex relented with Mr. Bors paying the fare.

Jose stepped over from where he had waited and greeted everyone. The Wild West Show took place in a pavilion but before entering, an authentic Indian village had been set up. The six visitors walked among the teepees and real Indians working for the show. The brochure stated that over one hundred Indians were in the show, including women and children, and mostly from the Lakota Sioux tribe.

Since none of them had ever been in the American West they marveled at the clothes each participant wore. Soon it was show time and the group passed the ticket counter and took their seats in the arena. What followed was three hours of gun fights, Indian raids, trick shooting and horse races through the arena. It was one exciting noisy act after another and the crowd loved every bit of it.

"Indians Brave! Indians Brave!" the French crowd yelled in unison at the native Americans chasing the settlers around the arena. Soon the calvary showed up and a rip roaring gunfight ensued. All the time the French yelled for the brave Indians.

Alex looked sideways at his friend and say something in Jose's expression. There was something clicking in the filipino at the crowd encouraging the indians in their fight. He glanced to his left and the two sisters sat entranced, large smiles showing. When Anne Oakley put on her display of sharp shooting, they were on the edge of her seats.

As the finale closed down the show, the crowd in the arena filed out with a buzz of excitement. Reaching the boulevard in front of the show grounds, Ann turned, her face flush.

"Since its dinner time I propose we find a nice restaurant. And dinner is on me," she announced. A small argument followed until she mentioned that the show tickets were worth more then a ride and dinner on any day. She spoke that she had not been so enthralled since she couldn't remember when. Mary joined in her sister's acclaim for the show's excitement.

As they walked to a nearby restaurant Alex asked, "What are your plans tomorrow. Perhaps we could go sail boats at La Jardin du Luxembourg. Its the park near my home and don't worry, they are miniature boats."

He noticed a frown for the first time since meeting Ann at his suggestion.

"I'm afraid we are scheduled to leave tomorrow," Ann said. "We are taking the train to Geneva and the Alps."

"Oh, I didn't know," Alex said.

Dinner was rather subdued as the four sat and ate. The two chaperones sat at a table nearby. Alex did noticed that Jose's thoughts were elsewhere so he carried the conversation. Finished with dinner, Jose excused himself for his walk to his hotel while Alex escorted the sisters back to their hotel. Again Mr. Bors paid the fare at Ann's insistence.

Leaving Ann alone with Alex on the sidewalk, Mary and the two chaperones stepped into the lobby to retrieve their keys. Alex turned to Ann.

"Is there time that we could see each other in the morning before you leave?"

"I'd like that," Ann said. "Our train doesn't leave until noon so we could meet here in the lobby at 9 am I suppose."

They said their goodbyes and Alex trudged back to his room. It would be a rustless night for him.

At nine he sat waiting in Ann's hotel lobby. Ann arrived with her traveling clothes on. The two clasped hands. Alex looked around for the chaperone but none appeared.

"Could we got sit in the park a bit?" Alex asked.

"Yes, I'd like that."

They crossed the street and walked into the 17th century formal gardens of Place des Vosges. Finding a park bench they sat down.

"Ann, I was thinking last night about returning to the States. And I was wondering if it would be possible for me to travel to Ohio to see you."

Ann's expression went blank at the question and she lowered her gaze to her hands folded neatly in her lap. Sensing something, Alex added, "Of course I would ask your father for permission to see you."

Ann did not answer and continued to stare at her hands. Alex sat and waited patiently but knew something was amiss.

"Alex, I didn't mean to lead you on. I was just having so much fun together that I didn't really think. But there is someone else. Back in Ohio."

"Oh," Alex uttered.

"I'm sorry Alex. But I want you to know I'll always think of you fondly when I think of Paris. And I'll look for your photographs. I know you'll be famous someday."

The two sat quiet for a long time before Ann announced that she needed to return to her room. She thanked Alex again for a wonderful time and the two parted ways. Alex stood and watched Ann cross the street and enter the hotel. He finally shook himself and started a long slow walk home.

A loud banging at his door announced morning. He rolled over in bed to ignore the intrusion. But it got louder before Jose yelled out his name. Alex climbed out of bed to let his friend in.

"Come on Alex. The day awaits us," Jose said as he walked to a chair and sat. Noticing the dejected look on his friend's face he asked. "Love not springing this day?"

"No, Ann is spoken for. She finally told me yesterday."

"I am sorry. She was a beauty. And full of spirit too. Someone is a lucky guy somewhere. But as you told me when I arrived, we are in Paris."

"I'm not much company today, Jose. can you entertain yourself?" Alex asked.

"Yes, I'm getting the Los Indios Bravos together. I thought of it last night at the Wild West Show. I'm meeting with my fellow countrymen. We writers will from an association. To take the American Indian spirit to fight for our freedom in the Philippines."

"Sounds great," Alex said. "I'll catch up with you later."

"Well, you my friend are an official member of the Los Indios Bravos but we will get started without you."

* * *

Ann Garner and her sister Mary continued on there Grand Tour of Europe accompanied by their chaperones. Having her ears pierced continued Ann's strive for personal freedom as she enjoyed hiking through the Alps. Upon returning to Geneva, she withdrew money at the bank before going to collect letters from the United States.

One letter from home stopped her cold. A Mark Gray, local business man, had died September 2 of meningitis. She collapsed on the bed devastated. The man she was destined to marry was dead. Her sister Mary found her sobbing on the bed.

The rest of their trip would be more a wake as the two sisters carried on completing their Grand Tour. Long forgotten was their gay time in Paris before Ann's world imploded.

Finally returning to Ohio, Ann attempted to return to her duties at her father's bank. As she struggled with her loss, eligible young men began to come around, eager to win favor. One particular local lawyer would be successful and on January 25, 1891 Ann was married. But she would often wonder what would have happened if she had returned to Paris to study French.

Chapter 6

Boston, Massachusetts
May, 1893

It had been a non-eventful crossing as the SS *La Touraine* maneuvered into Long's Wharf in Boston. Alexander Dull stood at the rail on the First Class deck and watched as downtown Boston inched closer. He saw the horse traffic on State Street and wondered if a wagon for his luggage would be available.

It had been four years since the Paris World's Fair and Alex had been living overseas for six years. He felt a certain strangeness coming over him as he got ready to return to his home town. Life in Europe had been all he had wanted it to be and he felt apprehensive about his choice to give up Paris.

The letter from his mother had arrived three months ago announcing the upcoming wedding of his cousin Rockwood Hoar. And although Alex had fond memories of time spent when he was young playing with Rockwood, a wedding certainly wasn't reason enough to give up his life photographing Europe to attend. It had been the tone of the letter from his mother that had gotten him packing.

Not mentioned, but implied, was that her monthly support of his life in Europe would be coming to an end. At the age of thirty, Alex knew it was time for him to make his own way in the world. Letters from his three brothers had certainly been more explicit in their comments on his lifestyle.

Now he would attempt to find a way to support himself with his photography, and not by opening a studio. As his friends had succumbed to studio work all seemed trapped in their work photographing the rich and famous if they were lucky. Providing portraits to the middle class paid the bills but did not provide anything more exciting. And Alex wanted more from his craft. He didn't really care about riches, although his mother's fortune had been nice, but he did care about making a difference.

His time spent with his friend Dr. Rizal had shown him a higher calling. Fighting for freedom for a subjugated people certainly was a worthy cause and Alex knew he needed to find his calling. That Jose had been exiled by the Spanish authorities to an island in the Philippines demonstrated the risk of speaking one's mind in an authoritative government. And although Jose had only provided the words through his writing, others were acting on those ideas.

The large passenger ship bumped gently into the fenders lining the dock and a slight bounce took Alex's thoughts back to the task at hand. He had rented a First Class cabin for the crossing mainly for the convenience of his cargo. Besides his two suitcases and satchel holding his camera gear, Alex had carefully packed about one third of his glass plates for the trip home. Leaving the remainder of his photographic negatives at a classmates studio in Paris, he had selected what he considered his best shots. If he could get them home intact, he hoped that he could begin publishing his work. And with publication, he hoped to begin getting paid for his photographs.

The ship's bursar walked up to Alex to announce that four stevedores would be in his stateroom in half an hour to move his luggage. First Class passengers would be the first to leave the ship before the hordes of second and third class passengers were allowed up on deck.

Alex had noticed the segregation of classes on the ship with the second and third class passengers confined to the lower decks. Called steerage, these classes were considerable cheaper in cost to cross the Atlantic from Le Harve, France to America. With so many European migrants heading to the United States, ships were loaded with poor families looking for opportunity in the New World. It drove home how lucky he was to be among the well to do of America.

"Thank you," Alex said and slipped a two French franc gold piece to the bursar. He wanted the best workers to handle his fragile cargo and knew he had to pay to get them.

"Right away Sir," the bursar said as he tipped the brow of his hat.

Alex walked through the companionway and found his cabin. Unlocking the door, he made a quick check to make sure he had left nothing. He double checked his luggage that it was all secure and just as he was sitting down at the small desk, a wrap at the door announced the movers.

"Right men, these large cases are extremely valuable and fragile. They are full of glass so please use the utmost caution."

"You're right sir. We'll take right good care." one of the stevedores said. "And I'll tell the derrick operator to be extra careful."

Alex had already checked and his heavy cases would be off loaded the same way they had been loaded. The ship had two masts with derrick arms that swung out for moving cargo. While primarily a passenger ship, goods that needed fast passage across the ocean were consigned to the ship. Alex's goods would be among the first off loaded and he followed the workers with their hand trucks out onto the open deck.

Other first class passengers were already lining up as the gangway swung into place from shore. Alex followed his luggage to the forward derrick and supervised the workers placing his load into the rope net laying on the deck. They gathered it up and cinched the corners into a turnbuckle, ready for the crane operator.

"Thanks men." Alex again reached into his pocket and withdrew five gold French franc coins and handed them to what he took as the lead worker. "And something for the operator there."

"Hey Pierre. Extra easy now," the stevedore yelled and held up the gold coin to get the message across.

Pierre gave a thumbs up and then doffed his beret slightly at the tip he'd just received. Lowering the cable down, one of the workers clipped in a shackle and gave the thumbs up. The delicate load lifted slowly off the deck as the cases and luggage all found a happy resting spot in the jumble. Once settled, the load swiftly went up as the derrick swung out over the edge of the ship. Pierre lowered the cargo until it almost reached the wharf.

Looking over the side, Alex observed more stevedores unclip the net after Pierre lowered it to the deck. The worker who Alex had handed the tip to yelled down.

"Look lively there on deck. Thems cases are fragile."

"Thank you," Alex said as the worker again doffed his hat and walked off. Alex hustled to the gangway and got in line with the others. He was soon on deck and locating five men to help move his load. Once through Customs, the men wheeled the four wheel freight carriage out to a jumble of people and horses on State Street.

Finding a wagon suitable, the men loaded his luggage and Alex switched to silver coins as he passed them around to each hand. They all touched their hats in thanks and disappeared back into the melee. Climbing up with the teamster Alex announced that they had a train to catch at South Station.

More movers and more silver coins later Alex's train pulled into Worcester's Union Station. Another set of movers and more tips and he stood at the street corner hailing a wagon. One more move and he would be home.

"Salisbury and Park Avenue please," Alex announced to the wagon driver.

"Yes sir."

It was a short two miles to his mother's home and Alex relaxed after so much stress in getting his photographic plates safely to America. The two horses slowly walked along and Alex noticed the hard wooden bench he sat on. Freight wagons didn't have the soft benches of the carriages and he felt each street imperfection, thinking of his fragile cargo. Passing by Institute Park the wagon crossed Park Avenue and Alex directed the driver to his house.

It was a large Victorian style two story home with a wrap around porch across the front. A driveway up the left side led to a covered portico where the teamster now pulled the horses to a stop. Afraid no one would be home to help unload his cases, Alex smiled as his three brothers all stepped out the side door.

"Finally back," Cornelius said.

"Good thing we all decided to be here today. Mother got your letter on the passage date and arrival time so we wanted to make sure you really came home," Max said. The others all smiled at the implication that Alex wouldn't show up at all.

"If you guys are finished, I've got my life's work here to unload. And don't drop it what ever you do."

Zachariah added, "You cut it pretty close little brother. Rockwood gets married in five days. Mother really wanted us all together you know."

"I made it, didn't I," Alex said, a certain exasperation showing at his brother's attitude. "Look, its been as stressful day getting my things here, so how about I just take a bath and go sleep for the rest of the day. We'll try this again tomorrow."

With all the luggage piled in the dining room just inside the side door, Alex disappeared up the stairs after giving his mother a hug. He apologized to her for just wanting to be alone.

He wasn't; sure what it was but he was suddenly feeling very foreign in his old home. He knew that living overseas all those years had given him a new perspective to life, and now it seemed his older brothers just wanted to put him in his old position of the younger brother. Always not measuring up to his siblings, aways not quite the go getter they were, not fitting in.

After a warm bath, he crawled into bed and noticed it was only four in the afternoon. But he didn't care. He needed space at the moment. Maybe tomorrow he would be ready.

Awakening in the middle of the night, his mind took over. His thoughts retuned to what had troubled his sleep now for months. Ever since the letters from Jose had arrived announcing his arrest and exile in the Philippines. *Why had Jose retuned to the Philippines?* he thought. Jose's letters over the past few years had shown him happy in Hong Kong, living with his family, practicing medicine. Jose had said that he had a small clinic on the street level of his building and life seemed good, at least in his letters.

Alex knew that Dr. Rizal had been popular with the ladies in Hong Kong, although Jose didn't elaborate. But Alex had witnessed him in Paris as he had gotten over losing his love interest in the islands.

Alex had stayed in touch with Los Indios Bravos, the association of Filipino writers in Europe committed to independence from Spain. Through them Alex learned more Tagalog and started to learn Cebuano, the main language of the southern Philippine Islands.

Rizal's writings continued to embolden the freedom fighters in the Philippines and Jose had formed La Liga Filipina. The Spanish authorities took note. Obstinately a civic group, La Liga Filipina advocated modest social reforms in the islands through legal means. The government disbanded the group and tagged Dr. Rizal an enemy of the state. He was soon deported to Dapitan.

Not allowed to leave Dapitan, Alex knew from the latest letter that Jose had started a school teaching English and self-sufficiency. All these events tore at Alex as he lay tossing in bed. His luxurious lifestyle in Worcester tore at him knowing his friend's predicament. An idea seeped into his thoughts. An idea that would risk much, but Alex knew that his life was meant for something more then what Massachusetts could offer.

The next four days Alex busied himself organizing his photographs. He carried prints of the plates he had shipped and after showing his family, he started searching where he might be able to market them. He received some interest from the local newspaper, the Worcester Telegram and Gazette, who would do a feature article in Sundays edition. Alex contacted his connections at Holy Cross College and the school arranged an exhibit of some of his works.

After Rockwood's wedding, Alex busied himself making frames and mounts for his showing. He had learned the skill working in his friend's studio on Paris and had thirty photos ready for the opening date. Having a U.S. Senator attend made the event a social must for Worcester. Alex had worked on his uncle and cousin at the wedding and had gotten a commitment from both.

At the day of his showing Alex stood waiting as the official start time approached. The hall his photos were hung in had been shuttered during his set-up and he was nervous no one would show. As the doors opened a small crowd waiting shuffled in to view his photos.

Alex had included a good selection of the Paris World's Fair since that continued to be talked about. The city had decided to leave the Eiffel Tower in place while tearing down all the other pavilions lent interest in the long closed event. Still the tallest structure on Earth, crowds of tourists visited the tower each year. Unknown to Alex at the time it would hold its tallest record for another forty one years to finally yield to the Chrysler Building in New York City in 1931. In 1893, the Eiffel Tower had become world famous and the audience in the hall marveled at Alex's photos of it.

He moved among the people answering questions as a steady stream of visitors entered the hall. A group of young men in suits entered and Alex noticed they were the first young people by themselves. He walked over to them and introduced himself. Finding that they all attended Worcester Academy he stated.

"Worcester Academy, hey. I'm a graduate myself."

"What year?" They all asked in unison.

"Class of 1883." Alex said.

They chatted a bit about life at the exclusive private school in Worcester. Many of the young men hailed from around the East Coast since the school catered to day students as well as boarding students.

One student in particular asked, "Did you play sports?

"Why yes, I was on the tennis team," Alex said.

Alex noticed a smile come over one eighteen year old's face but before he could ask why the reaction, his uncle, the U.S. Senator walked in. His cousin Rockwood and new wife joined a small group of dignitaries following the senator.

"Excuse me boys," Alex said. He turned and added. "Uncle, I'm so glad you could attend."

With his three family members close by, they asked to be given a personal tour of the exhibit. A number of visitors fell in at a respectable distance to overhear the artist talk. Alex noticed the gathering group and directed his talk at them as much as his uncle. Halfway through the tour Alex's mother walked in with his three brothers, interrupting the talk. They joined the family as Alex finished going through his photos.

"Thank you nephew," George Hoar said. "A most informative display. Your work is exemplary. I can see your mothers artistic style in your photos."

His cousin Rockwood and his new bride Christine nodded in approval. Alex looked to his brothers to assure himself that they were paying attention. Uncle George had provided the father figure in all four boys life's since their own father had been killed in the Civil War. Gaining his approval meant everything to Alex.

"I wrote down someone you need to see. You'll have to travel to Washington but I've taken the liberty to inform him you would be asking for him." Senator Hoar handed Alex a slip of folded paper. "Now, I'm afraid I have other business to attend while I'm here. So if you will excuse me."

"Of course uncle. And thank you again for attending. He thanked Rockwood and his wife and the entourage that had arrived with his uncle. He turned to his mother as the family group shrank and asked. "Would you like me to go over the photos you missed?"

Finishing with his family, Alex stood aside as his mother and brothers left. Noticing all the Worcester Academy boys had left but one, the one who had asked if he played tennis come toward him.

"Excuse me, my name is Gilbert Grovenor. I hope you don't find me impertinent to ask, but are you related to Colonel Paul Dull?"

"Yes, he is my father," Alex said.

"Then this is an honor to meet the son of Worcester's Medal of Honor hero of the Battle of Cold Harbor."

"Thank you Gilbert. Unfortunately I never knew him. I hadn't even been born when he died and my older brothers were infants. But why did you smile when I mentioned playing tennis."

"Perhaps we could play a match together."

"I don't know. I haven't played much at all since my junior year at Holy Cross. I'm afraid I wouldn't be much of a challenge now."

But Alex and Gilbert agreed to a match the following week, and although a bit one sided in the competition, it was a friendship that would direct Alex for most of his life.

Chapter 7

Potsdam, Germany
July 1893

The man once described by the Iron Chancellor, Otto von Bismarck, as the "best horse in the diplomatic stable" sat by the lake in front of his summer home. Sitting among the lakes of Potsdam, the elite of Imperial Germany all retired to the pastoral setting outside Berlin as the heat of summer hit. The center of Imperial power, Sanssouci Palace, sat a short carriage ride away. Built by Fredrich the Great, Sanssouci was the center of influence in was now called the First Reich.

The Iron Chancellor had resigned three years previous over disputes with the Kaiser. Wilhelm II sought a more aggressive role for Imperial Germany and the clashes with his Chancellor led to the resignation. Since then, Germany sought out more opportunities in the world to add to its stature.

And today, Paul von Hatzfeldt, horse extraordinaire in diplomacy would attempt a major move on the world stage. As Germany's Ambassador in London, he met every day with the elite of Britain. Charged with running the largest empire, Paul saw the day to day operations on a personal level. Imitating his fellow British diplomats he worked hard to gain Germany more land in the world. And today might be such a day.

A cool breeze came blowing off Templiner See as people in small boats enjoyed the summer weather. He would not be joining them today as he awaited his special guest. Remembering the work he had done before hand, he sipped a lemonade and waited.

A house servant arrived and announced an approaching carriage. Paul stood and walked briskly to his chateau and stepped through to the front entrance just as a carriage stopped. His servant opened the large front door and Paul walked briskly down the set of steps to greet his guest.

"My Archduke. So nice of you to join me."

"Ambassador. Thank you for the invitation." The Archduke Friedrich, Duke of Teschen said.

"And how is the Princess Isabella finding Potsdam?" Paul asked.

"Busy seeing family. Thank you for the distraction."

Paul had learned of the Archduke and Princess's visit and arranged a quiet meeting of the two men. At sixty two, Paul was in the prime of his diplomatic life. Knowledge of all the right people in Europe and a long history of associations over the years made him Germany's most connected personage.

The younger man before him, at age thirty three, was still learning the ways of European upper crust. And while he held a more exalted position as Duke of Teschen, Paul knew that the archduke would recognize that the power of the Kaiser sat right behind his ambassador. While these would be informal chats today, in the world of royalty, such informal talks often led to world changing events.

The two men took a spot under a large umbrella just feet from the slapping waves. It was a perfect setting as Paul offered the Archduke a drink from his pitcher of lemonade. They started with small talk of the archduke's family in Prussia. His wife, a princess in the House of Croy, held power in the Picardy region of France. But part of the family had connections to the Kingdom of Prussia from long ago and the Princess Isabella was close to its members. A lucky connection for Paul and Germany which he hoped to exploit now.

"My Archduke," Paul finally began the real reason for the meeting. "There is something I need to ask."

"Yes ambassador."

Paul noticed the body language of his guest and noted no change. He knew from previous negotiations to watch his counterparts body language, often more important than what they said.

"Your sister, Her Majesty the Queen Regent of Spain. I understand you are close."

"Yes, as her older brother she trusted me to watch out for her as we grew up."

Paul continued. "And do you get an opportunity to see her now that she is in Madrid?"

"Occasionally."

"What is King Alfonso now, seven years old?" Paul asked. He knew perfectly well that they both knew the age of the young king. Born after the ruler of Spain had died, Alfonso XIII wold not be enthroned officially until he attained his majority. Most considered that would take place when he turned sixteen years of age in 1902. Until that time, Queen Maria Christina ruled the Spanish Empire.

Born in Brunn, Moravia, part of the Austro-Hungarian Empire, the Queen Regent had strong ties to Vienna. Paul pinned his hopes of reaching a deal on the Germanic connections between Berlin and Vienna.

Before the Archduke could answer, Paul continued. "I imagine ruling the Spanish Empire is difficult for her majesty."

"She has made comments to that affect. Losing most of Central and South America has left Spain with an empire in name only. The pieces left are certainly not much of an asset for Spain anymore."

Hearing such words encouraged Paul's work. *If his sister had passed on such an attitude there may be an opportunity for Germany here,* he thought.

"I don't know if you are familiar with Count Marry y Colon, Francisco, 1st Count of Benomar. We met a few years back and broached the subject of German purchase of an island in Asia from Spain."

Paul noticed a slight change in body language at the mention of Germany buying Spanish territory. Such a statement would explain the real reason of the meeting to the Archduke. But in European circles, such topics were not uncommon among the elite.

"No, I don't know the man," Archduke Friedrich said. He seemed a little stiff to Paul. "And what did Spain say to your offer?"

"Very quiet on the subject I'm afraid."

"And you would like to bring the subject up again, I assume."

Paul liked the bluntness of the archduke. His life was made easier by those who could think ahead on any subject and reach conclusions on their own. With so much inbreeding among the royal families, that was often not the case. Great intelligence among the elite was not common.

"Yes, my government still wishes a port for shipping in Asia. The British, the French, the Dutch and even the Japanese have all made inroads there. We are forced to contract through these other powers for service to our shipping. Having a small island in east Asia would greatly enhance our position."

"And Germany is wiling to pay for such a concession?"

"As we offered the Count, we would offer you. Spain just needs to name her price and if it is a fair price for a suitable island, Germany will transfer gold to Madrid. And of course a suitable payment for those that helped facilitate such a purchase."

"An interesting offer Ambassador," the archduke said. "Please compliment the Kaiser on his record of paying for his acquisitions. I see the French have started another war in Indochina. I assume they are seeking more there."

"Yes, my sources tell me that France will take most of the province of Vietnam this time."

"And now the Americans are moving into the world. I see their hand all over this Hawaii thing."

Paul knew what the Archduke spoke. In January the local growers overthrew the Queen of Hawaii and declared a republic. That the United Sates Marines had assisted in the coup with the majority of America growers in the islands left little doubt that the islands would soon be part of the United States.

"And will they stop at Hawaii?" Paul asked "Once they break out from their North American strong hold, whats to stop them. Spain has Guam and the Philippines siting exposed without the resources to protect them."

Unsaid was the common knowledge that Spain was the sick man of Europe. Long holding a vast empire, wealth had flown into Madrid as silver and gold were transferred from the New World Those rich days were long past and now those lands were independent. Besides the Pacific Islands, Cuba and Puerto Rico comprised the empire now. And everyone knew the United Staes had long coveted the Island of Cuba. A short ninety miles away from the United States, many Americans considered it a natural fit to their country. Even as far back as President John Adams, the country had sought influence in Cuba. And if now the United States was turning to imperialism like the Europeans, where they would move to next was a mystery.

"And you would want me to broach the subject with the Queen Regent."

"Yes, your highness. I think it would be beneficial to both countries," Paul said.

Both man sat quiet as sailboats swept past their spot. Summer fun continued as power politics European style took place on shore. Soon the Archduke thanked the Ambassador for an enlightening meeting and promised he would get back with an answer.

Paul knew that whatever the answer, Germany was moving ahead with plans in Asia. Kaiser Wilhelm II wanted to add to his colonial empire and Asia was open ground. If the Spanish didn't realize the forces coming their way, Germany certainly did. And Germany would be ready.

* * *

Alexander Dull knew enough of Washington D.C. that nothing happened there during the summer. A southern city, the nation's capital was a hot, humid place to avoid until the cooler weather arrived. It was late September when Alex finally readied himself for his trip. Boarding the train at Union Station, his first transfer was in New York City. He caught a ride across the city to the ferry to New Jersey where he would continue on a train heading south.

Reaching the capital, he found a room at the hotel his uncle had recommended and the next day made his way to the Department of Interior. He asked for the name that had been given him and was ushered right away into an office over looking Dupont Circle. A man in a white shirt, his dress coat hanging on a hook to the side, greeted him. Behind him the open window let a warn breeze in.

"Mr. Dull, so nice to finally meet you. Your Uncle the senator has advised me of your coming."

"Thank you Mr. Meyer," Alex said. "I'm afraid I'm a little at a loss as my uncle didn't mention what this was about. Just that I should look you up."

"Quite alright. And please call be Walter. I hope we will be working together on something I find very exciting."

"Then please call me Alex. What do you have in mind?"

"The Department of Interior, if you didn't know, is in charge of most Federal lands, primarily in the West. Also under our tutelage are the native tribes out West."

Alex had read an account recently of the Ghost Dance War involving primarily the Sioux Tribe. Having been part of the Los Bravos Indian group formed by his friend Dr. Rizal while in Paris, Alex held a certain spot in his heart for the plight of the American Indian. His interest was being piqued by Mr. Meyer.

"I am aware of our native tribes, Mr. Meyer."

"Walter please. Alex, I think we have a splendid opportunity for you as it was explained by your uncle the senator."

"You know I'm a photographer." Alex didn't' know how he might be of assistance to the Federal government.

"And an accomplished one at that. Exactly what we need. Let me explain. Congress has set aside funds for an inventory of sorts for the Columbia River Basin

Indian tribes. We here at Interior thought a photographic record of each tribe would be the best."

Alex perked up at what Mr. Meyer was describing. His mind was already composing images that he would want to capture if this was really true.

"So, are there some parameters that you want covered?" Alex said.

"It's all up to you. Just cover the nine or so tribes in the upper river basin. Otherwise you are our eyes for the nation to witness our native peoples."

"You'll provide a list of the tribes you want then?"

"Right here. But I will suggest you travel as quickly as you can, if you accept this project, to Dalles City in Oregon. It is time for the fall salmon run up the river and Celilio Falls near by is a historic gathering spot for the tribes to fish."

"I can be ready to leave inside a week. I just need to gather supplies."

"You haven't asked the amount that the grant is funded for," Walter said. "It states that the department will pay one hundred dollars per picture up to fifty pictures. Half to be paid ahead of time for travel and supplies."

Alex'x heart leaped at the amount the government was paying. He quickly ran the cost of travel and supplies he would need and there would be enough left for him to accomplish something he had been thinking of late. Something that he had decided he had to do.

"That sounds adequate Mr. Meyer. And any provision if I provide more pictures than the fifty. I wouldn't expect more money but I might have more to say in my pictures."

"Walter, please." As a big smile came over his face. "We would love any and all pictures you wished to provide us."

"Thank you, Walter," Alex said, standing and extending his hand to shake his newfound benefactor. "Thank you very much."

After a week of preparation and four days on the train, Alex stepped off the train passenger car in Dalles City, Oregon. He was greeted by a western town of dirt streets and men in large hats wearing boots. Alex was tired from his trip and sought a hotel to get settled in. As he stood gathering his equipment from the freight depot, the Union Pacific locomotive blew steam and belched black smoke as it pulled out of the depot. Passenger cars rolled by behind him and soon it was quiet except for the clomp of horses moving down the street. He hired a carriage with a driver and asked for the local hotel.

He soon had a room in the Dalles City Hotel with a room overlooking the Columbia River. Alex had asked about hiring horses and had gotten the name of a livery close by. He would head out tomorrow with two horses, one to ride and one to carry his equipment.

Told that it would be about a three hour ride to Celilio Falls, he decided to camp out one night so as to have more time to photograph. That would also allow him the morning and evening light more beneficial to shoot in.

While Alex thought in eastern geography terms, he soon learned that western geography meant much longer distances. And with no good road network and few trains, many of the places he needed to get to were nearly inaccessible. From day one of his adventure he learned that what his mind had laid out to be an easy way to make some necessary money would be an adventure in survival.

After two days taking photos at Celilio Falls he moved across the river to the Indian village of Wishram. Another two days and he was ready for his next locale. People recommended hiring a guide to get him to the Warm Springs tribal area south of Dalles City. Leaving his extra photographic plates at the Dalles City Hotel, he headed out the next morning with a guide.

They were soon in wild country heading south and reached the small community of Hunt's Ferry where a rough ferry took them across the Descutes River. The country got more wild as they continued further south. Suffering from the long time in the saddle the two men arrived in Simnasho, the main village of the Warm Springs Indains.

"If you want, I can translate some for you." the guide said.

Alex had been told that the man he had hired knew many of the local dialects of the tribes in the area.

He continued, "As I told you, the Wasco and Warm Springs tribes moved onto this here reservation back in 1855. I speak Wasco real good, Warm Springs far to middlen."

"But you said there three tribes here."

"Yes sir. The Paiute tribe is up in Yakima. But they had trouble up there and the government moved the hot heads down here about fourteen years ago. Don't speak Paiute to well though."

"Two out of three will be fine I guess. Now, can we get a place to camp?"

"Sure thing Mr. Dull."

Chapter 8

Dapitan, Philippines
May, 1896

Three years of work and travel had brought Alex nearer to his ultimate goal. Lying on the north end of Mindanao Island, Dapitan sat on the Sulu Sea not far from Negros Island. A regular steam launch carried passengers and freight from Dumaguete to Dapitan on a regular schedule. In the mish-mash of tribal ethnic groups making up the Philippine archipelago, Mindanao Island held ten major groups with the Bisaya Tribe surrounding Dapitan. Speaking a form of Cebuano, the natives lived a subsistence life of rice farming and small animal farms.

Dr. Jose Rizal sat at his desk writing as the morning heat built. Most activity took place in the early morning and as the heat and humidity grew, a rest time in the mid-afternoon was required due to the conditions. Jose would write and do his medical work before the afternoon heat. As he finished up writing, an assistant that helped in his clinic knocked gently on his office door.

"Dr. Rizal, you have a visitor."

While patients and students were common, Jose seldom had visitors. The Spanish authorities had purposefully exiled him to Dapitan so he would be away from everyone. That anyone would make the journey to see him was rare. It was a four boat trip from

Manila to Mindanao which included crossing three islands where the roads were rudimentary.

Ever since his exile on July 7, 1892, the troubles had been building up north. Luzon Island was the center of the budding revolt against Spain. Called the Katipunan, a secret society of revolutionaries, it had gone active upon Dr. Rizal's exile. And though Jose had written extensively that he did not approve of their violent ways, the revolution continued to grow.

He looked up and said, "Yes, please show him in."

Jose stood and smiled as his friend Andres Bonifacio walked into his office. The two men embraced and Jose offered his friend a chair.

"What brings you all the way to Dapitan?" Jose asked.

"Are we safe speaking here Jose?"

"Yes, the authorities leave me quite alone as long as I stay put."

"News for Manila. Things are happening Jose. If you are willing to put your full support behind the Katipunan, we will rescue you."

"Andres, that is good of you to offer, but I am quite content here. If I escape with you I'd be a wanted man. All of the authorities would be after me. And you know my writings, I have only sought changes legally. No violence."

"As you have written for how many years now. And nothing. It is time to act. And if we must spill blood, so be it."

"What chance do you have?" Jose asked. "Peasants with bolos against armed Spanish troops."

"You know how weak Spain is now. Their empire is teetering on collapse. All of Spain's colonies in the Americas have fought for their freedom and now Cuba joins us in the struggle. The Americans are providing funds for the Cuban fight."

"But where are our friends. I'm afraid we are quite alone."

There was a pause between the two men as each thought carefully, the impasse in their actions evident. Andres spoke first.

"I shouldn't be telling you this. But under the circumstances I have no alternative," Andres said.

"The maybe you shouldn't speak."

"No, no. It is very important. The Katipunan has sent a delegation to the Emperor Meiji of Japan. We will be asking for funds and military supplies to continue the struggle."

"And who is to say in helping us that we won't trade one imperialist for another. Spain versus Japan as our overlords. What's the difference?"

"Maybe the world will take exception to Japan moving on our islands. Its a chance. And any chance is better then another three hundred years of Spain ruling us."

Jose thought of what his friend spoke. Yes, any alternative was preferable to Spain continuing its hold on his country. With another change, who could tell where things would take the Philippines. Jose even had dreams of Germany being involved in the Philippines.

He had raised a German flag over a hill in Manila a few years back just for that idea.

But to join the revolution fully meant being hunted. The authorities would turn the islands upside down to locate and execute him. As a writer and a doctor, he preferred his place in detention. He had freedom to teach at his school and tend his patients, all he really wanted to do in life. He sadly declined the offer of his friend. The two stood and said their goodbyes as Andres started his long journey back to Manila. They would not meet again.

* * *

It had ended up being an eighteen month project completing his grant for the United States government. Starting his photo assignment in October meant winter soon hit. Alex took the train back East to await spring weather. He developed the pictures he had taken and made enlargements but kept them safely in Worcester until his completion.

Once the snow melted and the spring floods subsided, he was back in the Pacific Northwest making his way to northern Idaho. After photographing the tribes in the Cour de Alene area, Alex headed south to Lewiston. Located where the Snake and Clearwater Rivers merge, as the former state capital before losing the title to Boise, Lewiston sat near the gold fields just north of town.

Alex headed east up the Clearwater to the land of the Nez Perce tribe. One of his assjgments to film, he was excited to be among the Nez Perce. During the winter he had had time to read up on the tribes he was filming and grew to admire their fight for freedom. The Nez Perce had put up one of the more memorable fights.

After Idaho, Alex had journeyed to the other tribes of the Walla Council, the Yakima, Umatilla and Walla Walla. Finished with his photography, he packed up his cases and headed back to Washington D. C. Turning in one hundred of his most epic shots, Walter Meyer raved at the quality and the majesty of the images Alex had produced.

Receiving his final payment, Alex soon headed west and caught a passenger ship headed to Hawaii. A short visit and some captured images of Oahu, Alex boarded a second ship headed to Manila.

Arriving in May of 1896, Alex made arrangements for passage to Dapitan. In his correspondence with Jose he knew of his friends exile. Knowing the language he quickly made passage to Mindanao Island. Standing at the wharf as he stepped off the boat, he asked the way to Dr. Rizal. A man with a caribou pulling a wheeled cart loaded up his luggage and slowly made his way to Dr. Rizal school. As the cart rolled to a stop, Jose stepped out onto the veranda and greeted his friend.

"I heard you were coming," Jose said.

"How ever?" Alex asked as he shoved himself off his perch on the cart.

"A runner beat you here with the news of a white man asking for me. A man with a tripod, all though they didn't call it that. I knew it could only be you."

"I did write you that I was coming," Alex said.

"I haven't received it yet. Mail can be rather slow out here in the provinces. But it is better to have you in person. Lets get you out of the sun and settled."

After embracing, the two men carried Alex's gear into Jose's house and dropped it in a bedroom. The room was small and sparse, a single twin bed in one corner, a wooden chair in another. The window in the grass thatchcd wall had no glass, just an opening. Alex dug in his luggage and pulled out a mosquito net.

"We will set that up after. First we shall eat my friend. You must be hungry."

The two men took up spots at a table under the open sided grass roofed hut. A woman brought food and drinks out and set them down on the table.

"So tell me, what motivated you to travel all this way. It can't be just to see me."

"Jose, when I heard the authorities had exiled you I knew I had to be here. If nothing else to photograph where you are being held. But I have to admit I was expecting something . . ."

"A little more harsh?" Jose asked.

"Well, yes, I guess," Alex said.

"No, this is quite pleasant. I have my school and my medical practice. The locals feel very honored to have me in their midst. The Spanish generally leave me alone as long as I stay put."

"I am happy for you then. I was very concerned."

"And here is my other joy," Jose said as a tall white woman with auburn hair walked into the compound from town. She carried two sacks with what appeared to be vegetables protruding from the top. Jose waved her over to where they sat. "Alex, my friend, I'd like you to meet my wife, Josephine."

Alex stood, a bit in shock. None of Jose's letters mentioned a wife. And certainly not such a beauty as the one walking up to him. Formal introductions finished, the three sat, Jose and Josephine close to each other on one side of the table.

"You never said anything in your letters," Alex said.

"Well, you know how love goes. I wasn't sure it would last and then when it did I became embarrassed that I hadn't said anything sooner. I apologize."

"No need to apologize. I'm just happy for you both. How and where? Tell me everything."

Jose told of meeting Josephine in Hong Kong when she brought her blind father in to his office. Many visits later found them in love and wanting marriage. Because of Rizal's writings the local priest would not marry so Jose's mother suggested a civil marriage. They had had a son who had died soon after birth.

"I'm so sorry to hear, " Alex said. "I know you would be wonderful parents."

Josephine finally talked and spoke of how often her husband commented on his famous photographer friend in America. "Did you bring your camera?"

"Yes, its in the house but I don't know how famous I am. But I'd like to move around the islands and record Philippine life. Jose, you never would guess what my last work was?"

"I got that letter. How I envy you working amongst the Indians of your country. Los Bravos Indians for real. How was it?"

Alex had written when he first got his assignment form Walter Meyer. Obviously his later letters had not arrived yet describing the conditions he found the tribes living.

"It was very sad to see them in the state the government has left them. Living in squalor on their reservations. I hope I captured a little of their suffering in my photos. I did my best."

"I'm sure you did my friend. You have a good heart my Los Bravos Indian."

The conversation stopped as the three sat quiet, thinking. Josephine spoke next.

"You didn't say how long you'd be with us?"

"How long will you have me?" Alex said.

"As long as you want," Jose said. "You can join me in exile here from your own country."

The two men laughed a bit at the comment but Alex knew that there was a certain truth to the statement. Alex had come away with contempt for his own government at what he had witnessed.

"It's like my own country," Josephine said. "I'm Irish and the British have tried to kill off the natives for decades. They put their big estates of transplanted English in our midst and watch us die of starvation."

Alex knew the starving the Irish had endured as they all fled the troubles in their home country and settled in the United States. He had see the discrimination they had been subjected to by the Americans as hordes of immigrants took low paying jobs and packed into substandard housing. While most seemed glad to be away from Ireland, Alex wasn't sure that America had been much better for them.

"Dr. Rizal," a young filipina dressed in a nurses outfit said. "Edgardo is struggling. Could you please check him?"

"Alex, excuse me. Duty calls." Jose stood and followed the young woman into the clinic nearby. Alex's gaze never left the two of them, Josephine noticing the interest her guest showed.

"Her name is Donita," Josephine said. "She's one of Jose's nurses. She has been with him since he first arrived here. First as an English student, and then learning nursing."

"She's very beautiful." Was all Alex could get out. He turned his head to Josephine as he felt his face grow hot. Embarrassed, he knew the redness would be showing.

"Yes she is," Josephine said. "She came to Jose from Cebu, just north of here. Her father is a fisherman and checks in with her when he makes his way down to Mindanao looking for a catch."

"But her appearance is very different then the other filipinas I have seen."

Josephine offered her explanation as she had learned of the Philippine islands. Located off the coast of South East Asia, Chinese people to the north and Malay people to the south, it had been a mixing pot of blood from both ethnic groups for centuries. The Malay had more of a square flat face while the Chinese generally had rounded features. The most beautiful woman in the islands had a mixture of the two, each blood modifying the strong traits of each. She further explained that added in the mix was three hundred years of Spanish blood, adding European features and blending them with the other two.

"I had no idea," Alex said.

"Well, legend has it that there is a lot of influence form the east also, the scattered islands between here and Polynesia. So add in that mixture, if true."

"You can't argue with the results."

"There is even an island just north of here. You must have crossed it on your way down, Negros. They are mostly gone now but the people historically on the island were black skinned."

"And all the languages. From my time with the Los Bravos Indians in Paris I learned Cebuano. Jose had taught me Tagalog. But I know there are many more languages here."

"More then I can comprehend. I just rely on Jose," Josephine said.

"Its as if all the American Indian tribes had flourished instead of dying from disease. If the Indians were the dominate population with a smattering of European interspersed then America would be a polyglot of languages, worse then the Philippines."

"I suppose you are right. I had never thought of that," Josephine said. She then excused herself and disappeared into the clinic. A few minutes later the woman that had drawn Alex's gaze emerged and walked over to him.

"Josephine asked me to come over and introduce myself. I'm Donita Calvero."

A little embarrassed, Alex stammered a bit. "Miss Calvero. I am happy to make your acquaintance. I'm Alexander Dull, but please call me Alex. Have you eaten lunch yet? Perhaps I can see if there is something for you."

"No thank you sir. Josephine tells me you are a famous photographer."

"i am a photographer, but I think the famous part is a bit premature," Alex said. "Would you like me to take your picture?" He immediately felt stupid asking, ashamed he resorted to his standard meeting offer for women.

"Yes please. My family misses me in Cebu and they would very much like a picture of me to remind them while I'm gone."

"Whenever you have time Miss Calvero."

"Donita if you will, Mr. Dull."

"Alex sounds better Donita."

"OK Alex."

Chapter 9

Cebu City, Philippines
August, 1896

A steam launch slipped past Bohol Island as it cruised north through the Cebu Strait. The weather had been pleasant since leaving Dapitan and Alex stood at the rail watching the jungle covered hills of Bohol pass. He turned to his left and saw the outline of Cebu Island. He carried his full photographic gear as he didn't know if he'd be returning to Dapitan.

Jose had received permission a few days earlier to make his way to the island of Cuba and tend to the victims of a yellow fever outbreak ravishing the island. Josephine would travel as far as Manila where she would stay with friends. She had pleaded to travel with Jose to Cuba but he had said the risk was to great.

Alex was also afraid for his friend. Yellow Fever was a unforgiving killer and willingly going into an epidemic took courage. He worried about his friend and debated what he should do. Jose had turned him down flat on his offer to travel with him. There was to much to document in his home country for Alex too leave now.

So Alex's plans had shifted to traveling through the Philippine islands recording life as he saw it. And in the two months he had been living in Dapiatn, his life had profoundly changed.

"Alex, we dock in half an hour. It is a short ride to my families home," Donita said as she walked up to him and joined him on the rail. "See that island there. That is where I live."

Donita held her arm out and pointed to an island coming into view on their side of the launch. Hazy at first, the low lying island became clearer as they moved into a narrow channel between it and Cebu Island.

"Mactan Island. We live in Lapu-Lapu City. It sits on the other side of the island. My father keeps his fishing boat there."

Alex and Donita had become very close in the two moths they had known each other and Alex's thought were of speaking to her father when they met. He knew he loved her and didn't see the nine year difference in their ages a problem. Jose had told him that in the Philippines age differences didn't come into love interests. But he needed to talk to Donita about things first.

Jose walked up and took a spot on the other side of Alex. At his arrival Donita excused herself and stepped inside the cabin. Things had been difficult between the nurse and her doctor ever since Jose had said no to her traveling with him to Cuba. Alex had been glad when Jose had said no to her nursing the yellow fever victims.

"Have you asked Donita yet?" Jose asked.

"No. Maybe tonight."

"Don't worry. Marriage isn't so bad. But we have known some women in our days, haven't we?"

Alex smiled at their escapades in Paris. He and Jose certainly had taken their pleasure with the locals and he knew Jose had continued with such things with the women of Hong Kong. While photography could attract women, being a doctor was even a bigger draw. That his friend had finally settled down to married life at the age of thirty five still amazed him.

"I figure if you can find happiness with one one woman, I guess I can also," Alex said.

"Donita is a very caring person who will take good care of you," Jose said.

The two men smiled at the statement at all it implied. The ship eased along side the wharf and slowed to a stop.

"But be aware what all filipinas want."

Alex laughed, "I already know. Lots of children.

* * *

The friends parted company two days later, Jose and Josephine on the steamer that would take them to Manila. There Jose would take passage on an ocean passenger ship that would take him to Barcelona, Spain. From there he would find his way to Havana, Cuba. Josephine remaining in Manila to await his return.

Alex and Donita had sent them off to tears and good byes, knowing the risk Jose was headed to. They had then rented a carriage that took them to the ferry to Mactan Island. There they rented another carriage to Lapu-Lapu City to the family compound of Felipe

Calavero. The couple was mobbed by family members as soon as someone spotted them arriving. Suddenly the dirt street swarmed with a hundred relatives, all speaking at once.

A man stepped forward and introduced himself. He spoke Cebuano. Alex didn't miss a beat in answering him back in his native language. "It is nice to meet you Mr. Calavero. Your daughter speaks of you all the time."

Felipe stood still as the entire crowd stopped speaking. That a westerner spoke Cebuano was a new experience for them. Even seeing a westerner on their part of Mactan Island was rare. Only in Cebu City did one see a Westerner, and then typically Spanish. That an American spoke their language had them stymied.

Donita spoke up. "Come on every body. Yes, Alex speaks Cebuano. So be careful what you say." She laughed as it was common when they saw a westerner in Cebu City they could say all sorts of thing about them safe in the knowledge that they wouldn't be understood.

At her encouragement, everyone spoke at once, overwhelming Alex. He held up his hands in protest. "One at at time."

"How old are you?" some cousin asked.

Alex had already learned since his time with Donita that this was the main interest. He had soon switched to asking them back how old they thought he was. Since their answer typically had him in his twenties, he would agree that they were close and leave it a that.

Alex had talked to Donita the night after their arrival in Cebu City and she had encouraged him to speak to her father. Asking Felipe to sit and have a coffee together, Alex asked for Donita's hand in marriage and received a warm agreement. Soon a marriage ceremony was being planed until Alex got the bad news.

Since the Catholic Church held sway over the entire Philippines, he would need to convert in order to be married. While he had attended a catholic college mainly to be close to home, he had been raised as a Lutheran. He felt that switching religions took something away from his life, even though he hadn't attended church in many years.

Donita didn't seem particularly religious. He had never seen her go to church while in Dapitan nor had she ever spoken of her religious beliefs. That night as they lay in bed under the mosquito net they spoke of their options.

"Donita, I just feel strange taking on a religion I don't believe in just to marry you. It seems sacrilegious that I am extorted into a religion where I don't really want to be."

"Then don't. It is fine with me," Donita said.

"But I want to make an honest woman of you. And our children need parents that are married. I'll have no bastards in my family."

"We can have a civil service. It is done here frequently. The Catholic Church is dominate of course, but not every one is a member."

"If that is OK with your family. We could be formally married in my church when we get to someplace that has one. Do you mind?"

"Alex, the priests run things in this country as much as the Spanish. They have done so for the entire time since they arrived. The Katipunan fight is as much against the church as it is against the Spanish."

It was the first time Alex had heard Donita refer to the revolutionary Katipunan. Such talk was dangerous and he began to wonder where her allegiances were. Being with Dr. Rizal certainly tagged her as Jose's writings were the basis of the revolution. But he had assumed she was just a nurse. Now, he began to wonder.

"Donita, may I ask something?"

"You want to know if I'm part of the Katipunan?"

"Yes," Alex said, nervous at the answer.

"I agree with Dr. Rizal on a peaceful changes within legal means. No violence."

"Thats good to hear."

"But Alex, even that attitude can get you arrested here. Just look at Dr. Rizal's exile."

Donita's words would be prophetic as events turned out. Upon reaching Barcelona, Jose was arrested and shipped back to Manila the next day. Word didn't reach Cebu until the ship had docked in Manila. Word spread quickly through the islands that Dr. Rizal was imprisoned at Fort Santiago. As soon as Alex received word, he and Donita were on the next boat to Manila.

Reaching Manila, Alex had Donita stay with friends while he made his way to the fort. There he found out Jose was on trial for rebellion and sedition. He located the court and used his Tagolog to gain entrance to the trial. Jose perked up seeing his friend in the audience when the jailers brought him in. He smiled at his friend as he sat down in front of the judge.

Alex spent the next three days witnessing a travesty of justice. Jose issued a manifesto disavowing the revolution and spoke in court of his noninvolvement with the current rebellion. The court read some of his writings and the judge took them as proof of Jose's involvement in the troubles.

Governor General Ramon Blanco had been sympathetic to Jose's position and had approved his traveling to Cuba but had been forced out of power. The Archbishop of Manila had pressured the Queen Regent Maria Cristina of Spain to appoint Camilo de Polavieja Governor-General which doomed Jose.

The court ordered Jose to be executed by firing squad. Alex left in tears as his friend was escorted from the courtroom. He received a letter from Jose a few days later explaining that Jose was content with his position and to not worry.

Chapter 10

London, England
June 22, 1897

The weather held threats of rain on this auspicious day as hundreds of thousand of excited people stood waiting. Seated in a reserved grandstand in front of St. Paul's Cathedral, the dignitaries waited for the official start to the celebration. Today the mighty British Empire would rejoice at the long reign of Queen Victoria.

At 11:15 am, the rumble of cannon firing from Hyde Park could be heard three miles away from the cathedral. Paul von Hatzfeldt, German Ambassador to Great Britain, reflexively checked his gold pocket watch and confirmed British punctuality. Seated around him were the various ambassadors of the other countries with embassies in London. As the largest empire on Earth, nearly every country had a representative in London. He noticed the Japanese ambassador two rows below him.

Looking in the direction of Fleet Street, Paul heard the procession before he saw it. As the marching bands trooped into view the crowd broke into singing "God Save the Queen". A phalanx of soldiers stood the length of parade route, their gleaming bayonets suddenly glittering as the sun broke through the overcast. As if clouds were willed away, the day grew sunny as uniformed men of various dominions marched by Paul's stand.

Carriage after carriage soon followed with the heads of the various Dominions riding past the cathedral, each leader dressed in their resplendent bright uniforms, medals flashing. Paul counted seventeen carriages until the royal carriage with the queen arrived.

Dressed in her perpetual black in mourning for her dead husband, now gone thirty six years, the seventy eight year old monarch sat in an open carriage with a parasol for protection from the sun. The carriage stopped directly in front of the cathedral as the Archbishop of Canterbury began the service of celebration.

Paul knew the queen's health precluded her from climbing the steps into the cathedral so the decision to perform the service outdoors, the queen siting in her carriage. The crowds looked on as the choir sang and the eulogies were read. After twenty minutes, the archbishop shouted, "Three cheers for the queen."

The crowd complied as they yelled in unison. The queen could be seen wiping tears from her eyes as the procession resumed its six mile route. As the last marching unit disappeared around the corner, Paul stood and made his way to the Japanese ambassador.

"Ambassador Shuzo, so good to see you."

"Ambassador von Hatzfeldt, a very moving tribute to the queen, don't you think?"

"Yes, I just wish our monarchs could have attended." Paul made reference to the fact that the British government had purposely not invited any other head of state to the celebration. Only the heads of state of her possessions were invited: New Zealand, Australia, South Africa, Canada and of course India being the most notable. Word had been whispered that the other monarchs of Europe had been excluded to avoid any conflict between the Queen and Kaiser Wilhelm II of Germany, her grandson.

Germany's continuance in expanding its empire in the world had been noticed in London. And the increasing size of the Imperial German Fleet had been watched carefully in London. Britain had always held as a policy that no one nation on the European continent should become too powerful. Spain followed by France had been the focus of British concern in the past. Germany now grew its scrutiny.

"Ambassador," Paul continued. "I wondered if we could meet in the next week to discuss a mutual issue our nations might agree on."

"Certainly Ambassador, would Wednesday be too early. I have a trip to Paris planned at the end of the week."

"That would be perfect. Might I suggest meeting at Friedrich House. Lunch?" Paul asked. Friedrich House was a small estate owned by the German delegation, an easy train ride to the Wembley section of the city.

"I'll see you then."

Paul stood as the Japanese Ambassador stepped down off the stand, greeting other dignitaries as he left. The seeds that Paul had planted some years back just might sprout after all. He smiled at the opportunities he felt just might come to Germany.

The rain had returned in force by Wednesday and Paul had the staff ready with umbrellas for his important guest. Seeing a carriage winding up the gravel driveway to Friedrich House he hustled two servants out the front door to met the Japanese Ambassador as he stood sentential in the front door waiting. Ambassador Shuzo stepped quickly as one servant held the protection from the heavy downpour. The two met just inside the doorway, both bowing slightly in Japanese greeting, before shaking hands European style.

"Typical English weather, Aoki," Paul said. He knew the man from when Aoki had been on the Japanese legation to Germany in 1873. Paul had been a junior diplomat then but had learned a smattering of Japanese. More importunely he had learned the Japanese way of doing things and the differences with European customs.

A servant took the ambassador's heavy overcoat and hat as Paul led him into a side dining room. A fire in the fireplace warmed the room from the wet chill outside and added to the atmosphere. Portraits of famous Germans lined the room projecting Germany's standing in the world. All for show to opposing powers.

"I do miss the summer weather in Tokyo, Paul."

"And I Berlin. But we do our best for our monarchs and accept our station."

Aoki recognized the Japanese cultural reference Paul had made to accepting ones position. He bowed at the courtesy as Paul directed him to a seat at the end of the table near the fire.

"Please. Perhaps drinks before we eat?"

Aoki nodded agreement and Paul reached for a red wine on the side board. He poured two gasses and handed one to Aoki. "To Emperor Mieji, long may he reign."

The men raised their glasses and drank to the Japanese Emperor.

"To Kaiser Wilhelm II, may he led Germany with wisdom and grace," Aoki said.

The two raised their glasses again to toast the German monarch before the two men sat down. First discussed was Japan's recent war with China. Paul passed on praise at the success of the Japanese forces in routing Imperial China. He knew he was treading on delicate matters as Germany had joined with Russia and France in the Tripartite Intervention after Japan had won the war.

Upon occupying Port Arthur, the Russians took exception to Japanese forces occupying the city. Japan had gained complete control of the Korean Peninsular and the island of what was now called Formosa. With three European powers arrayed against it, Japan backed off and relinquished Port Arthur back to the Chinese in leu of a larger cash indemnity.

126

Paul was aware that the Japanese had tried to enlist help from the British and Americans but neither power would become involved. Russia soon took advantage of a weak China and had occupied Port Arthur and were now fortifying the city.

Germany had gained concessions in Shandong Province from the Chinese as well as France and Britain also gaining concessions. That Japanese blood had been spilt while the Europeans took full advantage would affect future Japanese action.

The Sino-Japanese War sent shock waves throughout the world as the first Asian country to defeat another in a western style war. The other world powers took notice.

"I want to express my personal position that I was against Germany's involvement with the Russians," Paul said. He used his best diplomatic face to say it in hopes that his true feelings didn't show. Of course Paul was glad that Germany had finally gotten land on Mainland China to build a naval base and set up a trading port. But he fully understood Japanese sensibilities that how it had come about would set Japan on a path of not trusting the European powers ever again.

The Japanese would do what they needed to do to consolidate their new imperial gains and get ready to strike again. He was certain of that.

"Thank you Paul," Aoki said. He offered nothing more. Lunch arrived and spared the two speaking of the subject again. Talk shifted to the food as idle chit chat followed as they ate. Finishing, a servant poured more wine and withdrew, leaving the two men alone.

"Aoki, I wanted to meet with you on an entirely different subject. I am aware of your country's feelings over the Hawaiian Islands. That the Americans set up a coup to overthrow the queen and are now arguing about annexing the islands was a bit of a shock to us."

"Yes. And to us also," Aoki said. "We have interest in the islands as well and were rather shoved aside in our complaints over what transpired."

"It would appear that the United Sates is moving out into the world. This may be just their first step."

"I agree. And with the European powers grabbing everything they can, it is becoming difficult to know where each of our spheres of influence are."

Paul nodded agreement. "Exactly our feeling. Germany came late to the game and view another power getting involved as a competitor. That they didn't interceded on your behalf when the Russians pressured you seems to mean they are picking sides."

Aoki nodded and sipped his wine. Paul knew he was waiting for the real reason of the meeting. Two up and coming powers, Germany and Japan, struggling for space and colonies in the world. *Now with the Americans maneuvering for their share* Paul thought.

Paul continued. "And now Cuba. This McKinley fellow seems to be an imperialist at heart. He lets his citizens raise money in support of the Cuban Revolution and does nothing. A slap at Spain if you ask me. The United States has always had designs on the island of Cuba. I have read their history and as far back as their own revolution they had Cuba in their sights."

"Are your sources saying Spain may be in open conflict with the United Sates soon?" Aoki asked.

"They have a strong anti-imperialist faction in their government. Annexing Hawaii is a very contentious topic in their Congress right now. I'm not sure which way the government will turn. But suppose the Americans do attack Spain in Cuba. Do you feel they will stop there?"

Aoki took on a white complexion as he contemplated the question. Finally he asked, "Do you believe they would attack the Philippines?"

"They have their Asiatic Fleet. And currently they have no home port in East Asia to base it. It would be very advantageous of them to control Manila. Add in the Spanish island of Guam and they have a perfect support route right into China. And we have all read Admiral Mahan discourse on sea power. I don't think they would pass up an opportunity they may soon find themselves with."

Silence followed as both diplomats contemplated what a bold move by the Americans meant for their countries fortunes. The European and the Japanese were maneuvering for land, and now to have the Americans shoving their way onto the scene complicated the great game.

When the Japanese had backed down in the face of the three power threat it was all about tonnage. The Japanese fleet totaled thirty one warships with 57,000 tons. Russia, France and Germany had thirty eight warships already deployed in east Asia with a total tonnage of 98,000 tons. A two to one advantage to the Europeans meant Japan had to concede some of her gains. But Paul knew that disadvantage would be even more so with the American warships included. If he could offer Japan a friend in the equation, maybe he could succeed.

"Aoki, I can tell you that Germany has made diplomatic inquires to Spain about selling an island to us."

The Japanese ambassador sat up and stared at the news. The secret talks between agents of Germany and Spain had yet to produce any response by the Queen Regent, but Paul knew the seeds had been set in Madrid. Whenever Spanish pride was sufficiently humbled things might open up.

"Any response?" Aoki asked.

"Not at this time. But its an ongoing discussion," Paul lied slightly. Things had been quiet with all his sources to Madrid on the matter.. "But if things develop as we are discussing, I don't think Spain would last long against the Americans. Things may happen fast in the near future."

"What are Germany's intentions then?"

"I'm not at liberty to say. But we are very determined that if the Americans move on the Philippines, they will not have a free hand."

"And you tell me this because?"

"The Philippines has many islands. We only want a few of them. We are not greedy. If the Americans attack, they will certainly attack Manila. The

Spanish fleet is there as well as their garrison. We are content to let the Americans occupy Luzon Island. But beyond that, I think there are many islands for others."

Aoki's eyes grew wide at what he assumed was being proposed. "And are you offering an alliance to divide up the remaining islands?"

"Your fleet is the largest single fleet in east Asia. The British are second. If the Americans do what we think they will, a combined German Japanese fleet would force their hand. Just as you were out tonnaged in your conflict with the Russians, the Americans would be outclassed by our combined fleet."

"Is the Kaiser ready to put more assets into east Asia. I ask because the German East Asia fleet would be a junior partner in such an endeavor."

Paul knew that Japan at present would be the senior partner for any adventure in the Philippines. While Germany stationed protected cruisers in the waters, they had not committed any of its Imperial battleships.'

"You will need to watch for developments soon. That will tell you our level of commitment. And as we know, don't believe the news reports," Paul said. He smiled at the diplomatic inside joke that public news reports were hardly ever the real news.

Chapter 11

Berlin, Germany
July, 1897

After his meeting with the Japanese Ambassador in Great Britain, Paul von Hatzfeldt took the next train to Dover where he boarded a ferry to France. A second train had him on his way to Berlin and a meeting with the German Foreign Minister. He had sent a cable before leaving London to arrange a high level meeting in two days.

The next day he made his way to the Foreign Ministry building and an early morning meeting with his boss. As Ambassador to Great Britain, Paul held the number one diplomatic post in Imperial Germany. Good relations between the two empires was vital as Germany moved into the colonial world. Playing catchup to the British Empire took finesse and conviction, both attributes Paul held.

"I know you have been working on this Philippine thing for some time Paul. Do the Japanese seem interested?" The German Foreign Minister asked.

"They didn't come out and actually agree to a power sharing in case the Americans made a move on Manila, but he implied that they would certainly be open to such an alliance."

"And you've worked with the ambassador before? He can be trusted. This is a huge step that may lead to war between Germany and the United States."

"I am aware of the dangers sir. But I am equally aware of the opportunities that might arise. It is a once in a lifetime chance at acquiring strategic assets in Asia."

"I agree. I will call the Chancellor to brief him. Are you available this afternoon?"

"Yes, Minister."

Late that afternoon Paul and the Foreign Minister met with Germany's Chancellor. The meeting went well and at Paul's urging that speed was critical, the Chancellor contacted the Kaiser and asked for a meeting the next day.

Kaiser Wilhelm II sat and listened as Paul laid out his actions in attempting to acquire an island in the Philippines for a naval base and trading port. When he reached the point in his presentation of his meeting with the Japanese, the Kaiser took on a more focused expression. When finished, the Kaiser asked.

"Do we really need to involve the Japanese?"

"Majesty. If the United States moves on Manila, Spain will loose. Our ships have done courtesy calls to the Philippines and report weak forces arrayed there. The American squadron as it exists in east Asia will beat the Spanish fleet," Paul said.

The Chancellor added, "Your Majesty. The Japanese were embarrassed by our action joining Russia to remove them from Port Arthur. We are complicit in the Russians subsequently occupying Port Arthur. Taking joint action in the Philippines will place us in good relations again with the Japanese."

"And that is important? Why?" the Kaiser asked.

The Foreign Minister spoke, "Majesty. The British and the Japanese grow closer each year. They are negotiating new treaties as we speak. Japan is a rising power in Asia as witnessed by their defeat of China in their war. Germany would do well in courting an ally in those waters. And pushing a wedge between Great Britain and Japan in the process.

"I see," the Kaiser said. "Ambassador, you have had no word on our offer to purchase a concession from the Spanish?"

"None as of yet," Paul said. "Spanish pride is very strong and I didn't expect an agreement. But if a war should take the territory away, Spain would be open to a cash settlement in giving its rights away."

The Kaiser sat and processed what Paul had said. "So you believe the Americans would not force us out of the Philippines once we were there if the Japanese were also involved? And when Spain loses, we would be at the negotiating table parceling up the islands three ways."

"Yes your Majesty." Paul said. "We three get what we want with no bloodshed. Except for the American blood they might shed defeating the Spanish."

"Is our East Asian Squadron strong enough to deter the Americans then?" the Kaiser asked.

The Chancellor added, "No your majesty. We met with the Kreigsmarine Commander this morning for his assessment of what assets we would need to have in place if you approve this action. We need to act soon if those forces are to reach east Asian waters in time. It is at least a six month transit, if the British give us permission to use the Suez Canal."

They turned to their British Ambassador. Paul said. "Before I left I did check with Whitehall over a goodwill tour we were contemplating. They seemed agreeable to a transit by our warships. We would just have to do a formal request through their embassy here."

"Well, gentlemen, I have much to think about," the Kaiser said. "We will see where this may lead."

Paul left the meeting and was told by the Foreign Minister to stay in Berlin a few days. He knew the Kaiser would discuss what had been presented with his royal advisors and reach a decision.

Paul would be tied to Berlin for two extra weeks until finally called into the Foreign Ministry. He discovered a royal party would board a train for Wilhemshaven, home port for the Imperial German Navy. Things had moved fast since the Kaiser's first meeting and Paul found out on the train just how quickly things came together.

Prince Henry of Prussia, the Kaiser's younger brother, would be in nominal command of the squadron heading east. Labeled a good will tour of the globe, Germany would be sending two of its newest battleships around the world, calling at various ports of call. The first stops were scheduled for Bombay, India, Columbo, Ceylon, Singapore, Manila, Philippines and on to Tokyo.

For public consumption the press was handed a full list of ports that included Seattle and San Francisco in the United States, followed by a stop at Valparaiso, Chile, Buenos Aires, Argentina, Rio de Janeiro, Brazil and finally a stop in New York City before the squadron's return to Germany.

Everyone involved in the operation knew that the tour after Tokyo was a ruse. The battleships along with two protected cruisers and two light cruiser were to linger in east Asia in anticipation of American action. At the first sign of war, they were to descend on the Philippines Islands and secure preselected islands for Germany.

Japan, seeing the battleships committed by Germany, was expected to sally forth with its own squadron, possibly headed by its own battleships. With the Americans outgunned, they would be forced to accept the spilt of the Philippines or risk open warfare with two of the great powers.

The Kaiser's party moved by carriage and then by royal barge to the Kaiser's flagship, the newly commissioned SMS *Kaiser Wilhelm II* anchored in the roadstead. Signal flags flew up the halyards as the party took a spot on the open bridge. The Kaiser gave the Kreigsmarine Commanding Admiral orders to initiate operations. Soon ships could be seen emerging from the naval base, two large battleships at the fore.

With binoculars Paul could make out Prince Henry in his admiral's uniform standing on the bridge next to the fleet's admiral. While Prince Henry was in overall command, an experienced admiral would control the ships movements in a tactical command.

SMS Brandenburg belched black smoke as the battleship increased speed leading the squadron. At over 10,000 tons displacement and burnishing six eleven inch guns as well as smaller caliber weapons, the war ship represented Germany's move to world greatness. Following came the sister ship, *SMS Kurfurst Fiedrich Wilhelm*, commissioned the same year with similar characteristics. While not the newest of Germany's battleships, they had been in commission since 1891 and had proven trouble free after their initial sea trials worked out construction problems.

The Kreigsmarine was confident they would make the long trip with a minimum of problems. In line with the squadron leader, the two protected cruisers followed in line, *SMS Hertha* and *SMS Frey*a, sister ships fresh from sea trials. Displacing 5,000 tons, the two ships each carried fourteen six inch guns and although newly commissioned in 1897, the Kreigsmarine wanted to test the construction of such new ships. A long ocean voyage would be an extreme test for a new ship.

The final two warships, *SMS Condor* and *SMS Geier* were unprotected cruisers with 2,000 tons displacement and armed with eight four inch guns. Slowest of the six ships at 15 knots, the light cruisers were three and five years old and should be trouble free. Finally the support ships passed the review as the Kaiser saluted each ships colors.

The squadron contained two supply ships and a collier for keeping coal flowing to the moving fleet. While each port would provide coaling stations, an auxiliary ship allowed the squadron to operate away from such stations if needed.

Not in review but as explained to Paul by the Chancellor were four troop ships that were slowly moving across the Heligoland Bight to meet up with the squadron. Formed up in Kiel, Germany's other naval base on the Baltic Sea, the ships had transited the newly completed Kiel Canal and would join the squadron for the voyage east.

Paul was told the troops ships carried regular Imperial soldiers and the First Seebataillon based in Kiel. With its support marines, the 1st Seebataillon comprised over one thousand men of the eight thousand total troops on the four ships. When asked about questions that might arise why Germany was sending troop ships east it was related that trouble in the German colony of New Guinea required more troops to suppress.

* * *

Unknown to the Germans at the time but fully anticipated, the world capitals of the Great Powers were soon abuzz with news of a strong German Squadron setting sail for east Asia. The ships would attract constant attention as they made their way east and the first reports of the German squadron transiting the Suez Canal.

Permission had been obtained and each of the other powers had agents ready to count ships and report their passage. The troop ships came as a surprise to all but the British who had previously approved of them. But the British Admiralty sent cables to all their posts to be on the lookout for German ships and to report time and location as seen.

In Washington D.C. the United Staes navy took notice. Germany had never committed battleships to Asia before. Only Britain and Japan held such sizable warships in the area and the British only limited in number. They typically stationed two older battleship to their China Station while Singapore might have a battleship on station occasionally.

So if the Germans were to be believed that this constituted a goodwill cruise, the troop ships spoke otherwise. No news of conflict came out of German New Guinea and the other powers smelled a ruse, leaving the world to wonder what Germany was up to.

Various countries' agents in Japan noticed no unusually activity with the Imperial Japanese fleet. But if they had been more careful in their observation they would have seen an increased training regime taking place. It had coincided with the Germany's squadron leaving Wihlemhasven.

Japanese officials had noted Germany's first move in acquiring Philippine territory which confirmed what Ambassador Shuzo had reported in the diplomatic cable. Written in code, the Japanese Prime Minister had ben made aware of Germany's quiet offer of an alliance and now the proof of Germany's commitment was at hand. The Japanese would be ready.

Spain, the target of the world powers, took no notice of a German squadron sailing. Deep into a rebellion in both Cuba and the Philippines, Spain bled the death of a thousand cuts. The Queen Regent sat frozen in time as her young son grew to take over the duties of monarch. But at age seven, while he had many years to mature to the task, Spain itself did not. Time quickly ran out on the Spanish Empire as the wolves closed in.

* * *

The slow passage of the German ships allowed time to pass and most people's interest to wain. Month after slow month the ships moved from one port call to anther. The first of the year found the ships anchoring off the city of Singapore. The admiral ordered all coal bunkers filled before any shore leave was permitted.

The thousands of troops bottled up on the four ships had been lessened after Bombay with two thousand of the men transferred to berths on the war ships. It made the warships crowded but eased the load on the troop ships. The troops on the ships were issued shore leave on a staggered basis after coaling was completed. This kept the deluge in each port reasonable and the locals happy. Sailors were also given shore leave to experience the shore facilities of the British trading port.

On board, Prince Henry read over his cables from Berlin. The German consulate in Singapore acted as the base of operations for the visiting squadron. Believing it a goodwill tour, the consulate arranged dinners with local dignitaries on each battleship.

Prince Henry was the talk of the town as very few European royals made their way this far east. Tonight he would be entertaining the British admiral and five of his officers. The prince finished his report and called for his flag lieutenant who would take the report to the consulate for coding and transmitting.

At precisely the time *SMS Brandenburg* rang two bells, a launch flying the union jack swung into the side of the ship. Stairs with a landing platform had been provided and the British Admiral stepped lively from the launch and climbed the stairs. Reaching the top he saluted the German ensign flying on the battleships stern and then turned to salute Prince Henry.

The prince returned the salute and welcomed his counterpart aboard his ship. The five staff officers followed suit as the prince led the men to a room off the flag stateroom. He offered refreshments before saying, "Admiral Wilson, it is an honor to have you aboard my ship. I note the Victoria Cross there. Well done sir."

"Your royal highness. It is I who am pleased to join you. We don't get many princes of any realm in these waters. My men were excited to come out and see the *Brandenburg* up close. A fine looking ship. And a type we don't see in these waters often."

Prince Henry laughed. "You mean German battleships don't you. You have such ships here regularly. Yes, a new experience for Germany."

Admiral Wilson said, "We do see the occasional Japanese battleships here abouts. In fact I've been notified to expect two within the month."

Being news to Prince Henry, he wanted more information. "What ships would those be?"

"The *Fuji* and *Yashima*, both new out of British yards are transiting home to Japan, your highness."

"Ah yes. Similar to your *Royal Sovereign* class, if I'm not mistaken."

"You highness is correct," the British admiral said. "The Japanese industrial base isn't up to building proper battleships."

Prince Henry made a mental note to cable headquarters to get an update on the transit of the Japanese warships. He needed better knowledge of where they were. Ships of that quality were a match for his two ships and any potential adversary needed watching at the moment. Prince Henry was confident he had the strongest squadron in the region. His ships outclassed the older British battle ships they kept in the area. *But two new ships of the latest British design needed watching* he thought.

As they sat down to dinner, Admiral Wilson had more news for Prince Henry. "So did you see that the Americans have installed a new commander of their Asiatic Squadron. Just got the report from Nagasaki where the squadron is presently stationed. A Commodore Dewey. Know the man?"

Dewey was new to Prince Henry. He knew the American ships were in Japanese waters but a new commander might mean changes in the United States designs in Asia. He wanted more information and connived how he might get it from Wilson. The prince didn't have anything to worry about as Admiral Wilson opened right up.

"We got the report from Washington when he was promoted by their Assistant Naval Secretary. Seems Dewey jumped many spots in the promotion list, so this Roosevelt character definitely wanted his man."

Prince Henry knew the structure of the American government. Navy Secretary Long was a bit of a hands off leader, but his assistant was everything but. Theodore Roosevelt had earned a quick reputation in the new McKinley administration as his own man. The German Embassy had posted that Roosevelt had practically ignored his boss in maneuvering Dewey to the eyes of McKinley, forcing Long to acquiesce to the President's wishes. For a royal, it all smacked of typical ways as commanders used politics for advancement.

"So, what's your measure of this Dewey?" the Prince asked.

"Civil War veteran," Admiral Wilson said, "Was at New Orleans with Farragut. Dewey was at the helm of the *USS Mississippi* taking his ship in close to shore as the squadron took on the defensive forts protecting New Orleans. He was ordered to ram a Confederate ship and ended up forcing his prey aground. As a lieutenant he fought in two other main battles earning praise from his commanders."

"Sounds like a hard charger then," the prince said. "But it might take him a while to become familiar with the ways of Asia."

"Afraid not. He was captain of the *USS Juniata*, of the Asiatic Squadron, so he has served here already. It would appear that the United Staes might be getting ready for something here about."

"Certainly not a good will tour," the prince laughed slightly at his statement and the British smiled in agreement. *Yes, the American just might be getting ready for something* the prince thought. He made the quick decision that his stay in Singapore would be longer then planned. Engine trouble in one of the new cruisers just came to his attention.

The conversation turned to normal navy talk: food, ports of call, sea conditions, ship maintenance, everything not important versus what had been discussed. The dinner finished, drinks and cigars appeared as Prince Henry, his staff and his guests all mingled amicably. Strange behavior between potential adversaries. But all routine as each side sought out information about ones intentions. Having a strong German squadron in his harbor would certainly perk a British admiral interest.

Soon, the British were escorted to their launch and Prince Henry retired to his stateroom. He had much to digest from the evenings talk. Very important information.

Chapter 12

London, England
March, 1898

Sir Edward Malet, 4th Baronet, Member of the Privy Council, rode along The Mall headed to a meeting with the Foreign Secretary. Not informed of the nature of the meeting, Sir Edward stiffened as the carriage passed Trafalgar Square with its towering obelisk to Lord Nelson. As the driver turned down Whitehall the former ambassador to Imperial Germany developed a pit in his stomach as the carriage continued to Downing Street.

Since the government had sent for him they had provided the carriage. Now finding out that the meeting would take place at the Prime Minister's residence, Sir Edward sat up and straightened his suit. He had attended plenty of important meetings being a Privy Council member, but never on a Sunday. *Very unusual* he thought.

A servant opened the door to #10 Downing Street and Sir Edward stepped into the seat of power in the British Empire. Removing his overcoat, he took the stairs up to the conference room on the second floor. The Foreign Secretary stood and greeted his friend.

"Sir Edward. I am glad you could make it on such short notice."

"Of course Foreign Secretary. What is this about?"

"You'll learn soon enough, I'm afraid."

The statement did not ease Sir Edwards stress level. He did not have time for reflection as the doors to the conference room were opened and the two men walked in. Seated at the left side of the long table, the Prime Minister looked up from his paperwork. The two men took seats across from the Prime Minister.

The Foreign Secretary said, "Lord Salisbury, I know this is highly unusual but I believe the information I have received by cable last night warrants such haste."

"And you bring Sir Edward with you," Lord Salisbury said.

"Sir Edward may be able to shed light on what is happening."

Sir Edward squirmed a bit in his seat not sure what light needed illuminating. But he had been a diplomat long enough to know how to handle such meetings.

"Please continue," Lord Salisbury said.

"Yes, my Lord. Yesterday I was handed a cable from our naval commander in Singapore. You are familiar with the good will cruise by the German Squadron having left that port a week ago. They were scheduled to visit Manila next but the Spanish withdrew their invitation due to the growing troubles in Cuba."

"Yes, I know. We think the Germans are up to something besides a good will tour. So is Hong Kong next on their stops?"

"No sir. As reported there is a bubonic plague outbreak in the city and we have closed the port to all unnecessary shipping."

"Yes, I'm aware of the outbreak. Terrible business that."

"Well, it seems our German friends have returned to Singapore," the Foreign Secretary said.

"What," the Prime Minister blurted. "Why are they back?"

"The report from the Admiral Wilson claims that they have experienced mechanical problems in one of their new cruisers. They have requested anchorage while they make repairs."

"Most unusual. Are they requesting dry-dock space?"

"No my Lord," the Foreign Secretary said. "Prince Henry has stated they carry the necessary parts on their supply ships and can make repairs while anchored."

"Sir Edward, you were with the German all those years. What do you make of this?" Lord Salisbury Asked.

"My Lord, typically ships don't make a good will tour with what we estimate to be eight thousand troops aboard. They have something else planned."

"Exactly. You were with the Germans when they offered to buy an island in the Philippines. You think that could be their purpose."

"It very well could be my Lord," Sir Edward said "Tensions are rising in Cuba after this *USS Maine* sinking. The Americans have their blood up and we have the cable that the new American Asiatic Squadron Commander has left Japan. Could he be headed to Hong Kong to join the rest of his ships?"

The Foreign Secretary added, "There is more my Lord. I hadn't passed this information to you since it is routine information. At least up until this other news arrived. The two battleships we built for Japan have arrived in Singapore this week. Just two days after a cruiser arrived from Japan with a fleet admiral on board."

Lord Salisbury sat back and took in the new information. Having four battleships plus assorted cruisers from foreign countries in a British port at one time made policy makers take notice. The nearest British ships that were somewhat comparable were in Hong Kong under quarantine. And those two ships were older versions and not in the same class as the four newer ships.

The Foreign Secretary broke his thoughts. "My Lord, the admiral seeks guidance. Do we let the Germans make repairs or send them to another port?"

"Sir Edward, your advice."

"I'm afraid we have no choice. With the Kaiser's brother in command of their squadron, to send them away would be an insult. And Imperial Germany doesn't take insults well."

"Agreed," the Prime Minister said.

"But we can make it difficult on them so they will move on. I suggest granting permission but denying shore leave. Keep the troops on board ship. That will move them along. Troops stuck on transport are bad enough when they are moving, but sitting in port looking at the city they previously had fun in will cause trouble."

"Grand idea," Lord Salisbury said.

The Foreign Secretary asked, "But what of Prince Henry and his admiral?"

"They can visit shore of course. They need to contact their consulate for news. And notify Singapore I want to know immediately when both the Japanese and the Germans leave."

"And if the Americans show up in Hong Kong?" the Foreign Secretary asked.

"Yes. I think we need to put the Admiralty on notice that something may be up. They should get our ships ready."

"Yes my Lord. Right away."

Sir Edward stood and joined the Foreign Secretary exiting the conference room. The servant shut the doors behind them as the Foreign Secretary turned to Sir Edward.

"Are the German's capable of taking the Philippines themselves?"

"Yes, they have the fire power in the squadron in Singapore already to outclass anything anyone else has in the area. Add in their East Asia Squadron in China and only the Japanese could match them and thats' if Japan commits its entire fleet."

"And if Japan and Germany work in concert?"

Neither one answered the question as they knew if the two powers worked together, nothing in east Asia could resist them. Not unless Britain quickly sent considerable assets east. And even then the six month voyage might not make a difference as things would be over by then.

* * *

Prince Henry lingered as long as he could in Singapore with his mechanical problems on one of his cruisers. After two weeks he felt he could not gain any more time and had received permission to enter the port of Batavia in the Dutch East Indies. He knew of the plague in Hong Kong and wished to avoid that problem but he also wanted to stay in the southern portion of the South China Sea.

If the Americans made their move, and all indications indicted they were preparing for action, for Germany to invade and claim the southern islands of the Philippines meant he would be closer in Batavia. And he had to have a port with good communication to Berlin so he could get his reports on any action.

The last report he had received was that the Americans had moved away from Hong Kong when the United Sates had declared war on Spain. The battleship *USS Maine* had been reported sunk in Havana Harbor in February and Prince Henry assumed that such an act by the Spanish would be caus belli for the Americans. Upon reaching Batavia, Prince Henry located the German consulate and gained the news that the American Asiatic Squadron was anchored in Mirs Bay, a Chinese anchorage near Hong Kong. The British authorities had requested the Americans leave due to neutrality rules. War between Spain and the Untied Sates had been declared on April 21st. Further news stated that the Americans had painted their warships gray, covering their peace time white colors. Subsequent reports had Commodore Dewey purchasing supply ships from the British which led the prince to assume action was imminent.

Prince Henry toured each of his warships to assure himself each was ready in case of action. Satisfied that his crews were ready, he allowed shore leave on a short term basis. He needed everyone close at hand in case they had to leave quickly. But there were also many eyes watching so a semblance of a goodwill tour had to be maintained.

On May 2 news arrived that the Americans had won a decisive victory at Manila Bay. Prince Henry ordered all shore leaves canceled and sent marines through Batavia rounding up wayward solders and sailors. A cable to Vice Admiral von Diederichs, commander of the East Asia Squadron ordered him to proceed to the mouth of Manila Bay but not to enter. They were to check the American squadron while Prince Henry brought his squadron north.

Von Diederichs commanded ships that represented a stronger force then the Americans. The German cruisers *SMS Kaiser, SMS Irene, SMS Cormoran, SMS Kaiserin Augusta* and *SMS Prinzess Wilhelm* carried a total over 25,000 tons of displacement. With that displacement came the armament and armor accorded such warships. Dewey's ships carried a total displacement of only 17,700 tons. A clear advantage to the Germans even without the two battleships and additional cruisers under Prince Henry's command.

The next day the southern squadron set out from Batavia for Cebu City in the Philippines. The Prince had met with his Japanese counterpart while they were both in Singapore. Under the guise of a evening dinner between staff, the Japanese Admiral and Prince Henry had removed themselves from the festivities on board his flagship to a quiet conference room, a detailed map of the Philippines sat on a table.

The two men discussed which islands would be under which countries' sphere influence. Leaving Luzon Island and Manila to the Americans if they made their anticipated move, Germany took the second largest city, Cebu City. The Japanese took the third most populist city, Iloilo City on Panay Island. The two men then set boundary lines between German and Japanese interests.

Since Cebu City lay in the middle of the Visaya region, the islands of Negros and Bohol would be needed along with Cebu Island to protect the shipping lanes reaching Cebu City. The Japanese grabbed the nearby islands to Panay Island and added the island of Mindoro to the north. This put them in close proximity to the Americans on Luzon.

Prince Henry pointed out that since Mindanao Island lay between Cebu City and the existing German colony of New Guinea to the south east, the Germans would occupy Mindanao as well. The Japanese offered no complaint to the division. Palawan island was raised and neither country made any move to claim it.

It sat as an outlier in the Sulu Sea and along with Samar and Leyte Islands were left alone. It was assumed that the Americans would take Samar and Leyte as they sat close to Luzon. Palawan didn't raise much interest and would be just left alone by both powers.

Prince Henry set a course that would take the fleet north along the Borneo coast into the Sulu Sea, past Mindanao and into the Cebu Strait. His captain estimated a three day voyage as Prince Henry's excitement at Germany asserting itself in the world grew. What the Americans would do about such action didn't really cross his mind. He had the firepower to end any American threat and a willing accomplice in the land grab. *What could the United States do?* he thought.

The Americana were already at war with Spain. While not much of an adversary, would the United States risk war with both Japan and Germany over something that wasn't really theirs. Winning a navel battle did not constitute winning a war. Opportunity was at hand and Prince Henry was determined to scoop up his prize.

* * *

Captain Wilhelm von Mueller stood at attention in Admiral von Diederichs stateroom awaiting orders. His cruiser, *SMS Prinzess Sophia*, waited his return. At 1,868 tons displacement, his was the second lighest ship of the squadron and had been consistently used as a dispatch boat. Hence his station outside Manila Bay when Commodore Dewey led the Americans to victory.

After confirming that the Spanish fleet had been finished, Captain Mueller had made a dash to Hong Kong where he risked the plague in order to get the news cabled to Berlin. Returning to the mouth of Manila Bay with the entire squadron, he was now handed new dispatches for Prince Henry.

"Captain, you should beat our squadron to Cebu City so I suggest you await its arrival in the Cebu Straits so as to enter together."

"Yes sir."

"I'll assume his highness will have further instructions for me after he disembarks our troops in Cebu City. Secondarily, I want you to check in at Iloilo City to determine if the Japanese have acted."

"Yes sir," Wilhelm said. "Do you want me to check on the way to Cebu City?"

"Yes, his highness will want to know if our joint plans with Japan are in place."

Captain von Mueller saluted after tucking his packet of dispatches under his left arm. The admiral saluted back and wished him luck.

Wilhelm was soon motored across the ocean and climbed back aboard the *SMS Prinzess Sophia*. He gained the bridge and took his second in commend to the charts.

"Set a course for Iliolo City. We leave right away."

"Yes sir."

Wilhelm left to deposit his crucial dispatches in his cabin and by the time he returned his second in command had the course ready to implement.

"Take us out of line lieutenant," the captain ordered and watched as the helmsmen swung the wheel to starboard and increased speed, leaving the slow moving squadron patrolling outside Manila.

Entering Panay Gulf, the course changed to north north east as Guimaras Island loomed up off the starboard side of the ship. Easing his speed, Captain von Mueller had signal flags raised with the agreed upon greeting between the two erstwhile allies. Since both sides had limited interpreters on board each ship, a common flag standard had been set ahead of time.

Wilhelm lifted his binoculars, scanned the harbor and saw the Japanese squadron anchored, the two new battleships leading the line. Their guns had been trained outward to the open sea for protection in case of any enemy arriving. Seeing the correct answering flags on the lead ship, Wilhelm had the signal officer run up the next set of flags. The Japanese responded and the SMS *Prinzess Sophia* changed course to Cebu City. He could report a successful Japanese landing on Panay to the prince.

As he came around the southern tip of Negros Island, Wilhelm spotted the black smoke of warships steaming north,. He ordered the *Prinzess Sophia* on a intercepting course. Four hours later his ship pulled along side the SMS *Brandenburg*. Signal flags ran up the halyards as the signal officer read off the messages. Passing on the news of the Japanese occupation of

Panay Island, Wilhelm was ordered to fall in the van of the line. He reduced speed and the helmsmen adjusted their course to take up the rear of the German squadron.

Chapter 13

Cebu City, Philippines
May, 1898

Lapu-Lapu arose to another hot, humid day as the sun cleared the horizon and Olango Island to the east took the first rays for the day. Small fishing boats were already amongst the Olango Reef Flats throwing their nets out hoping for a good catch. Further out in the Olango Channel separating Bohol Island the larger boats drifter slowly with the current formed by the tides moving among the numerous islands.

One boat in particular held two men working, one fishing, the other maneuvering the boat by adjusting the two sails along with the rudder. A large dugout canoe, over thirty feet long, the boat had outriggers on each side made of three bamboo poles lashed together. Cross members of bamboo held the outside floats and steadied the craft. The fisherman worked hard pulling in his net, the fish dropping into the bottom of his boat.

The helmsman tied off his rudder and scooped up the fish, throwing them into woven baskets. He placed the full baskets under the small roof in the middle of the boat. Made of bamboo with a grass roof for protection from the rain and sun, the little open cabin offered relief for the two men. On longer sails the area was big enough that one man could sleep out of the elements.

Alexander Dull climbed over the bamboo cross member and took up the helm again. He swung the lateen sails inboard and the craft took on more speed. His father-in-law took in the remainder of his net and stowed it under the roof. He spoke to Alex in his native Cebuano.

"We have a good catch. Set sail for Cebu and we can sell them first thing."

Alex adjusted his aft sail as Felipe adjusted the forward sail. The twin masted sailboat pulled in the local breeze that blew up the channel as Alex set a broad reach to gain the south side of Mactan Island. A haze hung over the larger island of Cebu further in the distance and as they swung around Mactan and turned north in Mactan Channel, Alex saw something he had never seen before.

Large warships were anchored in the channel off Cebu City where only small local boats ever sailed. At the city's lone wharf, a large cargo ship was tied up and as they grew closer they could see a gangway spewing people down onto the wharf.

But it was the enormous battleship they were passing that held their attention. Alex immediately recognized the Imperial German Navy standard hanging loose on its mast on the rear of the ship. His mind raced as to the meaning of a fleet of German ships here in the Philippines. He held his course steady for the end of the wharf where they had always unloaded their day's catch.

When he wasn't off taking photos, he typically went out and helped with the fishing. He wanted to be part of the family he had married into and contribute where he could. Having been in country two years, his original money had been spent and now he now lived off what the land offered as his Philippine family had done for generations.

His family had grown by one as Donita had given birth to a son ten moths after they had married. So he more then anything wanted to be a productive part of the family as his now five month old son grew. His wife already talked of more children and made sure Alex held interest in her to make that happened.

It is a good life. Good food, good drinks, make babies he thought. *The Philippine way of life.* It was confirmed daily as he looked around him and saw the number of children playing, happy.

When he wasn't performing his other duties, he ran a school for the local children, teaching them English among other topics that were common in Western schools. Attempting to make a difference, his memory of his friend Jose Rizal kept him focused. That he had named his son after his friend aided his memory each day. Jose would not have died in vain as Alex strived to fulfill his promise he had made to Jose on their last visit in prison.

Suddenly a booming voice in German commanded Alex's attention. "You there. Swing away. This wharf is off limits to all but Imperial German business."

While Alex understand the man in uniform, he shook his head on how a local fisherman would understand the orders just given. He pulled in his sail and swung the rudder to make for the beach further up the channel. He saw other boats lined up on the beach and assumed the locals had gotten the message whether they understood it or not.

"What is this ?" Felipe asked.

"It appears we have been invaded by the Germans." Alex said. He knew his father-in-law had no concept of Germans. White people with guns were Spanish to him. But he kept the boat on course and swung into the beach, dropping the sails. The boat scrunched easily into the sandy beach and local residents hurried over to see the fish that might be available.

The crowd was abuzz with excitement as Alex listened as Felipe sold their catch or traded fish for other items people offered that the family might need. Soon empty of their morning's catch, Felipe adjusted the items traded in the baskets and made to push the boat off the sand.

"Hold on there," a German voice yelled.

A squad of soldiers appeared from behind the fishing shacks lining the beach. They marched right to Alex with an officer stepping forward.

"Come on dago. All Spanish are to be interned." The officer made it plan that Alex was to come with them. He saw the fear in his father-in-law's eyes as he stepped out of the boat. Alex spoke Cebuano to him and told him not to worry.

"Let's go. No talking."

Alex fell in line with the soldiers as they marched off the beach. The locals all stared at the events taking place but went back to their business. Power politics were alien to them as survival held their attention.

The officer led his men through the streets of Cebu City and into the central government building that until today, held the Spanish officials in this part of the Philippines. Alex, dressed more like a local with his straw hat that had protected him from the tropical sun, could almost pass as a local. His dark tan belied his European origin and it was more his height among such short people that gave him away. But now among the new German arrivals, his height didn't show, just his dark skin.

Northern Europeans considered Southern Europeans dark by nature so it was easy to peg Apex as a Spaniard. Hence the slur term dago used by the German toward the assumed Spaniard. Alex thought of barking out in German but decided to see what would happened living as a Spaniard under German auspices.

The German squad leader stopped in front of who Alex assumed was his superior officer. "I captured another one down on the beach major. Where do you want to put him? The prison cells are full."

Alex bristled at the idea that he could be thrown into prison. What would become of his filipina wife and son if he was locked up while who knew what would happened after that. While he had lived with the Germans and had been raised partially as a German, he had no knowledge of how they behaved as imperialists. And suddenly he had no interest in finding out.

In very clear concise German he said. "I am an American citizen. I demand to speak with my embassy."

The two men turned and stared. Before they could speak, Alex added. "I demand to speak to your Oberst now."

Alex wasn't sure what rank the men in front of him were but he knew colonels in any army held enough power to assure he was heard. He was startled slightly by the answer back.

"We can't accommodate an Oberst as we are a naval unit. Marines as you have in America," the one that seemed in charge said. He turned to his subordinate and said, "Take this man to the Kapitan zur See."

"Yes sir, right away,' the man answered. "Let's go." he directed at Alex and led the way out of the building.

The two men returned to the wharf area and gained the gangway up into the ship. Climbing up to the main deck, they found an officer directing the unloading of supplies. Deck hands busied themselves loading crates into a net that was immediately lifted over the side to another crew unloading on the wharf. The entire area buzzed with activity.

"Sir, the Lieutenant sent me here with this man. Claims he's American but speaks perfect German."

The Captain took a long look up from his clipboard at the dark man in front of him. He then looked at his midshipmen before he gazed back down at his shipping manifest.

"I don't have time for this. Take him to the battalion commander. Let him deal with it."

"Yes sir." Again Alex followed the officer into the ship as they maneuvered through companionways and climbed ladders. Higher in the ship the man knocked on a stateroom door. A command to enter moved them inside to stand at attention in front of a uniformed man at a desk.

"What is this?" the officer said and stared at Alex. His gaze took in his attire and colored skin before shifting to the midshipman before him. "Well?"

"Colonel, sir. My Captain ordered this man be brought to you. Claims he's an American. But speaks perfect German."

The colonel tuned back to Alex. Alex spoke first.

"And English. And French. And Cebuano. And Tagalog. And Chinese. And Japanese." He offered his complete language proficiency and spoke it in each language, not German.

"What's that?" the colonel asked/

Now in German Alex offered, "I said I am fluent in English, French, Japanese, Chinese, Cebuano, the local language here, and Tagalog, the local language on Luzon Island."

He knew he was stretching things a bit on speaking fluent Japanese. He had studied Chinese while in Paris which naturally led to learning Japanese. While he was certainly not fluent, he could get by in a pinch.

"Hmmm," the men mumbled. He sat back as Alex could tell the man was processing what he had just learned. It would be obvious to anyone but a moron that the stranger standing in local clothes and with a dark skin was not the typical wayward tourist. "That will be all midshipman. Tell you Captain thank you."

The officer saluted and left the stateroom. The Colonel offered Alex a chair in front of his desk as he wrote on a sheet of paper. He stood, steeped outside his stateroom and returned a short while later.

Sitting down, he looked at Alex and asked, "So, what is an American doing way out here in the provinces?"

Relieved that this man seemed to believe his story, Alex didn't still know what the Germans were up to yet. He would hold things close until he knew.

"I'm a photographer. I've been chronicling life here in the islands for over a year now."

"What were you doing on a local fishing boat then?"

"Colonel, I'm afraid I'm not a rich man. My funds have gotten depleted and that fisherman offered a room and meals for help on his boat. I'm an experienced sailor so I operate the boat while he fishes."

"I see. Let me introduce myself then. I'm Colonel Lettow-Vorbeck, of his majesties' First See Battalion. That would be similar to your U.S. Marines."

"Alexander Dull of Worcester, Massachusetts at your service colonel."

"Mr. Dull, if I might ask. Do you have any other clothes?"

"You mean Western clothes. Yes sir. I keep them safe for when hopefully I return home."

"Good, if I give you your parole do you promise to return here tomorrow dressed properly?"

Alex took exception at the word parole being used with his name attached. A parole was when a prisoner of war given permission to do something on his honor to not escape, but to return to captivity. If he was being considered a prisoner of war, was his country and Germany at war. The look of concern took the colonel.

"Perhaps a bad choice of words. You are not a prisoner of war. I just want you to be back here on the ship in the morning. And if I must, I can send an armed guard with you to assure me of your return."

Not wanting the Germans to know of his Philippine family, he quickly agreed to take his leave alone and return in the morning. "Will eight o'clock do, colonel."

"That would be splendid. Good day Mr. Dull. I'll have someone escort you off the ship."

Practically running back to Lapu-Lapu after taking the ferry across to Mactan Island, the colonel had given him a written pass in case any other soldiers should spot him lose in the population. After explaining to his wife and family what he thought was happening, he warned them that he didn't know how safe they would be with his presence known. He packed a small bag and told Donita that he would rent a room in Cebu City rather then return but would stay in touch.

The next morning, he rose early in his rented room. Taking a cold bath, Alex dressed in his best suit with dress shirt and tie. He knew he would suffer in the heat with such an outfit on but the colonel obviously had something that needed him looking as western as possible. Crossing the island in the pre-dawn darkness, he kept cool as he carried his jacket under his arm and kept his shirt open and loose. He ferried back to Cebu Island and walked the short distance to the wharf. Things were already bustling as the German's were learning early morning hours held reasonable temperatures for work versus the hot afternoon sun.

He showed his pass to the sentry at the end of the dock and gained admittance to the restricted area. Stopping at the bottom of the gangway, his letter again had him walking up onto the ship. An officer met him on deck and escorted him to Lettow-Vorbeck's office. The colonel was already up and working. He motioned Alex to a chair as he continued his reading. At eight o'clock, the ships bells rang out and the colonel stood.

"Mr. Dull. You look much better this morning. A bit dark but understandable."

"Yes sir. What are we up to, if I might ask?"

"With your language skills, I think we might have a job for you. I want you to meet the admiral."

The two men left the ship and stepped down the ladder onto the wharf and climbed into a motor launch. The seamen pushed off the piling and shifted the steam launch into forward as they set a course for what Alex assumed to be the flagship. Motoring along the line of warships, Alex marveled as the ships grew bigger and more menacing as they moved up the line.

Reading the names of each ship painted on their sterns the final ship announced itself, the *Brandenburg*, the home port of Wilhemshaven printed in smaller type below. The steam launch putted to a stop at the bottom of stairs leading to the main deck. Lettow-Vorbeck led as they stepped onto the platform and started the climb up.

The colonel reached the top and saluted the officer standing there, then turned to salute toward the standard flying on the ships stern. A junior officer led them through the maze of corridors and ladders finally stopping outside the Admirals stateroom. The seaman knocked.

"Enter."

The colonel and Alex stepped inside and were greeted by an officer dressed in white with a gold braided epaulette hanging off one shoulder. Alex knew enough of military tradition to recognize a flag staff officer. They were offered seats and then the man disappeared. An adjoining room's door opened and an officer that could only be the admiral by the amount of gold on his shoulders.

Lettow-Vorbeck stood and saluted. "Admiral, I'd like to introduce Alexander Dull. The one I sent the note on yesterday.

"I'm very happy to meet you Mr. Dull. You seem to be a remarkable man. And one that seems to good to be true out here."

"Thank you Admiral, I just wanted to . . ." Alex was cut short be the interior door opening again. A man in even a more splendid uniform than even the admirals stepped into the room.

"Prince Henry, your royal highness, I wasn't expecting you to join us," the admiral said as he and the colonel turned and bowed.

Alex was flummoxed as to what he should do. He knew of Germany's nobility but had never been around them. As an American he had no obligation to bow to another countries royal class and remembered that in the U.S. Constitution that Americans were forbidden to any royal claims. He stood upright.

The prince looked him squarely in the eyes, the room quiet as a certain tension held. Finally the Prince smiled and offered everyone a seat. He turned to the admiral and said, "Perhaps some refreshments. Mr. Dull looks to need a good meal."

"Right away your highness." The admiral stepped out quickly and soon returned.

Prince Henry turned his attention to Alex. "I assume German fare is suitable, Mr. Dull?"

"Yes, very. I grew up on it."

"You don't say," the prince said. "Worcester in Massachusetts I understand. German immigrants then?"

"Both sides of my family. We spoke German at home."

"Yes, you are flawless in your pronunciation. Did you spend time in the home country?"

168

"Yes, in 1887. I stayed with relatives after graduating from university," Alex said.

"Very good. Where is your family then?"

"Mostly Baden-Wurttenberg, Sir. I was in Heidelberg."

"Wonderful city. Did you enjoy your time with us?

"Yes, you highness," Alex said. He was warming up to the man and knew he better show a little more respect to him. It appeared by the forces arraigned that the German's had come to stay. The Kaiser's younger brother holding command assured Germany's interest in the Philippines. But part of him sank at the thought that now the local population not only had the Spanish to deal with , but also now the Germans.

"I understand you have asked to see your embassy? That might be a problem."

"I don't understand."

"Your country and Spain are at war if you haven't heard yet. The American fleet entered Manila Bay and inflicted a resounding defeat on Spain."

This was wonderful news to Alex. That his freedom loving country had thrown the Spanish out of the Philippines meant that the Filipino people would soon have their independence. Alex knew his country would do the right thing by the Filipinos and grew sad that Jose had not lived to see this day.

But as his thoughts drifted to a sadder time, he suddenly remembered where he was. If the Americans were here in the islands to free the locals, what were the Germans doing here?

"Prince Henry, might I ask you a question?"

"Of course Mr. Dull. But let me anticipate you. You want to know what a German Fleet is doing anchored in the Philippines?

"Yes, your highness."

"Very simple. We are here to protect German merchants from any instability."

"Oh." Alex said. He knew it was a lie as there were no Germans of any kind anywhere south of Manila that he knew of. And in Manila there might be a handful of German nationals. And if the fleet was here to protect them, why weren't they in Manila Bay?

"But Mr. Dull," the admiral said, "The reason we have you here today is something entirely different. I'm told you have exhausted your funds and might be in need of a paying position."

"Yes, I am quite broke I'm afraid. What did you have in mind?"

"As the colonel has informed us, you are quite capable in the local languages. You speak German so we would like to hire you as an interpreter."

Alex agreed to work for the German authorities. The colonel made the formal offer and the amount was very generous. Here in the islands it would let him live like a king. Alex wasn't sure what he was getting himself involved in, but he also knew he didn't have and option to say no. The Germans held power here now and to reject their offer would put him and his family in potential danger.

"That is acceptable. If I can be if service, I am glad to help as much as I can."

170

"Splendid,' Prince Henry said. As he said it, the outer door opened and three servants brought in a German breakfast of eggs, sweet breads and ham. Alex's mouth immediately watered as the plate was placed in front of him. He had not eaten such food in years and he suddenly realized that beside the money, other perks of working with the Germans might come his way. "Please Mr. Dull, eat up. I'm looking forward to a close working relationship here in Vasaya."

"Thank you your highness." But Alex's stomach turned a knot at the prince's mention of Visaya. That he had used the term for the entire region and not Cebu meant only one thing. Southern Philippines was about to see a change. A change that Alex had just agreed to help execute.

Chapter 14

Manila Bay, Philippines
June, 1898

"What the hell are you telling me. The German's have landed at Cebu? Jesus, how did this happen?" Admiral Dewey yelled at his flag officer.

"Reports are sketchy sir. Mostly rumor. We have no confirmation."

"Well, we damn well need to get conformation. If the Krauts are making a move on these islands we need to know."

"Yes sir. Shall we detach one of our ships to send?"

"With the German East Asiatic Fleet still siting outside the bay. No. We need every warship we have if they make a move here."

"Yes Commodore. There is a Spanish ship that didn't engage us in the battle. It escaped destruction and perhaps we could put a crew on her. The *El Coreo* sir. Five hundred ton gunboat. And the word is it is sea worthy. Maybe not for an ocean crossing but should make it down to Cebu and back without incident."

"Very well. Find an officer to put in charge and have him select a crew," Dewey said. "And I want that ship gone within the week. You hear me."

"Aye Aye Sir."

* * *

"Commander Dull, Caption wants to see you. Right now." The ship's second in commend yelled inside Cornelius's stateroom.

"Yes Sir. Right now." Corny pulled on his shoes from where he had been trying to sleep in his bunk. He checked his uniform in the mirror on the back of the door and pulled his tie straight. Even with the tropical heat, Dewey had held to strict naval bearing from his men.

Stepping onto the bridge to find the captain, he noticed that the U.S.S. Boston sat at anchor off Cavite Naval Base. Since the resounding victory over the Spanish fleet almost two months ago, the squadron had been sitting waiting for the troop transports that would bring the army. The Spanish garrison continued holding out inside the walled fortress of Intramuros.

The American squadron carried few troops for storming a fixed fortress and once the Spanish fleet was eliminated, cables to Washington requesting ground troops got things in gear. And that meant a long wait as troops were gathered in the States, boarded on transports, equipment shipped and all of it to steam across the Pacific Ocean. Word was that the troops would arrive in August.

"You wanted to see my sir,"

"Ah yes. Commander," The captain of the U.S.S. Boston said. "It seems that Commodore Dewey has a special mission and he needs a German speaker to command it. You are fluent in German aren't you."

"Yes sir, although not from living in Germany, but speaking it at home. Both parents were German descendants."

"Very good. You have seven days to get the *El Coreo* ship shape. Here is a list of the men assigned to your ship."

"The *El Coreo* Sir?"

"Spanish gunboat of 500 tons. She was in Cavite when the fighting broke out and is deemed seaworthy."

"Yes sir. Seven days though," Corny started to protest the short time to get a foreign ship with a new crew ready for what ever duty was required.

"If you have a problem mister I'm sure the commodore can find another."

"No problem sir. Thank you for the opportunity. Any idea what I'll be doing?"

"You'll received your orders in five days. I suggest you get moving Commander."

Cornelius saluted and practically floated back to his bunk, his mind racing at his first command, with all the things he had to accomplish to make that command a success. It was an opportunity but it was also a real chance that his navy career would go down in failure.

A quick look at the roster of men assigned to the gunboat had him reconsidering his promotion. Whenever crew were needed for a new ship, captains always dumped the worse sailors they had to get rid of them. The ones assigned to him from the *Boston* had a reputation for being sluggards and malcontents. He assumed the others from other ships in the squadron would be similar.

The only bright spot was a master chief from the *Boston* the captain had gotten rid of. Corny knew him to be an excellent non-commissioned officer. It just was the master-chief was a violent drunk whenever they were in port. Captains got tired of bailing their crew members out of jail. And his second in command, a Lieutenant Peter Gay was an unknown officer from the *U.S.S. Concord*. Coming off the American gunboat he at least would be familiar with small ship operations.

The week flew by as the *El Coreo* was surveyed and converted to an American warship. Coal was loaded and the propulsion system checked out. Cornelius had no idea why it had been in the shipyard but he found the ship generally capable. When he received his orders he doubled his efforts to assure his crew a ship that could complete its mission.

The day before they sailed, Cornelius called the crew together on deck. He needed to read the U.S. Navy's assignment of command to the men that officially authorized him as their commander. Captain's of warships, even small warships held enormous power over their crew. With the official speech completed, Cornelius gave his first speech as a Captain.

"Men, we have an important mission to do. We are a new crew. Many of you may have had problems on your old ships. That is old news. Consider you have a fresh start as of today to make yourself the sailor your country expects of you. We are a small ship so not many opportunities to hide. Everyone will be doing their duty. And if you need an incentive, we are heading out into the Philippine Archipelago where we might meet a Spanish warship that had been on dispatch duty. Our very lives will rely on all of us being ready if we have to fight. Thank you."

The master chief asked to address the crew and Corny nodded agreement. "And I'll be watching all of you real close. Ask any other *Boston* crew members. I stand no shirking of duty. That is all."

"Thanks Master Chief."

"Yes sir. Glad to be here. Independent action is always preferable to fleet work."

"I hope you're right Master Chief."

Cornelius kept the composure of a confident captain until he steeped into his small stateroom and closed the door. That was when it all hit him. The responsibility, the danger, the risk of failure. He pulled his thoughts together at a knock at his door.

"Enter."

His second in command opened the door and saluted as Corny looked up. His lieutenant looked barely out of high school but had checked his records and knew he had graduated two years previous from Annapolis. They would learn about each other as their cruise got under way.

"Captan, if I may? Could I set up gunnery practice for tomorrow?"

"Very good lieutenant. As soon as we clear the mouth of Manila Bay, and assuming the German Squadron has vacated their blockade."

"Are you expecting trouble breaking out Sir."

"No, that was a cynical remark. We aren't blockaded. It just sometimes feels that way. I guess if we really are blockaded we will be the first to know. Ready to start a new war mister?"

"No sir. One is plenty for me."

"Good, carry on."

Lieutenant Gay closed the door and Cornelius returned to his pile of paper work. Ammunition had been inventoried. Coal loaded. Food and water provisions stored. He pulled out his crew list and went to each individual's file to see if he had missed anything. *Where were the weak links if they ran into trouble?* he thought

Cornelius had done his best assigning his crew to where they looked to be their strongest. The U.S. Navy had a system of categorizing its men and Cornelius had to rely on that information and experience the best he could. But time would show who were the leaders among his crew. If he had time that is.

Leaving the next day was uneventful. The former Spanish gunship moved out smartly and gained the mouth of Manila Bay. The German Squadron held its position as it had now for over a month. He received no threats upon moving into the South China Sea and changed heading south. The German flagship ran right up behind him and as Cornelius trained his binoculars on the lead ship, he saw the officers opposing him scanning his ship. Shortly after the line of ships performed a one hundred and eighty degree turn one after the other and steamed back north.

"Sir, Ship sighted. Two points off the starboard bow. Three thousand yards out," one of the lookouts shouted.

Everyone on the bridge turned their gaze in the direction. Cornelius' binoculars picked up a warship steaming south, black smoke trailing behind.

"What do you make of her?" Corny yelled to his lookout.

"Can't tell sir. Appears to be a light cruiser. One thousand tons maybe. No standard flying."

Lieutenant Gay asked, "German dispatch boat heading to their southern forces Sir?"

"Most likely," Corny said. As he continued watching, he finally added. "Appears to be about two knots faster then us right now."

"Shall we follow sir."

"As long as he's going our way. Our mission comes first over any outlier ships."

The *El Coreo* clanked along steady. Cornelius had scrubbed gunnery practice with a potential adversary within range. He moved from station to station inspecting his ship. It was the first time he had seen it operate and he wanted to make sure they could finish their mission. His most concern was the engine room.

He opened the hatch leading to the boilers and the tremendous heat hit him. The crew were shoveling coal into the burners as the steam engines pounded out the steam. The noise and heat had always gotten to him and he knew he would have to relieve his crew often so they could find relief on deck.

He found his noncommissioned officer in charge of the engine crew and asked, "How is our ship Chief?"

"As well as can be expected. She's old. She Spanish built. She was rushed into service. But we'll make her work."

Cornelius thanked his chief and noted that all the gauges had English translations stuck beside each Spanish language gauge and valve. Two crew members he had been given were Spanish speakers and had spent days labeling everything on the ship. Cornelius made his way topside to the relief of an ocean breeze.

As their journey south grew in length, Coron Island off their starboard side came into view. They had been moving along Mindoro Island off their port side. The mystery cruiser ahead had become barely visible with the long telescope that had been given to the lookout.

"Sir, our friend has changed course. Appears to be gaining the island to port sir."

Cornelius checked his chart and assumed San Jose City would be the logical place the ship might be headed. He changed course to take the *El Coreo* closer in to shore so he might see better.

With two outer island off Mindoro proper, he couldn't get as close as he wanted. But he got close enough to see a warship anchoring in the small bay off San Jose. Cornelius climbed up to the outlook nest and took the telescope. Training it on the warship he saw sailors busy on deck anchoring the ship. As he scanned the length of the ship, two crew men walked to the stern and appeared to be attaching a flag. Cornelius watched as they pulled on the halyard and the standard ran up the mast.

Cornelius heart stopped as the Imperial Japanese flag broke out in the fresh breeze. *What were the Japs doing here?* he thought. He knew this was a game changer if he found Germans in Cebu City. He yelled out a course change to take them back out to sea before climbing down to the bridge.

He had a fitful sleep that night. Awake most of the time, he couldn't stop thinking about what he had seen, Japanese warships in Philippine waters. By morning he had made up his mind. When he entered the bridge he checked his ships location and knew they were making steady progress. Standing silent on one side of the bridge, the crew went about its business knowing their captain was deep in thought.

Cornelius scanned Panay Island off to port and as the ship reached the southern tip, he ordered a course change. Now moving north east up the Iloilo Strait, the *El Coreo* headed toward the third largest city in the archipelago. While this was not in his orders, he took the initiative to add to the information from yesterday.

Growing closer to Iloilo City, the lookout called out. "Warships in the harbor sir."

Everyone trained their binoculars toward the city but the morning mist and their weaker glasses left them waiting.

Soon the lookout added, "Holy shit sir. There are some big sons-a-bitches I'm seeing."

"Keep the comments down and report seamen," the master chief yelled.

But by now Cornelius could also see some big sons-a-bitches. Looming larger he finally could make out enough detail of the superstore to determine the class warship. But there were two of them. And as they grew closer smaller warships that had been hidden behind their lead ship added to the sight. Cornelius counted four cruisers, two protected, two light, to go with the two battleships.

"Royal Sovereign Class," Cornelius said.

Lieutenant Gay lowered his binoculars and turned to his captain. "The British are here also, sir?"

But nearing the lead ship the Imperial Japanese standard on the stern was very evident.

"Japs sir. Bloody Japs," the master chief said. "Where did they get those battle wagons?"

"British built, I'm afraid. Fresh from the builders yards. Obviously planned on their return to Japan to be here at an opportune time," Corny said.

The helmsman added, "Blimey, Commodore Dewey will shit his pants."

The master chief jumped right on him. "Stow it seaman or you'll be relived. We don't need to hear from your bile."

But Cornelius knew the seaman was right. His commander would shit his pants to have two first rated battle ships sitting in waters he had assumed was all his. He made a mental note of each ship anchored before giving the order to reverse course. By this time the rat lines on each ship were lined with Japanese seamen staring at the minuscule Americn warship turning its tail. Cornelius heard the jeering across the water as three thousand men all showed their contempt for the United States show of force.

And they were right to be confident Cornelius thought. At over twelve thousand tons displacement and carrying four twelve inch guns never mind the thirty four other guns of various calibers, the American Asiatic Squadron was nothing in comparison. What they might find at Cebu City made him more nervous then before. If the Japanese and the Germans were working in concert, the entire American fleet of battleships would be needed to clear them out.

The journey to Cebu City had the *El Coreo* clear Negros Island and then turn north up the Cebu Strait. Cornelius did the navigation so they would arrive in the morning. He ordered his warship to slow slightly to the required the measurements he needed to arrive on time. A second fitful night left him groggy in the morning. But as they gained Mactan Island in their binoculars, everyone waited for the report from the lookout.

"Ships at anchor, Sir. I make out two large warships and four smaller ones. There are other ships that appear to be transports."

Growing larger in their sights, Cornelius could make out the superstructure of the lead ship as it sat anchored. It appeared to be familiar but he needed to be closer to determine its nationality. As a cadet at Annapolis they had studied drawings of enemy ships to learn identification. Silhouettes of each adversary's ships were continually kept up to date and this behemoth rang a bell in Cornelius' mind. When he saw the flag on its stern, he knew.

Two *Brandenburg* class battleships of the Imperial German Navy sat in front of him with their assorted cruisers. Combined with the Japanese fleet, this meant impossible odds to the United Sates. Two of the great powers were making a supreme political move in Spain's collapse. What America thought it was gaining in its war with Spain had suddenly shifted to a totally different outcome.

Signal flags running up the flagship caught Cornelius' attention. He didn't knew German code so had no idea what the ship was signaling, but as he gave the order to drop anchor several hundred yards off the flagship, the message became clear. Before he could order the long boat lowered so he could be rowed over to the German commander, a steam launch appeared from behind the *Brandenburg*. It headed straight toward the *El Coreo*.

Cornelius remembered he had never raised the United Staes standard just in case he had run into a Spanish ship. The Spanish would recognize the *El Coreo* as one of their own and in that hesitation Cornelius hoped his ship would gain an edge. Now, he quickly ordered the Star and Stripes hoisted.

A ladder was dropped over the side and before Cornelius dropped over the gunwale, he spotted the flag flapping proudly. He lowered himself into the launch and the German seamen pushed off his ship and headed to the flagship. Not speaking the entire time, Cornelius stepped onto the gangway up the ships' side, reaching the top where he saluted the officer of the deck.

"Captain of the United Staes gunship *El Coreo* to see the captain." Cornelius said in German.

Startled by an American speaking his own language, the officer led Cornelius through the battleship to a door where he knocked. An answer had the officer opening the door and steeping aside. Corny stepped in to two men standing behind a conference table.

He came to attention, saluted and spoke again in German. "The United States ship *El Coreo* wishes to extend courtesies to the Imperial German Navy."

The two men saluted back and motioned Cornelius to a chair opposite them. The man Cornelius assumed to be the ship's captain spoke first.

"Welcome aboard the *Brandenburg* Captain. Refreshments?"

The officer with more gold on his shoulders and who Cornelius assumed might be the fleet admiral stared, quiet.

"Yes sir. Thank you."

"So what brings you to Cebu City?", the German asked.

"My commander had received rumors of Germans in the area and we were tasked to investigate sir."

"In a Spanish ship?"

"Spoils of war sir. A handy ship for dispatch work."

"And a German speaker to help. Very handy. Native German or immigrant?"

"My grandparents immigrated sir. Both sides of my family. Spoke German at home growing up. I'm afraid my speech might be a bit rusty Sir," Cornelius said.

As a servant brought refreshments into the stateroom the officer that could be the admiral finally spoke. "So captain. What are your intentions here?"

"With all due respect, I would ask you the same. We are at war with Spain, so any territory of theirs is fair game."

"Agreed captain. We are only here to protect German nationals from the ravages of war."

Cornelius knew such a statement was crap. It didn't take two battleships and two squadrons of cruisers to protect the few Germans in the Philippines. *And the Japanese are they protecting Japanese interests?* he thought.

So he asked, "Again with all due respect, we steamed into Iloilo City on our way down and the Japanese have a similar fleet to yours sitting there. Are they protecting Japanese interests Sir?"

The two men looked at him with an intensity that Cornelius took as anger. He knew he was not being polite with his questions but he knew Commodore Dewey would want as much information as possible. Washington and the national government suddenly was on the brink of an all out war with two more powerful adversaries.

"We don't know what the Japanese are doing. Why would we? I assume they are concerned for their citizens' interests in the Philippines like we are."

Cornelius hadn't touched the sweetbread before him. The officer of lesser rank said. "Captain, if you are of German heritage, I'm sure you'll find the stollen and dampfnudel excellent. Our cooks are first rate on board."

The mention of dampfnudel brought childhood memories flooding back. His mother made the sweat dessert rolls often as it was a delicacy associated with southern Germany, his family's traditional homeland. He took one along with a cup of coffee and bit into the roll.

"Than you. Yes, just like my mother's."

The lesser ranked officer added, "Well, there you go. Mother's cooking and the fatherland."

But he didn't wear the uniform of the Fatherland. He wore a U.S. navy officers uniform and at the moment he represented his country. A country that might find itself in a lopsided war if he wasn't careful.

"So, is there anything else I should report to my commander other then Germany is protecting its citizens in Cebu City."

The higher ranking man turned to grab a rolled up chart. He flipped it open and placed two weighted bags on the ends to hold it open. Cornelius immediate saw the red marks on a map of the Philippine Archipelago. Two flags sat over areas within the red lines, one Japanese one German.

186

"Maybe this would help," the ranking officer said. "We will be protecting all the citizens on these islands: Cebu, Bohol, Negros, and Mindanao. The Japanese have expressed their desire to protect their citizens on Panay and Mindoro Islands. You Americans can protect your citizens on Luzon Island."

Cornelius noted that three main islands were outside any red line. He asked, "And Samar, Leyte and Palawan?"

"The Japanese and us don't know of any of our citizens on those islands so they are on their own."

Cornelius studied the map intently trying to memorize all its details. His effort was thwarted by the commanding officer.

"Captain, we have made a copy of the map for your commander so there is no accidental mistakes. We wouldn't want anyone straying into another territory and being injured by friendly fire."

"Thank you sir," Cornelius said. It was all he could think of as he rolled the map handed him. Finished, he stood, saluted and left the room. An officer outside the door escorted him to the waiting launch. He saluted again as he left the ship, his mind racing.

Upon gaining the bridge of the *El Coreo* Cornelius demanded a report from his second in command. He had left orders that the lookouts were to record all that they saw in enemy strength, including any troops they observed. The lieutenant handed a written assessment to the captain as Cornelius ordered the anchor raised. They needed to make time back to Manila to report these huge developments.

As soon as they had cleared Cebu harbor, Cornelius locked himself in his cabin and busily wrote his report. He knew it would be a report that might set a bomb off in Washington. His little ship strained as it raced at top speed back to the squadron. *And to what fate then?* he wondered. *A bigger war? A serious war with advisories that wouldn't be push overs like Spain had been so far.*

Chapter 15

Washington, D.C.
July 15, 1898

The nation's capital simmered under sumer heat as the humidity level left many scrambling for relief. As Washington D.C. emptied many headed to the mountains of West Virginia for relief. The rich and privilcgcd headed to fishing lakes on Michigan's Upper Peninsular or the fog bound Maine Coast.

Some however weren't as fortunate The poor, lacking resources to escape suffered through each day. The powerful were stuck beside them in the great buildings of the federal government. The nation was at war and the leaders remained in the city to direct the forces arrayed against Spain.

The first good news that had arrived in May of Dewey's defeat of he Spanish Fleet in Manila Bay had offered some relief from the oncoming summer weather. Congress had met and promoted Commodore Dewey to Admiral rank for his stunning victory. The entire nation joined in the celebration of the first ocean fleet action by the United States in its history.

That was followed a month later by news of Captain Henry's Glass's capture of the Spanish island of Guan in the middle of the Pacific Ocean. The protected cruiser *U.S.S. Charlotte* now sat on America's newest possession halfway between the Hawaiian Islands and the Philippines islands.

Yesterday news arrived by telegraph from Tampa of Admiral William Sampson and the main American fleet's defat of the Spanish Fleet in the Battle of Santiago de Cuba. Dispatches sent from Cuba with the same warship back to Florida announced the thrilling charge up Kettle Hill and the defeat of the Spanish army defending Santiago. The war was practically over as Spain could not reinforce its forces in Cuba without a fleet to protect its transports. While many Spanish troops remained in Havana, they were isolated and at risk to the Cuban revolutionaries.

President William McKinley looked again at the reports the War Department and the Navy Department had handed him yesterday. A reluctant warrior, McKinley had dithered as tensions rose between Spain and the United States, at least in the eyes of his distractors. For those that knew the man, elected in 1896, the former congressman and Governor of the State of Ohio was a measured man. Slow to react as he weighed all his options.

McKinley lead the proponents of a strong protective tariff. America had thrived behind its tariff wall as foreign goods fought for market share against American made goods. With the disadvantage of high tariffs, foreign producers couldn't compete and American had factories hummed with activity.

But the Panic of 1893 during President Cleveland's administration caused the worst economic downtown since the United States founding. It led to McKinley's election and a return to strong tariffs that had been weakened under Cleveland. McKinley now realized that with the surprising victories the United States had sustained, a burgeoning overseas market for America goods was at hand.

Congress had passed legislation forbidding any Cuban annexation. Not mentioned in the law were the other parts of the Spanish Empire. The Philippines, Guam and Puerto Rico had not been considered by Congress at that time.

The Newlands Amendment had just passed on July 7 and the President had signed thus making the Territory of Hawaii an official part of the United States. Adding Guam and the Philippines in the Pacific and Puerto Rico in the Caribbean, America entered the imperialists age along with the European powers and the Empire of Japan.

McKinley's Secretary of State entered the office, breaking the president's thoughts. William Day had been appointed in April taking over for the ailing John Sherman. Sherman had been a U.S. Senator from Ohio and was appointed to McKinley's cabinet ostensibly to make room for Mark Hanna to be appointed in his stead. Hanna was the wealthy industrialist that had been instrumental in McKinley's election.

"Good news Mr. President?" Secretary Day asked.

McKinley held up his reports from his military and naval commanders and smiled. "Couldn't be better. We can get this thing done and get our troops home. These casualty reports out of Cuba are sickening. We're losing more men to yellow fever then to the enemy."

"We were afraid of that when we decided to hurry our campaigning. We could have waited to the winter but you know how the public is."

"Yes, very inpatient as always," McKinley said.

"But those boys have sacrificed for something bigger then themselves, sir. Have you thought any more about what we discussed?"

The previous meeting between the President and his Secretary of State hadn't gone well. McKinley moved his position to claiming all that they could in conflict with his secretary that held the mindset it should all be returned to Spain excepting Cuba.

The President, though slow to action, now saw the deaths of his boy's as justification to keep the lot. He felt that their parents needed to know their sons had died for something greater then freeing a bunch of Cubans. Their families wanted something to show for their supreme sacrifices.

"Bill, I'm still weighing my options."

Secretary Day certainly knew McKinley's penchant for slow decisions. Everyone in Washington knew of the president's way of doing things.

MckInley changed the subject. "I recieved two frantic calls from War and Navy this morning. They have requested a meeting today."

"What's up, sir?"

"They didn't say. But by their tone it is urgent. I want you to join me."

Eating lunch before their meeting, the two men finished eating and pulled cigars as both men attempted a brief relaxation period. But the tension of the upcoming meeting permeated the room. The talk during lunch was of routine politics as each man avoided the larger topic. And now the unknown of what information McKinley's other two cabinet members held kept them quiet.

Cigars finished, Mckinley led his secretary back to the conference room to find Secretary of the Navy John Long and Secretary of War Russell Alger already seated waiting. Both men looked nervous as their Commander in Chief walked into the room. MckInley took a seat across the conference table from his two war leaders as Day sat down next to the President. McKinley's Chief of Staff quietly stepped into the room and took a seat at the head of the table. He placed down a notepad and pen .

"Gentlemen, you have my full attention," McKinley said.

"I guess I should go first Mr. President," the Secretary of the Navy said. "Yesterday I received a cable from Hong Kong. It held news that I knew you would want immediately. Our signal staff decoded it as its quite lengthy, but I'm afraid its bad news sir."

The other men at the table took on a noticeable strained expression. With only wonderful news of the war this was the first bad news. Mckinley directed John Long to continue.

"As you know now, my Assistant, Theodore Roosevelt, initiated action in the Philippines without my or your knowledge. Those island hadn't been discussed as we focused on Cuba. But we all rejoiced in Admiral's Dewey's victory there."

"Good God man," McKinley said. "Spill out with it. I know the history. What happened? Dewey run into trouble. Spain have more ships in the area we weren't aware of. What is it damn it."

"Sorry, Mr. President," Long said, now flustered. "It's the Germans and the Japanese sir."

"What about them. We've gotten the reports from Dewey on the German Admiral, what's his name?"

"Otto von Diederrichs, sir"

"Yes, yes. We have the reports of Diederrichs being provocative with his squadron after our victory. Did he do something stupid?"

"It's not Diederrichs, Mr. President. I'm afraid we are dealing with a second fleet, this one is outfitted with battleships."

"What? The Germans have battleships in East Asia. You said their East Asiatic Squadron fully matched to our squadron if their was trouble."

Long grew more nervous. "And thats not all. The Japanese have committed a fleet to the Philippines, including their two newest battleships."

McKinley's stress level reached a new high. "Are they working in concert? Christ, four battleships against what we have. How did this happen?"

"It would appear that they had this planned for some time," Long said. "Our Captain Cornelius Dull on the captured prize *El Coreo* was sent to investigate rumors that the Germans had landed in the southern Philippine Islands. Seems Captain Dull speaks fluent German and came away with a map of the lines of demarcation between us and the Empires of Germany and Japan."

"What?" McKinley exploded. "Those son-a-bitches are sneaking in and grabbing things we fought for. This is cowardice."

"Whatever you want to call it, they seem to have the upper hand," the Secretary of State said. "Did the dispatch contain the areas of occupation John?"

The Secretary of the Navy nodded that he had that information and reached under the table for a rolled up map. He placed it on the table facing the President and unrolled it. He threw two weights on the edges to hold it open. "I had our map staff draw out the lines as transmitted to us in the cable. As you can see, the Japs are here and the Germans are here."

McKinley stared at the map of the three zones of control. He ran his finger along the red lines marking the three areas deep in thought. He looked up at his secretary.

"Do we know how many troops they've committed to occupy there areas?

"Hard to determine, Mr. President. Captain Dull had his crew attempt a count while he was on the German flagship. But who knows how many troops they have placed on which islands. All he could report was Cebu City had a large number. Soldiers and German Marines as he had instructed his officers to mark the uniforms for him."

"And Captain Dull doesn't know Japanese per chance?"

"No Mr;. President. Captain Dull took his warship into Iliolio harbor but did not stop. He just listed the warships that were anchored."

The War Secretary finally spoke. "This changes everything. Our troop ships aren't scheduled to arrive until August. And here the Germans and Japanese already seem to be there in force."

"It doesn't matter what troops we have in the Philippines. With four battle ships already there to our none, we won't be in a position to challenge anything. If they defeat Dewey's squadron, which is assured by the way, we lose the Philippines for good."

"Mr. Long," McKinley said. "We have battleships sir. And as Admiral Sampson just showed, very capable ones."

"But Mr. President, they are in the Atlantic. It took the *U.S.S. Oregon* two full months to round Cape Horn to join the Atlantic Fleet for battle. How long would it take us to move Sampson's fleet to the Philippines? With the lose of the *U.S.S Maine* sir, we have five first line battleships."

"And the Germans?"

"Our intelligence says six sir. Two of which are already in East Asia waters."

"And the Japs?" McKinley asked.

"The two reported. And brand new from British shipyards Sir."

"Shit, this is a nightmare," The War Secretary said.

McKinley turned to his Secretary of State. "Bill, What's your opinion of how the British will take this?

Maybe if we get a little help on our side we can retrieve the situation."

"Good idea, Mr. President. But remember Japan and Britain have been negotiating a closer relationship. Evidenced by two British built battleships flying Japanese colors."

"Maybe. Or maybe not." McKinley said, "They are also jealous of the other great powers challenging their world position. And especially when Germany asserts itself. When the Prussian army defeated France in 1870 I know the British took notice. They watch the continent powers closely. Why don't you make inquires."

"Yes Mr. President?" the Secretary of State said. "I'll look into it right away."

* * *

"Wherever did you get this?" Sir Edward Malet, 4th Baronet and member of the British Privy Council asked.

The British Foreign Secretary said, "It arrived by cable two days ago. Information was reproduced on this map. What do you think?"

"I think the great powers are all maneuvering for the carcass of Spain. Easy pickings at hand."

"Sir Edward. This is quite serious. The Americans are searching for an alliance against the Japanese and Germans in their move on the Philippine Islands. Reports say four first rate battle ships are sitting holding their interests."

"And the Admiralty has what in East Asia?"

"Two old battle ships," the Foreign Secretary said. "No match for two brand new Royal Sovereign Class battleships we conveniently just finished for the Imperial Japanese Navy. God, this is a nightmare."

Sir Edward asked, "And you said the German's have two battleships there also?"

"Yes, with escorting cruisers. Eight in total between the two. Plus the regular German East Asian squadron with their cruisers. The Americans are desperate."

"I would say so. Their piddly little squadron is no match if they decide to assert themselves."

"The Admiralty has told me even if the Americans move their Atlantic Fleet to the Philippines, five against four would be a near thing. And that leaves the U.S. East Coast open to German warships. Germany still has four battleships waiting in home waters."

"I can see why they want us as a partner, " Sir. Edward said.

"What do you think then, Sir Edward. The Prime Minister has ordered me to find a consensus among his advisors."

Sir Edward didn't offer an answer and instead bent over the map on the table. He looked closely at the red lines the Foreign Office had drawn on the map. His fingers drew along each line, lost in thought.

"Maybe we have an opportunity here."

"What are you talking about?"

"The demarcation lines. They don't seem to include these islands here," Sir Edward held his hand over the Islands of Leyte and Samar. Then he shifted his hand and held it over the island of Palawan. "Nor here. Did the map maker get this wrong?"

"No, the cable was very specific in naming the main islands under each power's control. Those three islands were not listed."

"So, can we take it then they are up for grabs?"

"Sir Edward. Are you suggesting Britain join the mob and grab the spoils of Spain?"

Sir Edward looked carefully at the Island of Palawan. "This island is very convenient. I can't believe the Germans haven't claimed it. It controls both the Sulu Sea and the South Chine Sea. And there appears to be a decent harbor here at Puerto Princessa."

"I see your point," the Foreign Secretary said. "And with our new territory of Sarawak on Borneo that we signed under the Madrid Protocol in 1885, it would gain us a strong position to block both the Germans on Mindanao and the French in IndoChina."

"We would be breaking the Madrid Protocol though. We agreed the Sulu Archipelago belonged to Spain."

The Foreign Secretary smiled. "From the looks of things, Spain isn't long for any territory in Asia. We might want to send a flotilla to protect British interests on Palawan. The Americans will be looking for a peace conference soon from the reports of their war with Spain. I think we need to have a seat at that conference."

"You think you can convince the Prime Minister to send ships?"

"I meet with him this afternoon. I think you can be assured that warships will be leaving Singapore within the week."

Chapter 16

El Nido, Palawan Island, Philippines
August, 1989

German Captain Wilhelm von Mueller tried to sleep as the SMS *Prinzess Sophia* steamed heading northeast through the South China Sea. Escorting the fleet's collier back to Manila from Singapore, the captain had important cables form Berlin. The fact that German and Japanese forces had occupied parts of the Philippines was now known as each great power scrambled for more land.

Giving up on sleep, the captain pulled on his boots and sweater for the night time coolness on the moving ship. Hotter then hell during the day, Captain Mueller had relaxed the dress code of his seamen. Steaming this close to the equator the tropical sun blistered everything that sat under it. He had erected awnings were he could and worked his engine crew on one hour rotations for the heat.

Stepping onto the bridge, his crew took notice and straightened their stance. The Imperial German Navy relied on discipline, like most navies, and each man wanted to be as alert as possible. Especially when their captain was around. As soon as he slipped the strap of his binoculars over hsi head, the lookout yelled.

"Ships off our stern."

The captain and his Executive Officer both stepped over to the rail and trained their glasses aft. Just visible in the moonlight were the smoke of ships, running lights illumined on the bow. As they stared, the first ship revealed a second and then a third. Soon a squadron of warships was plainly visible as they grew closer on the same bearing as the Germans. With the collier trailing the cruiser and determining the overall speed, the slow transport allowed the faster ships to overtake them.

As daylight illuminated the ocean, the squadron began passing the lone German warship within hailing distance. Wilhelm spotted the Union Jack snapping in the breeze on the lead ship. He wrote down each ships description as it passed: armament, probable displacement, speed. When transports followed, he surmised which ones held supplies and which one was a collier.

If the flotilla was headed to Hong Kong or China Station, it was off course. Hong Kong lay to the northwest and these ships were bearing northeast. He decided he would follow as best he could. His country needed information if Britain had designs on the Philippines.

The ship's bursar brought him a mug of coffee and some sweetbread for breakfast. Captain von Mueller kept a careful watch on the slowly disappearing British squadron as it out paced his slower coal ship. He debated detaching the slower freighter and pursuing. But he had his orders and though the British ships destination was hugely important, he followed his orders. But he did change course and took his ship in closer to Palawan Island.

The island lay along the natural route between Singapore and Manila so he wasn't ignoring orders. He would just adjust his routing a bit so he could play a hunch. The *SMS Prinzess Sophia* had been in these waters for a number of years and the captain was familiar with many of the good anchorages. When not doing other work, each of the German ships in the East Asia Squadron had done survey work for future needs.

Navics were always gathering data on sea conditions, channel depths, safe harbors in storms and any other information that would help a navy operate in an area safely. And in his survey cruises he had discovered a wonderful anchorage just ahead. *If the British knew of such a spot, they might be found there* he thought.

He checked his chart and replotted his presumed position. He yelled out a new heading to the helmsmen and the cruiser slowly changed course. The collier moved in unison as it continued to follow. Wilhelm stepped out onto the deck and lifted his glasses. The northern tip of Palawan grew more distinct as the ship drew closer.

"Take it in closer," the captain said.

The helmsmen did as ordered while the captain scanned the area with his binoculars.

"Make signal to our companion. Slow speed and maintain your course. We will return."

The *SMS Prinzess Sophia* raised signal flags and the collier acknowledged the captain. The cruiser swing into El Nido as it passed two outlying islands. As soon as they rounded a point, the British warships could be seen in the act of anchoring. The German cruiser slowed as it lingered, observing. Soon, long boats were lowered over the side and troops were seen scrambling over the transports sides and into the boats.

Captain von Mueller had seen enough and directed his ship back out of the large bay and into the South China Sea. He picked up the collier steaming on its original heading and took up its escorting duties. Captain von Mueller descended to his stateroom to write his report. The long fourteen hour steam back to Admiral von Diedrerich's squadron would be torture. And he knew he would then be dispatched to Prince Henry's fleet with the news. The British had chosen sides.

* * *

President McKinley screamed at his Secretary of State. "What the hell do you mean the British have taken Palawan. Where's the damn map? I don't even know where this damn Palawan is for Christ sake."

"Right here Mr. President," William Day said. "It seems they noticed the island wasn't inside anyones zone of influence. And they are tied to Borneo down here." The Secretary of State swept his hand south pointing out where British interests already lay. "They have been here in Sarawak for quite some time. Palawan seemed to be unattached. It fits with their strategic position in East Asia."

President McKinley looked hard at the map. "What about these islands? What are they, Samar and Leyte it says here."

"No news of yet. sir."

"Well, what are we waiting for. I'll get the Navy Department on the phone an order them to get Dewey on the ball out there. We need to claim those islands and let all these other bloodsuckers know their ours."

"Yes sir." Secretary Day said. "We don't know what's on those islands sir."

"Who the hell knows. But I want them. If this is a land grab, we need to assert ourselves."

"Mr. President, our ploy to get the British to align themselves with us against the Germans and the Japs seems to have backfired."

"Mr. Secretary, no words were more obvious."

"So what is our plan now, Mr President?"

"Hell if I know. Lets get Alger and Long in here and see what options we have."

"If any, Mr. President."

The next day, William Mckinley met with his cabinet over the developments with the war with Spain. Concerned mostly with his War and Navy secretaries, he addressed them.

"Russell, John. I need your best ideas on where we need to proceed," Mckinley said.

John Long, Navy Secretary went first. "Mr. President. As we discussed, we are at a complete disadvantage now. Your phone call yesterday wanting a contingent of ships and troops to go occupy Samar and Leyte weakened us. Admiral Dewey only has part of his squadron now available if there is trouble. I'm afraid is would be a bloodbath."

"And our troop ships should be there by now Mr. President," War Secretary Alger said. "But as you already know the Philippine Revolution had liberated all of Luzon Island but Manila proper. The Spanish will be on their last supplies and are fearful of reprisals at the hands of the filipinos. They have three hundred years of oppression to pay back I'm afraid. Spain has asked for our parole to evacuate their citizens from the city before a massacre happens."

"Are the other islands part of the revolt. Tell me the Japs and Germans are having problems with the locals."

"No Mr. President. As best as we can determine the revolution was confined to Luzon Island. As we know, the Tagalog and Ilcano tribes that make up most of the population on Luzon are the hot heads. The Visayan tribes down south where the Germans are haven't been involved."

"Lucky us," the President said. "Any other good news."

Secretary of State Day spoke up. "As you remember, Mr. President, my position all along was except for Cuba, everything should be returned to Spain at the conclusion of the war. As you saw in the Senate battle for Hawaii, the Anti-Imperialist's constituents hold sway over a good portion of the members. I can only imagine the fight we will have on our hands attempting to annex the Philippines now. With three other imperialist powers grabbing a portion, that puts us squarely in their camp. We would have a hard time taking the high ground of protecting the Philippine people until they are prepared for independence."

Navy Secretary Long said, "Mr. President. Even Secretary Day spoke of retaining a naval base in Manila Bay as a price for our victory. We control the entire Island of Luzon. With Samar and Leyte Islands it is more then we had hoped for. And remember, Luzon is the economic engine for the entire country."

"But what of this revolution," McKinley said. "Do we suppress it? Will that fly with our voters. We have an election this fall. If I loose control of the House, then the Democrats could be trouble."

"A bunch of natives with machetes are what my commanders say," War Secretary Alger said. "Shouldn't be too much trouble for our boys sir."

"Yes, I agree. Along with Guam and Puerto Rico, we have something," the President said. "Bill, set in motion a peace conference with Spain."

The Secretary of State asked "And our fellow partners in the Philippines? Shall we involve them sir.?"

"They're involved already so I guess they need to be notified. I suppose we will be sitting around the table together. I don't like it but don't see any other option. We will see how the voters take it in November."

* * *

The delegates to the peace conference between the United States and Spain began arriving at the end of September. President McKinley had started the process in August when he called the French Ambassador to Washington to propose a ceasefire and subsequent talks. The French offered Paris as a site for the conference to take place.

Trouble started early when the United States attempted to keep the talks between the two specific belligerent countries, which would have excluded Japan, Germany and Britain. With their forces siting on Spanish soil in the Philippines, ostensibly there to protect their citizens property from damage, pressure was brought to include them in the talks. The argument delayed the start but it was Spain who finally invoked their right to have the other countries present.

Heading the American delegation was William Day, former Secretary of State, who had resigned and been replaced by John Hay. Four other members of the American delegation were either senators or a retired diplomat.

Spain's delegation was headed by Eugenio Rios, and was joined by four of his countrymen. Paul von Hatzfeldt, German Ambassador in London headed a five member German delegation while his friend, Sir Edward Malet, 4th Baronet, and member of the British Privy Council headed their five member delegation.

Prince Shuzo, Japanese Ambassador in London headed a two member delegation. He had been joined by the Japanese Ambassador to France since the short time didn't allow any representatives from Tokyo to attend. The French added their diplomat Jules Cambon as moderator.

The Philippine Republic, as it had declared itself, had sent a representative. Felipe Agoncillo had made the trip to Paris after a stop in Washington where he was rebuffed in meeting with President McKinley. He was similarly being rebuffed in gaining a seat at the conference table.

At the opening session on the first of October, Spain demanded the return of the city of Manila to Spanish control. The Americans had finally landed troops and had quickly captured the city. Actually, a scheme had been worked out ahead of time to avoid the city's capture by the Filipino rebel forces. The Americans would attack at a specific time, the Spanish would put up token resistance to fulfill Spanish honor, and then quickly surrender the city. The Americans complied and kept the local forces for entering the city.

At the demand to its return, the American delegation flatly refused. The next month saw talks revolve around Cuba. The primary point hung on the four hundred million dollar national debt of Cuba. Eventually the Cubans were granted freedom and the debt absorbed by Spain. Guam and Puerto Rico were ceded to the United States while the three Great Powers sat waiting for the main event.

The disposition of the Philippines drew everyone's attention as Spain first demanded the return of the islands. The four powers that controlled the islands refused such a demand which brought the United States to make the demand that Germany, Japan and Great Britain leave the islands. This was refused also.

Talks were stymied as the Americans held an election. President McKinley had campaigned in the off year election around the country. He spoke on behalf of Republican congressman running for office and whenever he mentioned the Philippines, the crowd would roar its approval for retaining the islands. Clearly the American public voiced a desire to step out onto the world's stage. November 8th brought the answer as Mckinley held his majority in the House of Representatives from what had been anticipated would be a loss. The delegation in Paris took the message that it implied that America would hold out for at least its portion of the islands.

Now finished with the opening moves, the delegates hammered out an agreement. For Spain, there would be payments in gold for their relinquishing all claims to the Philippines. The amounts to be paid took a week to determine The Americans, receiving the largest island of Luzon, would pay twenty million dollars to Spain. They added Samar and Leyte to their zone of control to go along with the neighboring Luzon.

Germany receiving the most islands, but of a rural subsistence economy, would pay fifteen million. Japan receiving two islands would pay ten million and Great Britain would pay five million for its lone island. The official map with zones of demarcation was signed as numerous small islands had not been specifically named in the text. Now known as the Treaty of Paris, the official map would settle claims over the other seven thousand island making up the Philippine Archipelago.

Felipe Aggoncillo was stunned by the results of the conference. He had kept abreast of the proceedings by a sympathetic member of the American delegation. The United States had a strong anti-imperialist political faction which held a strong position in the U.S. Senate. The treaty would have to obtain Senate approval and Felipe now made his way back to Washington D. C. to continue his fight for independence.

Meanwhile on Luzon Island, the standoff between the forces of the Philippine Republic and U.S. troops grew tense. As reports of the peace conference reached the Philippines, Andres Bonifacio, 'father of the revolution', began plotting his next moves. With his country now divided between four Great Powers he saw opportunity in the natural rivalry between them. Bonifacio would see if his previous delegation talks with Emperor of Japan would bring fruit. Little did he know that another power would be his benefactor.

Chapter 17

Lapu-Lapu, Mactan Island, Philippines
January, 1899

"But Felipe, you play a very dangerous game," Alexander Dull said to his father-in-law.

"I know my son, and I don't want you involved."

"But you are involving me. And Donita. And the entire family if you are caught."

"So it may be. But my country needs me right now. Just as you told me your father answered the ultimate call for your country when the need was great."

Alex stopped his arguing. Felipe was right that the Philippines needed all its citizens to help to gain the country's freedom. The final Treaty of Paris had been signed on December 4 and the results were quickly dispersed around the islands. The filipinos were confused on how their country, on the verge of beating the Spanish in their rebellion, had suddenly acquired five overseers. And like Felipe, many had had enough and were joining the struggle.

Traditionally, the revolution was confined to Luzon island as the tribes that lived there were more forceful in their desire to rid themselves of Spain. Luzon held the money interests of the islands while the neighboring islands lived a subsistence existence that was little affected by Spanish rule. Life was simple out in the provinces. It was those hotheads on Luzon that had the time to think.

Now Felipe joined the Kapiaana that guided the revolution. Using his large fishing boat he had agreed to run money and weapons to Leyte Island. It paid well as it was being financed by the new German masters in Cebu. Felipe didn't really consider the reason for Germany's magnanimity, he just knew the rebels needed support. And while things were tense but quiet around Manila, everyone knew a boiling point was not far off.

Alexander lifted the trap covering Felipe's cargo. Wooden boxes wrapped in a tarpaulin for seawater protection filled his boat. Alex pried open one box. He wanted to confirm what Felipe was hauling and stopped when he saw the contents. He lifted one out of the rack and examined it.

"My God. These are Japanese Mausers."

"Good rifles, no?" Felipe asked.

Alex looked around to make sure no one was near them. He placed the rifle back in the box and hammered the lid tight. Stretching the tarp back on tight, he turned to his father-in-law.

"The Germans are sending Japanese rifles to the rebels. When they are captured the Americans will think its the Japs helping."

"That's OK, no. If all the powers begin fighting amongst themselves, may be we Filipinos can have a chance."

"But what if the Americans are doing the same to the Germans? Or the British to the Japanese? We could end up with fighting on all the islands."

"Good. Kill them all."

"But Felipe. If the great powers turn the islands in a war zone, it will be Filipinos that will bear the brent of the deaths. Wars always kill more civilians than soldiers."

"God will provide."

Alex had learned that this was a traditional response in the islands. *God would provide an answer to life's problems. It kept life simple and uncomplicated. No one thought to much about the future here, just live for today's needs. God would take of the rest* he thought.

As an American, and even more so as an educated American, life needed a path. Some thought as to where you wanted to be in the future. If you didn't set a goal, nothing ever changed. From his friendship with Dr. Rizal, they had talked of the Filipino attitude and how educated citizens had to make sacrifices that at times seemed pointless. As he stepped out of the loaded fishing boat, he made a determination that he would have to do change his way. A peaceful way. In honor of his martyr friend.

Alex didn't have long to wait. On February 4th the uneasy truce between the American and the Philippine Republic forces ended. Near the main water supply for Manila the First Nebraska Regiment patrolled its defensive line that kept the Filipinos from entering the city. With the peace treaty being discussed in the U.S. Senate some felt that McKinley wanted a provocation to help pass the treaty.

Others argued that Emilio Aguinaldo, recognized as the fist president of the newly independent Philippine Republic on January 21, 1899, wanted to force the American's hand. He knew the results of the Treaty of Paris left the Americans the new masters on Luzon Island. The struggle against Spanish rule now became a struggle against American rule. The start of the Philippine-American War would answer the question on who ruled the Philippines.

But for Alexander Dull the war would be a back drop. Peace prevailed in his portion of the world as he went about helping the Germans set up a government for their portion of the Philippines. Now officially called New Prussia, the Germans had committed to spending money on schools, roads and water systems among other infrastructure projects. German traders soon began arriving setting up copra operations and coffee plantations. Tea cultivation had been started as well as jute for ropes.

Alex watched as the simple farm and fishing life of the islands began to change. Money drove up prices of goods and more shops opened providing a wide variety of items. Not sure he welcomed the changes, Alex continued his language interpretation duties. His new friend Captain Wilhelm von Mueller had become a close friend and confidant.

The *SMS Prinzess Sophia*, having the shortest draft of all the German warships, had been made the official island government vessel. Alex would move through the islands translating for various German officials that had been assigned to establish local governments. Local Filipinos were appointed captains of their barangay, or villages. Each captain had an elected board of five members.

New Prussia had been divided into provinces much along the lines of the old Spanish system. Provincial governors had been appointed and Alex worked in translating the German division of power between the locals and Berlin. It generally came to everything but foreign affairs under Filipino control. Goods imported and exported were taxed and were under German control, along with immigration of foreigners.

The two battleships had long ago left Philippine waters and along with Prince Henry had sailed to the German commission at Tsingtao in China. The original East Asia Squadron had followed the prince back to China while the four cruisers sent with the battle ships remained in New Prussia. More ships would be sent as Germany's territory expanded.

"Alex, good to see you," Captain von Mueller said as Alex enter the captain's stateroom.

"Where are we headed this trip?"

The two men traveled extensively throughout New Prussia establishing German rule over the area. The Governor-General recently appointed by the Kaiser continued Berlin's policy of locally controlled government and Alex was happy to assist. The more experience the filipinos gained in self government the sooner they would attain self rule.

"Zamboanga I'm afraid."

Alex's heart sank at the mention of Zamboanga. Located in the middle of Moro territory, the local Muslim population had taken the attitude the the new Germans were just like the old Spanish, more westerners and Christians to fight. A long four hundred year struggle continued and Alex knew that he could do little.

"You do know my Tausug is weak," Alex said.

Among the one hundred and seventy languages in the islands, Alex had mastered some, knew a little of others. But Tausug, the language of the Sulu Archipelago, was more related to Borneo then the Philippines. In fact, the entire area around Zamboanga had ties to the Sultan of Sulu and even more to the Brunei Sultanate. History had this area of the Philippines moving between sultans over the many years up until Spain arrive. The issue was finally settled between Britain and Spain with Britain dominating northern Borneo while Spain gain exclusive rights to Sulu.

Now the Germans were asserting their control over the area and the locals had been resisting. Many of the troops shipped east with the battleships had also left for China as trouble seemed to be building. The entire East Asia area simmered with the great powers laying rule over a smorgasbord of old alliances and kingdoms. Much like the Balkans of Europe, the area abounded in old feuds between many different peoples, all speaking different languages and worshipping different gods.

"I know Alex. I tried to explain that but you know what they say. Do your best."

"Easy for them siting here in Cebu City."

Alex's easy relationship with Captain von Mueller carried on through the summer of 1899 as the two worked the various islands of the new German territory. Alex provided language interpretation and von Mueller the transportation and security. Different German officials had been assigned to different islands with a small contingent of soldiers to enforce the German edicts.

The locals on a whole accepted their new masters well and continued their rural life fishing and farming. The Germans began building schools and as teachers arrived from Germany, began language lessons. More and more Germans became fluent in the local language and Alex's work began to wain.

The only places that German rule was being contested were in the Moro sections of Mindanao Island. Between allegiance to either the Sultan of Sulu or the Sultanate of Brunei, the locals continued to look south for leadership and not to Cebu.

The Governor-General of New Prussia wisely let the Moro population alone as he worked hard on building a new colony in the rest of the Visaya region. Time would be on his side to move on the Moros after the rest of the islands were assimilated. Alex's trips became fewer and fewer as his skills were no longer needed.

Felipe Cavato, Alex's father-in-law continued working with the German's in moving war material to the rebels on Leyte and Samar Islands. The war on Luzon between the Philippine Republic and American forces continued to grind down the local forces. The Americans were making steady progress moving northward on Luzon Island into Ilocano tribal territory.

The Ilocanos and Tagalog tribes were the main support base for the revolution. And unlike the tribes on the other islands, the tribes on Luzon fought for their independence. But American firepower and military training worked against the locals as battle after battle were lost to the new colonists. It became bad enough that the President of the Republic, Emilio Aguinaldo, had to declare guerilla war on Nov. 13, 1899.

Alex met Captain von Mueller in Cebu City a week after the announcement. They sat in a sari-sari shop and took coffee together. As good friends, after Alex lost his work translating, they would continue to meet and discuss island affairs whenever the caption was in port.

"How is it going with the Moros, Wilhelm?"

"Don't ask. They are a tough group and it will probably lead to all out war to bring them around."

"That's what the Spanish discovered. I heard the stories while living in Dagipatan on Mindanao with Dr. Rizal. They will not submit to any Western power."

Captain von Mueller wanted to change the subject as he knew the Moro problem wasn't going to be solved soon. He asked, "What do you think of Aguinaldo's decree to switch to guerrilla war?"

"I'm sadden by it. It was what Dr. Rizal feared. A lot of locals will die because of it, I'm afraid."

"You know what happened with the Spanish in Cuba when the locals wouldn't submit. The Spanish invented the way to end a guerilla war."

'I know. Concentration camps. Move all the locals into camps so they can be controlled and not give aid to the guerilla. Unfortunately they starved or died of disease outbreaks."

"Or fortunately if you were Spanish."

Alex knew of the tens of thousands of women and children that had died in the Cuban Revolution. It was one of the moving factors that lead to the United States declaring war on Spain. The American public had read the stories of Spanish atrocities and opinion grew to support the Cubans.

That America might use the same tactics abhorred Alex. But it seemed to satisfy his friend.

"Kind of ironic my friend, don't you think?"

"Ironic in what way, Wilhelm?"

"Think about it Alex. You Americans go to war to liberate a victimized people only to turn around and victimize people yourself."

His friend was right and Alex knew it. He had spent many waking hours thinking on what his country was doing in the name of freedom. President McKinley had issued his 'Benevolent assimilation' decree back in November of last year. Alex couldn't reconcile benevolent anything with what seemed to be happening on Luzon.

But Wilhelm wasn't finished. "And now we receive word that your General Arthur MacArthur has issued orders for martial law. The screws are ratcheting up as they say."

"Yes, I'm afraid so. At least it continues to be quiet in New Prussia."

"And no word from the Japanese islands. I assume things are quiet over there also."

Alex hadn't heard of any trouble on Mindoro or Panay islands. Only that the Japanese were busy building schools and introducing Japanese to the students as teachers arrived from Japan. Four powers, three new languages, it all overwhelmed him as he saw the Philippines devolving into four separate countries. He thought of his friend Dr. Rizal and how he would take these developments.

Alex and Donita's family continued to grow as their second son was born the first of the year. His money from working for the German authorities was safely tucked away for emergencies. He went back to fishing with his father-in-law as photography was put aside. He had run out of glass plates and didn't want to spend his money on more supplies. With the war continuing on Luzon he knew he and his family might need to leave quickly. His father-in-law's business of shipping material to the rebels had gone unnoticed so far. If discovered, however, he and Donita could be implicated.

Alex and Captain von Mueller didn't see each other the rest of that summer and it wasn't until late September that they finally met. News of President

McKinley's assassination in Buffalo, New York had filtered down to the outlying islands. As Alex got ready to bicycle across Mactan Island to meet his friend, Felipe caught him.

"Alex, you need to know something bad is about to happen on Samar. You've warned me about my activities and I've told the Germans I won't be transporting guns anymore."

"What is it Felipe?"

"I don't know, but on my last trip they were very excited. They had something planned, I could tell."

Alex knew that the war against the Philippine Republic had taken a blow when President Aguinaldo had been captured in Isabella Province in North Luzon. As things began to wind down on Luzon Island, however, the rebels on Samar Island in particular became more active. And with the arms Germany had smuggled into the rebels, things would be more deadly.

"Felipe, its about time. You know you put the entire family at risk."

"I know Alex, but its something I had to do. I couldn't sit and let others fight for my freedom. But I am done."

Alex was relieved that one threat to his family had ended. But he wondered what the Samar Island rebels had planned. Things had been bad enough with atrocities on both sides as Luzon was subdued. Little did Alex know then that Samar would redefine atrocities.

It wasn't until he met with Captain von Mueller in October that he learned what his father-in-law had warned about. Sitting down across from his German friend, he saw the sadness in the captain's eyes.

"What is it Wilhelm?"

"Very sad day I'm afraid."

Alex's heart sank. The news in the islands continued to be bad as scattered elements of the Philippine Republic continued the struggle on Luzon. He waited for his friend.

Wilhelm continued, "The rebels on Samar just attacked your soldiers in the village of Balangiga. Forty eight troops of the 9th Infantry were slaughtered mostly with machetes. The rest of the soldiers escaped by sea."

"My God. This will earn Samar an attack for sure."

"You don't know how true you are Alex. We have friendly personnel in your army and they smuggled out the orders from your American commander General Jacob Smith. I understand he's been given a free hand to clear out the perpetrators of this attack."

"How free a hand do you mean?" Alex asked.

"Read this," Wilhelm handed a paper to Alex.

Alex read the message and glanced at the General's name at the bottom. It read :

'I want no prisoners. I wish you to kill and burn, the more you kill and burn, the better it will please me. The interior of Samar must be made a howling wilderness.'

"I can't believe a U.S. Army officer would issue such an order."

"It gets worse. Word is an officer asked what age limit on the killings should be observed. Your general replied ten years old."

Alex sat stunned. The United Staes was making war on everyone over the age of ten on Samar, and not war, but extermination. No rules against harming civilians. Everyone would feel the wrath of America.

Wilhelm added, "They've started calling him 'Howling Wilderness Smith' for his orders."

Alex thoughts turned to his father-in-law and his decision to stop trading with Samar and Leyte. He soon learned that the Americans had cut off all trade to the island. The more he thought about it the more he knew he had to do something. He went home and talked to this father-in-law. He put his last unexposed plates in a crate and checked his photography equipment. The two men left three days later sailing for Leyte Island. At Leyte they learned of the blockade of Samar to the north and how they could defeat it.

Landing at what had once been Balangiga village, only charred remains showed where once a thriving village stood. Alex and Felipe unloaded their supplies and Alex soon met a local. As he and Felipe told them what they wanted to do, the man disappeared. The next day a small cadre of men showed up carrying the rifles that Felipe had delivered over the past year. As Felipe sailed away, Alex and his new helpers disappeared into the jungle.

Alex was determined to photograph what was happening on Samar. He soon learned that he would have no trouble finding atrocities to take pictures of as the American soldiers had started what they were calling the 'March Across Samar.' Alex knew the reference to Sherman's March to the Sea in the Civil War, Sherman's intent to make Georgia howl.

From his guides, Alex learned that hundreds of villages had been burned and that any locals were shot on sight. His decided to photograph some of this destruction and pushed aside his fear of being captured. While he held a certain safety in that he was an American, being caught with the rebels wouldn't help him if the troops shot first and asked questions after.

The group spent the next four days avoiding detection as they moved through the jungle. Alex took photos of villages that had been burned, especially where they found ones were locals had bee shot. Capturing images of women and children dead among the ruins filled Alex with rage at his government.

As they neared the village of Basey the leader of the rebels explained that the soldiers had been very active. The next day a scout came to them to report soldiers ahead at a village. A Navy officer had been killed on a beach nearby and the Americans seemed extra blood thirsty. Alex asked if they could move closer and the rebel leader agreed.

Soon they were on the edge of the jungle, a village being burned a short one hundred yards away. Alex set up his tripod and attached his box camera. He slipped in a glass plate and aimed it toward the village. As he did, soldiers dragged the inhabitants out of the village and shoved them against a wall of one house. Other soldiers stood in a row nearby and raised their rifles.

Just as they pulled the trigger, Alex snapped his shutter, capturing the moment of impact. As the executed civilians crumpled to the ground, a second group was shoved to the same spot. Alex quickly changed plates and readied himself. He clicked the shutter as the second volley rang out. Swapping plates he waited. A third group was brought out and readily shot.

The remaining buildings were put to the torch and any remaining animals in the village shot. Caribou joined pigs and chickens as the scorched earth edict was carried out. The soldiers gathered in lines and soon marched off.

Alex and his guides moved into the village as he set up his camera for a close up. Capturing the bloody pile of bodies, he swung his lens to the burning buildings for another shot. With his dry plates exhausted he instructed his rebel leader that he needed to return to Cebu as quickly as possible. Alex knew that such shots of the war in the Philippines would result in the American public revolting to what was happening in their name.

Chapter 18

Washington D.C.
January 26, 1902

The ongoing Philippine-America war had killed thousands of locals over the ensuing two years. Senator George Hoar entered his office full of hope. The hearings were to start today and as the leading anti-imperialist in the U.S. Senate he held out hope that if the rumors of atrocity taking place in the Philippines were proven true, that it would lead to America giving up its quest for empire.

For the young new president, Theodore Roosevelt, the hearings were crucial. Sworn in as the twenty-sixth president after President William McKinley's assassination by an anarchist in Buffalo, New York, his administration came under scrutiny as to the war in the Philippines.

Livid reports led to sensational cartoons of American atrocities being committed in the name of bringing peace to the islands. The facts seemed to play out differently as report after report filtered down of American troops wantonly executing locals, men, women and children.

And then the news of a massacre at Balangiga on Samar Island showed that the war was far from over. The capture of the revolutionary leader Aquidiou had the United States hopeful that the hostilities would soon be over. The killing of forty eight Americans in a gruesome attack with machetes stirred the public.

The ensuing pacification of Samar became public as worse atrocities were metered out on the island in retribution. When the reports of wholesale slaughter of Filipino citizens on Samar reached America, the U.S. Senate could no longer stay motionless.

"Senator, there is a visitor here to see you," Senator Hoar's chief of staff said.

A young man, thin but tall, stepped into the senator's office. He wore a loose suit looking as if he had borrowed it from someone much larger. His face was gaunt and pasty.

Senator Hoar stood and walked from behind his desk. This was one of his star witnesses in the hearings.

"Mr. Riley. Good of you to come over early. We have reviewed your letters and just want to follow-up on some items."

The letters were ones Charles Riley had mailed to his mother while a private in the 26th Volunteer Massachusetts Regiment out of Northhampton, Massachusetts. As a local boy, his mother had read in horror at the description of what her son was doing in the Philippines. Fighting on Luzon in the race to capture Aguilido, Riley had witnessed the early aspect of the war.

Contracting dengue fever, the private had almost died and had eventually been sent back to the United States debilitated from the disease. Hence his emaciated look.

"Private Riley. When your mother brought your letters to my attention, we knew we had to have you testify to what has been taking place in the Philippines."

"Thank you Senator. I just hope I can hold up. I'm afraid I'm still plenty weak."

"And I assure you that I will call a recess immediately if you falter. But I believe our country needs to hear from one of its heroic soldiers what the high command is committing overseas. We have no right to be subjugating other people in the name of American empire."

"Yes, sir."

"Sorry. I just get so riled up over our country becoming just another imperial power. We are better then that and I aim to see that we come home immediately and end this empire building scheme the president desires."

"I'll do my best sir."

"I know you will son. Did your mother make the trip with you like we asked?"

"Yes sir."

"Good. we will seat her right behind you. I want the other senators to see the mothers of our brave boys dying in foreign lands." Senator Hoar bristled at the thought of some brave young American wrapped up in this wild crusade. And now with blood on their hands at the orders of their superiors.

The hearings, soon to be called the Lodge Committee, named for its chairman, Senator Henry Cabot Lodge of Massachusetts, would investigate the rumors and charges flying around Washington. Private Riley's testimony was only the beginning.

On March 12, 1902, Major Waller's court martial trial began and the interest shifted to its outcome. When the Marine officers voted on April 11th for acquittal, more court-martials ensued.

But a story in the press in mid-March brought the nation's attention to the Army Commander, General Nelson Miles. In an interview, he blamed the administration for covering up attempts by he Army to investigate the atrocities in the Philippines.

Focus then shifted to Manila where 'Howling Jack' Smith's court martial had begun. The news reports were building as the headlines screamed of more and more killings by the Army. 'Cruelty and Barbarity Will be Investigated' yelled the Atlanta Constitution in sync with many American newspapers.

But by May the trial of General 'Howling Jack' Smith ended in a whimper as the board voted to admonish Smith with no further punishment. The man who had ordered everyone on Samar killed over the age of ten walked away a free man.

All this time the Democratics attacked the Republican administration of President Roosevelt. With the fall congressional elections looming, the Democrats tried to ride the war news to a victory.

Their hopes of wounding Roosevelt ended on Memorial Day. The President traveled to Arlington National Cemetery and gave a rousing speech on heroic war dead and all they had fought for. His rally round the flag speech swayed the country and the following days the mood of the country swung to other things.

On June 3, 1902 the U.S. Senate passed a bill granting Philippine Civil government to the filipinos. All the Republicans but one voted in favor. Senator George Hoar the one voice joining with the Democrats against imperial America. The anti-imperialist league had fought hard but failed to move America away from empire building. On June 4th, the U.S. Senate begin work on the Panama Canal bill which passed within two weeks. American stepped firmly onto the stage with the other world powers.

* * *

As all of this took place in Washington, D.C., back in Cebu City a hospitalized Alexander Dull awoke to sun filtering through the gauze curtains over the window. His body ached intensely as he felt the pain of just moving his head to the right. Beds full of patients lay filled the room, a nurse nearby tending patients. The nurse looked up and saw Alex's open eyes.

"We have a live one doctor."

Alex saw a man in a white coat appear from his left and pick up his wrist to check his heart rate. Next the doctor took a table light near the bed and swiveled it into Alex's face. The doctor pulled his eye lid up and examined his pupil.

"Well, another one saved by Robert Koch and Dr. Thomas Latta," the doctor said.

"I'm glad doctor," the nurse said. She had moved to assist the doctor in his quick examination.

The doctor turned to face Alex and said, "I thought we'd lost you son. Your nurse here wouldn't give up on you though."

Alex tried to speak but his throat was dry and constricted. The doctor noticed his inability to speak so took a notepad on the table and handed it to Alex with a pen.

Alex wrote why he was in hospital.

"You contracted Cholera. Your friend brought you in two weeks ago very near death."

Asking who had brought him in, the doctor answered, "Captain von Mueller. Said he had found you off the Comotes Island in a local craft. The natives flagged him down when they knew you were so sick. And good thing they did. Thousands are dying."

Asking who the two people the doctor had mentioned, Alex got his answer.

"Robert Koch isolated the cholera bacteria, Vibrio Cholerae."

Not really caring what the stupid disease was really called Alex wrote a question about the second name.

"Dr. Thomas Latta. He discovered the saline drip." The doctor then reached over and shook the tube protruding from Alex's arm. Alex turned to the pull on his body and noticed the glass bottle hanging over the left side of his bed. He then noticed all the other patients in the ward with similar hook-ups.

"Cholera does its deadly work by causing its victims to shit themselves to death. The bacteria dehydrates the body to the point where you die. The saline drip gives your body life saving liquids to keep you alive until the bacteria runs its course."

The nurse chimed in. "There are thousands of deaths in the islands. It started in Manila and spread quickly with all the soldiers moving about the Philippines. The German authorities tried to do a quarantine and have been somewhat successful."

"Captain von Mueller reported you had been on Leyte which would have been ripe for the disease with the Americans coming over form Luzon. We have had only scattered cases so far."

Alex wrote a thank you on the paper and the two medical staff nodded their acceptance. They ambled off to other patients as Alex laid back and thought. *What became of my photos taken on Samar?* he thought. He almost died getting those pictures and became concerned that they had been lost.

The next day he began the road back with his first food in three weeks. German potato soup with everything mushed into pulp felt wonderful as it went down. The nurse ladled another spoon full into his mouth giving him his voice back.

"I had important luggage with me in Leyte. Did they give you anything to store for me?"

I'm afraid we only got you. You'd have to check with Captain von Mueller about anything else."

A week went by and Alex could finally stand and walk short distances. His muscles complained at the energy it required to move but he was determined to get out of the hospital as quickly as possible. Released two days later, Captain von Mueller was there as he made his way to the room he rented in Cebu City.

"Alex, so good to see you alive my friend."

"Wilhelm, I understand I owe you my life."

"You were pretty bad when those natives sailed up to our ship. We were on quarantine duty at the time, keeping any locals moving from the American zone to the German zone."

"Did you get in trouble taking me across the boundary?"

"I told them I found you alone in a local boat off Banacon Island near Bohol. Not to worry. I'm good."

Alex had to know, "My photography equipment?"

"Its in your room, safe and sound."

"Thank you." Then Alex remembered his family in Lapu-Lapu. *They must think I'm dead by now* he thought. It had been close to two months since he first left for Samar Island. He made excuses with his friend that he needed to lay down and Captain von Mueller told him he would see him later. Later that evening Alex grabbed a ferry and then a cart ride across Mactan Island. His wife, Donita screamed with joy as he stepped off the cart at the Calvero family compound.

It would be a week eating and trying to gain his physical strength while he considered what his life held. Alex knew with the photos he had captured on Samar that his fellow citizens back home needed to know the truth. With the money he had earned from translating for the Germans authorities, he decided he had to return to the United States. When he developed the glass plates of his Samar adventure, he was convinced the images could change the situation in the islands.

Little did Alex know that events were passing him by in America. The Lodge Committee closed its hearings on the day he and Donita and their three sons stepped aboard the steamer bound for Singapore. With Manila still under the grips of the cholera epidemic, shipping avoided the port. They would have to travel to the British colony and then take a steamer to San Francisco.

Four months later they arrived in the United Sates as San Francisco celebrated New Year's Day. With the arrival of 1903, Alex hoped that the world, and especially Asia, might settle into a tranquility.

Boarding a train across the country, Alex and his family arrived in Massachusetts where Alex's mother met her grandchildren for the first time. As it was still the winter break for Congress' recess, Alex found his uncle at home in Worcester.

"But uncle, I have photos of the atrocities that took place on Samar. I risked my life getting them."

"I'm sure you did Alex. But it's all a dead issue now. The U.S. Senate, in all its wisdom, has moved on. The Panama Canal was approved and Roosevelt held the Republicans in a majority Congress in November. It seems the American public is totally enamored with our new possessions."

"Could we at least put my photos on exhibit. Maybe we can get the public rethinking this whole sordid mess."

"Alex, as your uncle, I would advise you put those atrocity pictures away. The Philippines is a raw scab right now and peeling that scar tissue off could be very dangerous for you and your family. Powerful people from the President on down want us to have colonies around the world."

"But uncle, it's not what America stands for. It's not what my father died for, at least."

"You are so true about that. We need to be smart and play the long game. Right now empire seems bright and wonderful to most. Our flag flies around the world like those other Great Powers. If we play it right, a day will come when empire isn't so wonderful. Then maybe we can bring out those photos and remind people what the price of empire really is."

"I'll take your advice, as always."

Senator Hoar smiled at his nephew. "But I think an exhibit of life in the Philippines would do wonders. I'm sure you've captured the essence of life in the islands. Show the American public those. Show what level of development our colonies are and what we will need to spend to bring them into the new 20th century. I'll make the arrangements. You get your photos ready."

Alex sat in despair at what his country had become. And even more so for the results in the Philippines. He thought of his friend Dr. Rizal and despaired at Filipinos ever gaining their independence.

A showing of his Philippines pictures, minus his war atrocity shots, opened at the Smithsonian Museum two months later to great fanfare. People wanted to see what they had gained in the recent war.

A meeting of an old friend during the exhibit had Alex off on a new adventure. Gilbert Grosvenor had been hired by a new magazine, the National Geographic. Grosvenor had remembered Alex's first exhibit at Holy Cross College so many years ago and upon attending had offered Alex a job.

As Alex and his old friend walked among his photo exhibit, Alex added commentary to each picture. At one photo, Gilbert stopped and stared.

"What is it?" Alex asked.

"This picture isn't in the Philippines. It looks like Paris."

"It is. That's a picture of my dear friend Jose Rizal and I on the Eiffel Tower during the Paris World's Fair. He is considered the father of the Philippine Revolution."

"No, I recognize him. It's this woman here I was wondering about. She looks familar," Gilbert said.

The statement had Alex thinking back many years to the beautiful woman he had gotten to know at the fair. His mind raced to remember her name.

"Ann Garner I believe, if I recall right."

"Ann sounds right, but I know her as Ann Eisele."

Alex asked, "So how do you know her?"

"She is married to Federal Judge Lawrence Eisele of the U.S. Court of Appeals here in Washington.

237

Eisele was a close friend of President McKinley who appointed him to the bench. His wife is an old friend of the former First Lady."

"I had no idea. We had a fun time in Paris and then she and her sister left to complete their European tour. I never heard from her again."

Gilbert smiled and said, "Well, it will certainly be interesting if she shows up to your exhibit. Her husband may have a few questions for her."

Alex marveled at what a small world it really was but had no time to ponder if his photos would result in marital problems. He and Gilbert worked out an photographic assignment and Alex was busy preparing.

Alex soon returned to Massachusetts to get Donita and his family firmly settled in Massachusetts, He worked hard in the ensuing months improving his Japanese language skills and studying Japanese culture. Just after Christmas, with his supplies packed, Alex left Donita and his sons with his mother in Worcester and headed back to Asia on assignment.

He would do a photo shoot of Japan. Its rise in world stature with its newly acquired territory had the public clamoring for more information on the mysterious country. Alex's knowledge of Japanese eased his arrival and transition to Japanese life .

A week after his arrival, Japan attacked the naval Inuits of Russia at Port Arthur. Opening hostilities with a surprise attack, the Russians were initially stunned and Alex had a new calling. He worked his connections and by April 1904 he was imbedded with the Japanese army laying siege to Port Arthur.

Alex had missed the Boxer Rebellion in 1900 when eight of the world's powers had sent a naval and military force to subdue the rebelling Chinese. He was determined to capture the gruesome images that wars create. Alex took photo after photo as Japan conducted frontal assaults on the Russian defenders. Gruesome casualties in the thousands left Alex stunned at the futility. But through it all he held firm in documenting the entire event.

By June he had had enough and with dwindling glass plates for his camera, he made his way back to Tokyo where he made passage for Seattle. The train deposited him in Worcester once again and a peaceful Fall in New England. The trees had not yet begin to turn color, but the evening chill hit him as he stepped off the train onto the platform.

Gathering his luggage, he hired a carriage to take him the short ride to his mother's house where his family waited. Unloading in the vestibule, his brothers stepped outside to lend a hand. Their mood seemed very subdued to their brother retuning from the war and Alex asked, "What's wrong. You don't seem very happy to see me."

Alex's mother stepped outside and asked her youngest son to come inside while the three brothers moved his luggage into the dining room. Sitting down in the parlor, Alex looked a this Mom. He could tell she'd been crying.

"What's going on Mother?"

"It's Uncle George. He died two days ago in Washington. His body will lie in state in the rotunda in the Capitol building for two days and then be sent by train for funeral services and burial here in Worcester."

Alex slumped and put his hands over his face. Tears flowed though his fingers as he began sobbing. The man that had acted as his surrogate father all these years had died.

"At least you got home in time to join us for the services,"

He lifted his head up and looked at his mother, tears streaking his face. He attempted to say something, but his voice failed him. His mother moved to sit next to her son and hold him. He leaned his head to her shoulder and continued to cry. It was the arrival of Donita and his sons that caused him to pull his composure together.

As all four boys ran to their Dad, he noticed his wife standing in front of him. His tears stopped as he smiled at his wife. He stood and took her in his arms, kissing her, four boys clinging to his legs.

All three older brothers entered the room to support their younger brother. None of them had married which left Alex and Donita the sole job of carrying on the family line. That Alex had married an Asian had certainly diversified the strong German blood lines.

Rockwood Hoar along with his wife Christine arrived at the Dull home that afternoon. After welcoming his cousin home form Japan, Rockwood accepted condolences all around. He outlined the funeral and burial plans for his father before they all sat down for dinner together. As they regaled with stories of the late Senator, little could anyone know the son would die within the year.

Chapter 19

Maastricht, Germany
August 2, 1914

"Listen Major, I'm putting you in charge of this civilian. Keep him out of my way."

"Jawhol, colonel," Major Otto von Mueller, second in commend of the 3rd Royal Prussian Magdeburg Jagerbattlion, said. As part of Heinrich von Kluck's First Army, von Mueller's regiment sat in its staging area outside Maastricht. There they awaited orders.

Standing in front of the two Imperial German officers, Alexander Dull waited. As the battalion's colonel turned and left, he knew he would have to be careful. He had arrived in Germany three months prior, sent by his employer, the National Geographic magazine, to capture the view of a peaceful Europe.

Naturally, Alex had located his old friend from his Philippines days. Captain Wihelm von Mueller had become Admiral von Mueller in charge of the First Battlecruiser Squadron in Wiilhemshaven. The two old friends recounted their lives since their last meeting in 1902. Alec thanked the Admiral again for saving his life during the deadly cholera outbreak.

Austrian Archduke Franz Ferdinand had been assassinated in the Balkans on June 28. The month of July had been spent with the various powers of Europe making demands on each other, war clouds growing as bellicose neighbors all aligned with allies. During this time Alex worked hard on getting imbedded with a unit that would be at the front if war broke out. His experience in the Russo-Japanese War helped convince the power-that-be that he had the experience to handle a war setting.

Admiral von Mueller passed Alex off to his cousin, Otto von Mueller with praise for Alex's trustworthiness in the affairs of Germany. That Alex had helped Germany colonize its holdings in the Philippines seemed to hold sway with high command.

"Are you sure you want to be with us Mr. Dull?" Otto said. "We are a Jagerbattalion so will be in any battle that comes."

"Exactly where I want to be."

"It's your life. But I'll remind you, shells and bullets don't distinguish civilian from soldier. You accept that risk?"

"I've been there before. The Japanese made the same concerns known to me before they sent me to Port Arthur. And that was a slaughter like the world had never seen."

"And you captured it all with your camera?"

"You might have seen my pictures in the December 1904 edition of my magazine. It was well read at the time and I got many compliments at my images."

"No, can't say that I saw them. But I guess someone higher up saw them to let you march with us. You'll have to handle all your gear yourself. My troops are not here to be your porters."

"Understood. I've purchased three horses to carry my gear."

The day turned ominous as Germany made the demand on Belgium for free passage through their country to strike at the hated French. Great Britain had made a commitment to Belgium, guaranteeing their neutrality. The French needed help in defeating the stronger German Army in an invasion and knew the British would make their combined forces stronger. On August 4th, at a lack of an answer from the Belgians, Germany declared war and attacked Belgium.

Alex set out on the long march toward Paris the same day. Since he moved with the headquarters, his actual time spent near fighting was limited. As the 3rd Battalion fought its away across Belgium, Alex typically caught the after effects of each battle. Dead soldiers and horses would be scattered about as he set up his tripod and heavy camera. Glass plate after glass plate were exposed to the carnage of the First Army's march.

By September 3rd, von Klick's army sat on the northeast quarter of Paris. To the left on the flank, the German 2nd Army held the line near Chateau Thierry. The next day the British and French forces launched an attack along the Marne River. The Battle of the Marne sealed Germany's dreams of a decisive quick victory in the west. With Russia mobilizing quicker then expected, the Germans were now in a two front war. Unable to knock the French out early, the war would settle into a statement in the west as Germany began shipping troops east to deal with the advancing Russians.

Alex took the train with his unit as far as Cologne where he parted ways with Major von Mueller. News reports in the local papers announced fighting in the German colonies around the world. Japan, an ally of Great Britain, had attack German territory and with the British fleet controlling the oceans, Germany knew its colonies were on their own.

When Alex read the news, he thought of Japan taking the area that had been called New Prussia. The Visaya tribal area of the Philippines would once again change overseers and Alex wondered what that meant for Donita's family still on Mactan Island. He booked passage to Boston and was safely back home for Christmas and his eight children. Donita, after giving him four fine sons, had somehow switched and he now had four beautiful daughters.

Over objections by his mother, he had purchased a large home near by to raise their large family. But Donita grew worried about her family as news from the islands slowly drifted to America. Japanese authorities were not as forgiving as the Germans had been and were now requiring Japanese taught in all the schools.

A long simmering feud began between Alex and his wife. Adding to the stress was the knowledge that it became harder to send support money to her family when the Japanese took over. Where the Germans were very efficient at international bank transfers, the twice per year money transfer Alex did to his wife's family were stopped due to difficulties with the Philippine banks.

The winter of 1905 found the couple repeatedly arguing over how they could support her family and if they should work toward bringing them to the United Sates. Immigration was possible as immediate family members but letters suggesting such went unanswered from the islands.

"Alex," Donita said. "What are we going to do? I'm am worried about my family."

"I know you are Donita. But we can't seem to get the banks to cooperate. What can I do?"

"We could travel there and take the money in person. That way we could start the immigration process while we are in Manila with the American officials."

Alex had heard this argument of traveling to the islands before. Seeing first hand what was happening there would fill in for the letters that did make it through which were vague in their description of life under the Japanese. He had tried to get reports from Washington from official channels but even the government lacked information.

"I'll check with Gilbert on an assignment to east Asia. Then I can divert over to Cebu City and check on your family."

"But I couldn't go with you if it was work related."

"Donita, we have eight children that need to be cared for. You have your responsibilities here at home. I could never ask my mother to take care of our family for the months we would be gone."

Alex knew his wife missed her family and life in the Philippines. Each New England winter had been torture for her as she could never get warm enough. Years ago before the last two girls arrived they had talked of returning to the Philippines to live. Alex was glad they had never chosen that route. Life under Imperial Germany would be tolerable, life under Imperial Japan was now looking much worse.

Alex began the search for a project that National Geographic would be interested in while checking on assignments they had planned. Nothing held their interest at the moment and he continued his regular photographic work locally. His European war photos had been a big success and while there was talk of his return to the front, he personally wished to avoid anymore wars. The images he had captured had shaken him to the horrors of it all. He longed for more human stories such as his Native American photo assignment so long ago.

He was working in his darkroom when a knock on the door startled him. The family knew not to disturb him while he was working so he yelled out. Donita announced a visitor and that he should finish up.

Fifteen minutes later after putting his work away his work he emerged from the darkroom. His cousin Rockwood's widow sat in the parlor chatting with Donita. He walked across the room to give her a kiss on the cheek.

"Alex, I didn't mean to disturb you," Christine said.

She had been a widow now for close to ten years and had stayed close to the Dull family. While she and Rockwood had had one daughter, the large Dull family had been a surrogate sibling group.

"Thats fine Christine. I needed a break. It is good to see you. I notice a bloom to your face. Something we should know?"

"That's why I came. I have someone new in my life and after dating these past six months, we are talking of marriage."

"That's wonderful news," Donita said. "You've been alone much too long now."

"The problem is Louisa, I'm afraid." Christine said. "She knows I've been dating but I've tried to keep the two separate. At her age she is very emotional about missing her father."

Everyone knew Louisa had just turned seventeen, a difficult year in normal times. To be a teenage girl without her father's guidance was doubly difficult.

"What can we do to help?" Alex asked.

"I thought a group excursion might could ease my friend's introduction into the family."

"Great idea. With the summer weather a trip maybe to the water would be wonderful. I know my children have been antsy since school got out."

"Would a trip out to Sholan Park SSLT be too much?" Christine asked.

Sholan Park was an amusement park on Waushacum Lake just north of Worcester in the town of Sterling. The Leominster train made the excursion simple and a date was set. The following Saturday everyone met at Worcester's Union Station. Alex carried his camera while his oldest son Jose carried the tripod. Donita had the food divided among the other children as Christine walked up with Louisa.

Alex looked at her as to where her date might be and before he could ask, a man in a suit walked up. Alex was taken back a bit by Christine's friend. He knew local politics well enough to recognize the U.S. Congressman from the Springfield area.

"I'd like to introduce Frederick Gillett," Christine said. She went through the long list of names introducing everyone to Fredrick. As she finished she added, "Oh, here's our train."

Eleven revelers boarded the passenger car and settled in for the short forty minute ride to the park. The steam engine chugged out of the station as the crowded car bristled with amusement park attendees intent on a fun day near the water. Soon the train was crossing the causeway across the newly completed Wachusett Reservoir that fed Boston fresh water.

Switching from the main line at Sterling Junction, the short line to Leominster swung off and soon stopped beside the park. On one side of the train sat West Waushacum Pond while a smaller portion called the Quag sat on the other. The railroad had built a causeway and bridge between the two. Sholan Park

SSLT sat on the isthmus formed at the north end of the causeway.

Alex led everyone to the entrance and paid the entrance fee over the objections of Fredrick. They found a table available under the picnic pavilion and set up their food. The children soon left with Donita and Christine for the games, leaving Alex alone with Fredrick.

"Congressman, this is a surprise."

"Mr. Dull. Thank you for sharing you family to ease the news for Louisa."

"Alex please. If we are to be related, I guess first names are appropriate."

"I agree, please call me Fred."

"So tell me how did you and Christine meet?"

"We met many years ago when Rockwood and I were in Congress together. Rockwood's death was a tragic loss. To die so early at fifty-one. Your cousin and I had become close confidantes in Washington, He even took me to one of your exhibits in the capital. I was impressed with your work."

"Thank you. I too was shocked when Rockwood died. And so soon after, my uncle. We were very close."

"Rockwood would often talk about his extended family. How his father took over for your deceased father. Your father was a great hero as all of Massachusetts knows."

Alex sat and reflected on the two father figures he had had, now both gone. One he never knew, the other a major influence. Both men watched as the children and women all moved to the line for the steam launch that patrolled the lake. They waved back at the ten waving at them.

"Alex, I wanted to ask you, how is Donita's family in the Philippines?"

"I had hoped you could shed some light on conditions there. We can't get money through to them and letters are sporadic since the Japanese took over the German's territory."

"Very troubling indeed. I'm afraid out people in Manila don't have much contact with the Japanese territory. There is tension between us over this whole German land. The British seem OK with it, although I believe they are starting to wonder what will happen after the war."

Alex recognized a potential opening. He asked "Has there been talk in Washington on changing the status of the Philippines. President McKinley did promise the Filipino people a 'benevolent assimilation', I believe the term that he used. Eventual freedom after the island were assimilated and educated. Have we reached that stage? It's been seventeen years now."

"Alex, you ask good questions. I'm afraid after the Spanish-American War we got wrapped up in acquiring colonies. It revolved around the navy and its need for coaling stations mostly. After the fighting with the Philippines rebels, America wanted to forget the whole sordid mess."

"But now we have oil fired ships. The need for those overseas ports have disappeared."

"I know. But the navy still clings to having their bases. They argue it helps with our trading. Keeps us safe and all that."

"We don't have bases in Europe and we trade just fine. Nor in Africa nor South America. None in the Indian Ocean at all and we trade just fine there. Only Easy Asia we have bases."

Fredrick sat and stared as the stream launch swung around and made for the underpass of the railroad bridge that would take their route onto the Quag. Alex realized he was battering the congressman.

"I'm sorry, Fred. I didn't mean to turn this into a political lobbying event. You came here to relax and meet my family. My sincerest apologies."

"I understand. You are married to the Philippines and would naturally be passionate about its independence. I guess we will have to wait for the fighting in Europe to be resolved. The winners will determine much."

When America entered the European War two years later, Alex got an assignment to cover the United States forces as they trained and deployed to France. The ensuing two years had seem Fred and Christine marry and settle in Washington. Alex and Donita had not been able to travel to the Philippines as letters from the family continued sporadically.

Things on the islands under the Japanese seemed stable although money transfers were still difficult. Alex had worked around the problem by contacting a friend in Manila. The friend would receive the money through United States banks in Manila and then personally travel to Cebu City to deliver the support to the family. His friend reported that the Japanese were accommodating on his annual visits and that the family appeared well.

Alex could travel knowing things in the Philippines were safe for his family but knowing he would be involved at the end of the war with any independence push for the islands. When the war ended in November, Alex returned safely to Worcester determined to find another line of work. Being away from his family tore at him and covering wars had worn him out. The trench warfare he had witnessed and recorded was the worse yet. *Shear madness* he thought.

Chapter 20

Washington D.C
March, 1921

The next six years saw Alex's life transformed. After his rerun from the fighting in France, he moved his family to Washington where he took up a teaching position at Georgetown University. Settling into academic life, his classes on photography and journalism were popular with the students.

At the suggestion of the university president, Alex began work on a doctorate which he completed in 1920. Now a full professor in the School of Journalism, he enjoyed his life as he returned home each night from instructing young minds.

His photographic work transformed also as he acquired a Gaflex Century Graphic, the standard flash camera of newspaper reporters. As a venerable camera, it had been around since 1912 and continuously showed improvements. Alex's model had the latest Carl Zeiss lens and offered him an excellent instrument for capturing local events.

While a professor, he still attended news worth events with his camera, often selling his photographs to newspapers and magazines. As the national capital of the United States, world events happened frequently a short two miles from campus.

May 19, 1919 saw Alex's connection to potential news stories take an upward turn. Congressman

Fredrick Gillett had been elected Speaker of the House of Representatives with the enormous power that ensured. On March 4, 1921 things changed further. Warren G. harding was sworn in as the Twenty-Ninth president thus ending the progressive era of Woodrow Wilson. Republicans held sway again in Washington after a huge victory over the unpopular Democrats.

The U.S. Senate held a 59 to 37 seat advantage while the House of Representatives showed the Republicans with a 303 to 131 advantage. The only portion of the country voting Democratic was the South as America voted for a return to isolation after their foray into the European War.

Alex greeted his older brother Maximilian as he arrived in the nation's capitol. Max had been a confidant to the Governor of Massachusetts and when he had run on the ticket with Warren Harding, the new vice-president had asked Max to be his Chief of Staff.

"Congratulations brother and welcome to Washington," Alex said as Max stepped in the front door. "Donita," Alex yelled. "We have a special guest."

Some of Alex's children still at home greeted their uncle as he was led into the dining room. Donita soon showed up with refreshments for everyone as the two brothers sat down to drinks.

"So brother," Max said. "You said you had a room until I got settled. I've been much too busy to look for a place so if its OK, I'll stay."

"You are welcome as long as you want. With Jose and Felipe off at college you can have their room." Alex's two oldest sons were both attending college,

Jose at Notre Dame, Felipe at the University of Virginia. Paul, the third son was at George Mason University in nearby Fairfax, Virginia.

"Have you heard what our newly confirmed Secretary of State has proposed. Nothing less then an end to war."

"Ha, I wish him luck on that," Alex said. "I've seen enough of war for my lifetime and don't plan on attending any more."

"Well, brother. Maybe he can do something about the build-up to war. Borah's resolution set the stage."

Alex was familiar with Idaho Senator William Borah's senate resolution that called for the limiting of warships by country. When the Secretary of State jumped on Borah's idea, Borah switched positions fearful that any agreement would commit the United States to the hated League of Nations.

The peace Treaty of Versailles had officially ended the European War. Signed in 1919, the U.S. Senate had rejected the pact due to the terms setting up the League of Nations which was viewed as an encroachment on U.S sovereignty. Hence, the U.S. officially was still at war with the Central Powers.

That changed in August when negotiations between Germany and the U.S reached an agreement resulting in a separate peace treaty. Alex followed the changing politics as he went about his summer getting ready for Fall classes. A knock on his office door broke him away from his paperwork.

Opening the door, an elderly man, tall and thin with a gray beard stood before him. His bald head emphasized his broad smile as he asked,"Dr. Alexander Dull?"

"Yes," Alex answered.

"i'm Daniel Carter Beard. You may have heard of me."

"The illustrator. Of course. Come in please. Have a seat." Alex picked up a pile of papers and moved them from the only chair in his office. "Excuse the mess. I've been getting ready for Fall term. What can I do for you?"

"I've been an admirer of your work Mr. Dull. I'm surprised we haven't met before this."

"Alex please. Yes, I've enjoyed your illustrations in Mr Twain's books."

"The call me Uncle Dan. As the illustrator for Mr. Twain he confided in me many times. One of his concerns was the growth of the American Empire."

Alex was familiar with Mark Twain and his role years ago in the Anti-Imperialist League. Active in the aftermath of the Spanish American War, they sought to keep American from joining the other European powers in establishing colonies around the world. Their effort had been for not and the movement had whimpered to a close, especially after Mark Twain's death in 1910.

"Mr. Twain was a leading light with his writings on freedom around the world. A true lose for all of us."

"But perhaps his spirt lives on."

"What do you mean, Uncle Dan?" Alex asked.

"In 1905, Mr. Twain wrote a moving story called *The War Prayer*. His publisher at the time rejected the story and because of his contract, he could not publish it anywhere else."

"You bring me this information for what purpose?"

"I've heard that the Harding Administration will hold a conference to limit war. I think its time to release Mr. Twain's story to the public. It is very moving in calling for an end to war and for all peoples to be free from oppression."

"A worthy goal. I'd be happy to support you if I can."

"I believe you can. You have been one of the leading photographers of the effects of war. Perhaps we could include some of your images in any release."

Alex thought of all the scenes of war that he had photographed. Images popped into his head as he sat and thought, so many he suddenly had a headache.

"I'm afraid most of photos have been copyrighted and published already. At least the good ones."

"Perhaps you have a few that never made it into publication. New images that could add a sense of reality to Mr. Twain's words."

"Do you have permission to print Mr. Twain's work?"

"His daughter Clara is the only surviving heir of his three children. I've contacted her and she supports our efforts."

As Alex continued to roll through his images in his mind, certain images long forgotten and never published became clear. *They certainly showed the grim reality of war and were especially pertinent to America* he thought.

"Uncle Dan. I think we can work something out. Can you come back in a week as I'l need to search my catalogue for what I'm thinking of."

They agreed to meet again in a week and Uncle Dan took his leave. Alex dropped any pretext to preparing for his classes and headed home. He immediately climbed the stairs to access to the attic. Pulling the ladder down, he climbed to the large attic and all the things stored there. He flipped on a single light, sat down and pulled the first crate close.

Knowing now why he should have spent the time organizing all his glass plates, he began to go through them one by one. Wooden crate after crate followed as he searched for what he wanted. As the time advanced, he became nervous that somewhere in all the moves the images had been lost. Two hours later he pulled up a glass plate and there it was. Holding it to the light bulb, he saw what would move people.

Sitting in the crate were the next five plates that showed the entire story. A story that could only help sway public opinion. Images that had been hidden all these years on advice of his uncle. But Uncle George was dead now and America had changed. It had just fought its latest war and through Wilson's mismanagement of the peace process had brought a public desire for isolation. It might be the chance that the Philippines needed. He longed that he could make a difference and fulfill his old friend's dream of an independent Philippines.

Over the next week, Alex printed large images off his glass plates. He carried them in a carrying case to his office where Uncle Dan showed up. He pulled the five images out and handed them across one at a time, holding the most lurid one for last.

"Yes, I believe this will work," Uncle Dan said. Then Alex handed him the next. "Yes, this one too."

Uncle Dan's excitement grew as each photo was passed across. Upon the fifth photo, he stopped. Alex watched as he stared at the image.

"I don't know Alex. This one might be too much. Are these really American troops?"

The two men sat as Uncle Dan began to sweat on his upper lip. He pulled out a handkerchief and wiped his bare brow and then his mouth.

"I had no idea. These have never been published. I would have remembered them certainly."

"My uncle was a U.S. Senator at the time. After the Philippine War ended and the Senate quickly annexed the islands, he suggested it wasn't the time to publish them. They've sat in crates ever since."

Uncle Dan sat silent for a long time. Alex could see the man struggling with his conscience as to the fate of the images. Too gruesome could turn the public off to their goal. But being too easy would not attract the attention they needed.

Finally Uncle Dan seemed to decide, "I say we do it. Right between the eyes. Grab them with the images and let Mr. Twain convince them with his writing."

Two weeks later a pamphlet was released and it took the country by storm. Within a week it was the talk of America as newspapers across the country reprinted both the photos and the writings. Suddenly Alex found himself in a maelstrom of controversy as both sides took positions.

Some thought bringing America's war atrocities back into light was un-American. The other side rejoiced that the reality of war was front and center, even American bad behavior.

The Washington Conference to limit warship construction had been announced to begin the first of November. The ensuing two months meant the pamphlet calling for freedom around the world and an end to war had time to sway people one way or the other. Alex got a call at the end of October from his brother to meet him in his office.

Alex drove his automobile the two miles to the Blair House where vice-president Coolidge had set up his offices. Announced by the guard at the front desk, Alex was escorted to Maximilian's office on the second floor.

"Alex, good of you to come."

"It sounded like I didn't really have a choice," Alex said.

"You didn't I'm afraid. It seems President Harding is not happy with you little pamphlet. It's causing quite a stir."

"Good, that's what we intended."

"You do know that Secretary Hughes has his hands full just getting the Great Powers here to discuss things without your inflammatory rhetoric stirring up expectations."

"People's expectations needed stirring."

"Is this about the Philippines by any chance?"

"Max, those islands are stuck under three rulers right now. The Versailles Treaty didn't address the Philippines. Other former German territory was divided up, but not the Philippines. And we stated that our goal was freedom to the Filipino people after we had assimilated them. I think twenty two years of assimilation is enough. They need their independence."

"This conference isn't about those issues. I can tell you on strictest secrecy that Secretary Hughes is going to propose a building limit on warships as the first step. No land decisions are involved as much as you would like."

Alex stared at his brother. He din't care what the upcoming conference would be concerned with, there were always issues simmering under the surface and once the powers were in a room, who know what would come out. He decided he'd take his chances.

"Are you telling me something I can't do? Are you censoring me?"

"No Alex. I'm just warning you that you may be stepping into issues that will catch up to you."

"Sounds like a threat."

"Little brother, Just a word to the wise. Be careful."

"Thanks. I can watch out for myself."

The two brothers parted as Alex headed back to his campus office. As he reached it and closed a window from the cool fall air outside, he felt a chill. But it wasn't from the weather. He knew Washington could be viscous and he had seen plenty of people destroyed by attempting something impossible. His thoughts of Jose Rizal being executed by firing squad pushed any fear from him as he knew whatever his fate, it wouldn't be death.

Chapter 21

Washington D.C.
November 6, 1921

A tradition had been started at the Dull residence when Alex and Donita had moved to Washington D.C. Being stable home owners in the nation's capital, there was a standing invitation to any and all family members for Sunday dinner. Donita, being a filipina, was devoutly Catholic and would attend church every Sunday morning. Also being from the Philippines, she had a cultural need to gather the family together and feed them.

Typically Alex's cousin's widow would show up one week a month with her husband, attempting to maintain a connection with her late husband's family. Now that Alex's older brother was Chief-of-Staff to Vice-President Coolidge the Sunday gatherings would have his company a couple times each month.

But this Sunday it would be a trifecta. It portended a rare appearance of Alex's second brother Cornelius. He had served as a U.S. Naval Commander in the European War in charge of destroyer flotilla. Stationed off the coast of Long Island it had searched for German submarines. Recently, Cornelius had been nominated by the president to the rank of Rear Admiral. While he was stationed at the Navy Department since the end of the war, in the succeeding three years he had made Sunday dinner just once before.

Alex busied himself helping Donita ready dinner when the front doorbell rang. He wiped his hands off on a towel and excused himself, leaving his four daughters helping their mother. As he opened the front door he was warmly greeted by his oldest brother Maximilian.

The two brothers embraced and Alex led him into the parlor. As he moved to sit, the doorbell rang a second time. Upon opening the door, Fred and Christine Gillett greeted him warmly, a hand shake from the Speaker of the House and a kiss and hug from Christine.

"Alex, we have so been looking forward to dinner today," Christine said. "I've come to learn that the only people you can truly trust in this city is family."

Alex glanced at her husband who nodded agreement to his wife's statement. Fred clapped Alex on the back as the three joined Max in the parlor. Again, as he began to sit, the doorbell rang a third time. Everyone in the room looked up, not expecting anyone else.

Cornelius Dull entered as Alex opened the door and gave his younger brother a hug and slap on the back. Seeing the others, he happily walked over and greeted each of them. Finally seated, Alex spoke.

"Well, this is a first. All the Washington family here at one time."

Christine said, "I hope its not too much for Donita. We don't mean to impose."

"Trust me, its no imposition to a filipina. They are quite familiar with feeding large family gatherings of which this would not count. In the Philippines, large is large."

"Maybe I'll go see if I can help then."

Christine stood and headed to the kitchen, leaving the men alone. A certain tense silence ensued in her wake until Alex finally spoke.

"A big event this Friday. Entombing the unknown soldier. I understand President Harding will give the eulogy."

"A fitting affair after so much loss in Europe," Max said. "Are you attending Fredrick?"

"Yes, wouldn't miss it. I have many veterans of the European War in my district. And its remarkable how many from my district were killed. Our Massachusetts regiments were in the thick of things."

Everyone nodded agreement. They all knew of young men from Massachusetts who had been killed in the fighting. A few stories of those killed passed between them before Max asked, "Cornelius, are you privy to what the Secretary of State will propose at the upcoming naval conference. As an admiral I figure you'd know."

Cornelius laughed and said, "Are you kidding. I assume the chief-of staff to the vice-president would know such things. Doesn't President Harding keep his cabinet informed."

"No. He essentially lets Secretary Hughes run international affairs. The President concerns himself with domestic problems."

Each turned toward the House Speaker. Max asked, "Anyone inform the house leadership?"

"Quiet as a tomb at State," Fredrick said.

"You mean all three of you have no idea what's going to be proposed?" Alex asked.

The three all shook their heads that they knew nothing.

"I can share a little bit of the thinking," Cornelius aid. "Nothing that isn't already out there."

Everyone knew Cornelius's current assignment in the navy was work in the intelligence division. He remained mum on any details but by his advancement to admiral they all knew he would be at the top of the information chain.

He continued. "It comes down to three powers. The other six attendees are their as observers essentially. We are looking to contain the Japanese. They are too expansion minded in our view and with their growing fleet, we look to put some limits on that."

Alex knew enough of Japanese affairs from traveling there to ask, "Are we pushing to break the connection between Japan and Britain tied to their alliance? It's due for renewal next year."

"Very perceptive little brother," Cornelius said. "Yes, the British see Japan as a threat and would sooner trust us for the future. But the British want to avoid an arms race with us because you know who would win."

Max asked, "So what's in it for the Japanese. If the other two large powers are stacking up against them, why be here at all?"

"Everyone looks at Japan as an emerging power. But their industrial base is minuscule compared to the United Sates or Britain," Cornelius said. "I'm certain they want a limit on building ships so they can keep up. Plus I'm sure they want international approval of some kind on their expansion into Korea and Manchuria."

Alex could hold things in no longer. "And what about the Philippines. Nothing was settled at the Versailles Conference. Will nothing be done at this one?"

Everyone looked at him knowing his connection and emotional ties to the islands. Each was hesitant to answer.

Fredrick spoke first. "Alex, you should know since marrying Christine I've been reading your uncles papers. His speeches during the consideration of America's annexing colonies around the world are very moving. His eloquence over our values of freedom and the obligation to spread those values wherever we could are inspiring."

"So, are they inspiring enough to do something?"

Alex knew that the Senate controlled all international treaties. Any agreement coming out of the Washington Conference would have to obtain passage there. The House of Representatives had no say directly in any treaty. But where it held considerable sway was in financing any endeavor. All money measures came out of the house and the man who controlled everything within the House of Representatives sat before him.

"I'm sorry Fred," Alex continued. "I spoke out of anger just now. Thank you for at least considering Uncle George's position."

"That's fine Alex. I know the Philippines is very dear to you, as it should be. And being part of the family, by marriage, I want to honor Christine's side of the family if I can. Rockwood was a good friend and confident and I miss him."

Alex asked "Can I ask then, do you have something specific in mind?"

"Nothing specific at the moment."

Max and Cornelius sat and watched what could be national policy being birthed before them. But Alex knew an opening when he saw it.

"Any idea of withdrawing from the Philippines and giving the islands their freedom?"

"And give the Japanese a free hand there?"

"No, we would leave if Japan and Britain both granted independence and left."

"And what about Guam, Puerto Rico and Hawaii?" Fredrick asked.

Max finally joined in. "I know the administration is looking at all cost savings they can find. Empire building has been expensive. While President Harding hasn't pushed real hard on the subject as he's focused on the domestic side of things, I can unequivocally state that vice-president Coolidge is

269

all on board with cost cutting. He would gladly grant independence and come home."

Fredrick turned to Alex and asked, "Alex, you lived among the islanders. Are they ready?"

"Is any people ready. Were we ready when we broke with Britain?"

"I guess I need to be more specific then," Fredrick said. "Can we trust the Japanese to not co opt an independent Philippines if we left? Siam is the only independent country in East Asia not occupied at least partially by a Great Power."

"The Philippines certainly sits in a strategic part of Asia athwart the shipping lanes of East Asia," Cornelius said "Any one country controlling the archipelago would control all movement along the coast. I just don't see the Japanese giving up their position there."

Alex said, "I do. To remove the threat of an American Fleet based so close to their interests I think the Japanese would deal. They think they have an ace in their hand. They have been very active building schools and importing teachers from the home islands. Those teachers teach in Japanese. From letters from my family, the children are being taught Japanese as their second language. German has been forgotten on Cebu Island while the Japanese offer free high school eduction. But the price is knowing Japanese."

"So in the long view, you think the Philippines will naturally fall under the sway of Japan," Fredrick said.

"I think Japan thinks that. Its up to an independent Philippines to counter that influence."

"And you think a poor country can stand up to a vastly more affluent country?" Max asked.

"Yes, if America continues to trade with the Philippines," Alex said. "Money from around the world would boost their economy and international trade with all nations would keep them independent. We don't necessarily need to be there as colonizers, but we could still be there as businessmen. Its what we do best."

"Your argument has merit," Fredrick said.

Alex then said, "And there is one more thing, and its huge. If Japan continues its expansion and we are a threat to their shipping lanes, can we avoid war. A war that would see the United Sates losing thousand of our young men fighting over Asian territory. Is it a vital national interest to loose blood and treasure if the Japanese take over Manchuria and in our present position attack our bases in the Philippines."

Before anyone could answer, Donita entered form the kitchen and said, "Let's eat."

* * *

November 11 would be the most solemn day held as dignitaries stood quiet as the casket holding the 'unknown soldier' was carried to its final resting place. A three level marble tomb had been constructed under

Congressional approval to recognize the unknown dead of the European War. The remains of one dead soldier had been moved from France aboard the *U.S. Olympia* to the United States who would present all of America's unknown dead.

President Harding stood at attention as the pall bearers moved one slow step at a time in perfect unison forward, placing the casket atop the tomb. Moving carefully to a line abreast, the honor guard stood at attention as the President stepped forward to provide a eulogy.

The nine nations that had agreed to attend the Washington Naval Conference stood among the dignitaries as the president spoke. Declared Armistice Day for the end of the European War, all across America citizens honored those that had fought in all the wars of the country, especially recognizing the French veterans. It set the mood for everyone that would soon be discussing the first limitations on war.

Ten days later, Secretary of State Charles Evan Hughes stood before the representatives of Japan, Britain, Italy, France, Belgium, China, the Netherlands and Portugal to address the attendees. The regular opening remarks completed, Hughes finally released his proposal which had been kept secret.

The crowd in the Memorial Conference Hall were generally stunned as Secretary Hughes handed out his proposal. The United States would decommission or not build 30 warships if the other powers agreed to terms. Great Britain would agree to remove nineteen vessels and the Japanese would remove or not build seventeen.

Overall, the agreement would limit the main naval powers to a ratio that made the U.S. and Britain equal with Japan slightly smaller in total battleship tonnage. Aircraft carriers were limited on a similar ratio of tonnage. An agreement limiting cruiser tonnage was not forthcoming but the powers did agree on a maximum size of cruisers. Submarines, a weapon the British wanted banned, were left unlimited as no agreement could be reached.

Alexander Dull sat in the press section with his Graphic Plus camera at his feet. He held press credentials for the Washington Star, currently the newspaper of record for the city, that had been published since 1852. Alex's reputation for capturing historical events with his camera let him work part-time. Covering the conference had been a priority of his since it had been announced and had worked with the university on shifting his teaching duties while the conference took place.

After the noon lunch break, the cameramen of the various world's papers covering the conference were called forward and allowed an opportunity for pictures of the delegates before the conference resumed. Alex hung back as each photographer was allowed one shot. The others, all carrying similar press cameras with flashes, took their one photo and moved back to their seats. Alex finally stepped up last and with an extension on his flash and a light diffuser, moved in closer, snapping his shot.

While the others captured the entire scene in a glaring image, Alex worked on a softer subdued image that he knew would show a more thoughtful repose to the members. While his diffused flash lacked depth and delegates in the back would fade to black, the center of his shot would have a fine lighting worthy of a great photo minus the glare the others tended to capture.

Siting back down, he changed films and readied for his next opportunity. Meanwhile he listened to the arguments as each power recited their concerns for what Hughes had proposed. Each recognized that the United States could out produce anyone else at the table and for the U.S. to be willing to limit that production was an opportunity for change.

Alex attended each day and slowly an agreement on ship tonnage was reached. On the fourth day, he was handed a note as he left for the day. The Secretary of State requested a meeting with him that Saturday which was an off day for the conference.

The next day he drove his 1919 Budd-Dodge two door sedan the short distance to the office of the Secretary of State. Parking on the street he entered the front door and was met by a man who escorted Alex to the secretary's office.

"Mr. Dull, so glad you could join me," Charles Even Hughes said as he stood and held his hand to Alex.

Alex dutifully shook the Secretary's hand and sat down where he was directed. He looked around at the office having never been in such a powerful position before.

"Thank you for the invitation Mr. Secretary. I'm not sure what warrants me meeting with you though."

"I thought we could chat a bit. How do you think our conference is going?"

Alex was a bit taken back that the man would ask him his opinion. As a photographer he was not someone typically consulted on world affairs.

"I'm generally impressed with what you have proposed. If you can get some agreement, the world will be better off."

"I'm getting good feedback from the other powers. There are numerous little meetings between staff you should know. Everyone attempting to get what is important to them out of any overall treaty. I must say, we have some very diverse interests. Not all ship tonnage I can assure you."

Interesting to know but Alex still had no reason why he would be consulted on such topics. He nodded to the secretary his acknowledgement of the ways of international diplomacy.

"As you might imagine, all sorts of issues are raised when nations meet. It can become a little like making sausage, as they say. Lots of ingredients mixed into one final product. And some things you don't want to know get mixed in."

"Yes Mr. Secretary, I suppose it is a bit like sausage."

Still, Alex wasn't grasping where this conversation was leading. He soon found out.

"I asked you up here today for a reason though," Secretary Hughes said. "The pamphlet you put together with Daniel Carter Beard."

Alex's stomach churned at the mention of the pamphlet. It continued to create news as its message of peace versus war carried through the American public.

"Mr. Secretary, I can explain."

"No explanation necessary. I know Mark Twain was a leading opponent to American taking on the trappings of empire. And your work in the Philippines filming our troubles there certainly complement Mr. Twain's writing. You have a filipina wife I understand."

His stress level increasing by the topic of discussion, Alex said, "I do, Mr. Secretary."

"And her family still lives in the islands?"

"Yes, in the Japanese controlled portion, formally German, sir."

"I see," Hughes said. He then sat and thought for a bit as Alex waited for what might come next. The time dragged in as both men remained quiet. Finally the silence was broken.

"Are you at all worried about their well being?"

"Things have gotten harder to accomplish under the Japanese. Money transfers don't work. Mail arrives very slowly and sometimes not at all. My wife worries about their situation, Mr. Secretary."

"The reason I ask is this conference is mainly about the Japanese, the British and us. The three of us all have interests in the Western Pacific. And we are seeking different agendas at this conference. The ship tonnage limits are more a side issue."

"I had no idea, Mr. Secretary. Is the Philippines one of those issues?"

"It might be. And I wanted your opinion since you are connected to the islands as well as have spent time with the Japanese during their war with Russia. You speak Japanese I understand?"

"Yes, as well as several other languages. What's at stake for the Philippines?" Alex's interest grew at the thought that his islands were possibly in the discussion among all the powers.

"As you know, the Philippines were not part of the Versailles Treaty. No consensus could be reached as to their status at that time so the status quo was left in place."

"Yes, I had hoped that the end to the war could settle things there."

"Well, its seems one of the Japanese interests at this conference is being recognized as a great power. That includes the other powers recognizing its territorial acquisitions over the last many years."

Alex's heart sank at the mention of formalizing Japan's status. He looked at the Secretary for more.

Secretary Hughes obliged. "But they are more concerned with other places then the Philippines. Their control of the Central Pacific islands they captured form Germany is one. Korea the other. Manchuria and their concession port in China are third."

"And the Philippines?"

"They are being a bit coy on that subject. They've tested the waters so to speak on all the powers leaving the islands and granting independence."

277

"And what would be our position on that?" Alex asked. His stomach was practically twisted into knots at the implications.

"There has been a push from the House of Representatives to move the administration on cutbacks in international duties. As you know, they set the national budget and if the House won't fund our overseas commitments, then we need to look at alternatives."

Alex thought to his talk with Fredrick Gillett before Sunday dinner and thanked himself for the topic they had discussed. If true, Fredrick had provided the catalyst to move the country away from empire.

"If there is anything I can do to help that idea reach fruition, you only need to ask," Alex said.

Chapter 22

Washington D.C.
February 6, 1922

The Washington Naval Treaty was a hard fought affair but eventually the nine powers involved agreed. Britain and the United Sates would be limited to a total tonnage of battleships of 525,000 tons. Japan received 60% of their number and could maintain battleships with a total of 315,999 tons. Japan considered this a win since it put them as the dominate navy in the Western Pacific since the America and Britian had two oceans to defend.

But most important to Japan was the recognition by the other powers of its status as a major world power. As the only Asian country so recognized, Japan had made major leaps forward since its closed society had been first forced opened by American Commodore Matthew Perry and his warships in 1854.

Removing the Americans from home basing in the Western Pacific had been a small price to pay for giving up Japanese positions in the Philippines. It also pushed Great Britain back to Hong Kong and Singapore thus leaving the North Pacific to Japan. Guam remained an American possession but it out in the Central Pacific surrounded by Japanese held islands. The other matters in the treaty were small loses such as relinquishing their concession Port of Shandong back to Chinese control.

America continued to insist on what they called 'An Open Door Policy" for China. The policy demanded no outside power holding Chinese territory and all were free to trade with the new Republic of China. This meant the Chinese had freedom to develop as a free nation.

With a date of June 30th set for an official hand over to an independent Philippines and a withdrawal of all outside forces, Alex and Donita made plans to travel home. It had been too many years since they had seen Donita's family.

Since Alex's mother would turn 80 years old, someone had to be found to watch over the younger girls, the youngest being 12 years old. Christine Gillett gladly offered until Jose said he would stay home after graduating from the university to take care of his siblings. Christine then agreed to check in often to make sure everything was doing well.

By mid June, Alex and Donita traveled across the country by train and met their steamship bound for Honolulu. A mini vacation on Oahu for two weeks had them ready for the next journey to Manila. Reaching the Philippines as the rainy season set in, they hired an airplane to fly them to the new Cebu City airport where they made their way to Lapu-Lapu. The entire Calvero extended family met them as their carriage pulled to a stop in front of the family compound.

A Philippine family celebration for the next five days afforded all the relatives to travel to Lapu-Lapu to see the Americans. Alex pulled out his wallet as pig was followed by goat followed by many fish dinners were cooked and served. Neighborhood children, hearing the Calvero family was celebrating, lined up to be fed each day. The Philippine hospitality sign was out and all took advantage.

Finally Alex had had enough and the celebration stopped. Now just immediate family events kept them busy. And not without Alex using his camera to capture each event. It had been a long time since he had been out of the country and he was enjoying his photography again. While sitting around with his brothers-in-laws one evening he began to understand what they had been through

"Tell me again how it was? We have been worrying about you for some years now. Whether we could get money to you or not. How the Japanese were treating you. We just didn't really know."

"Manor Alex. You should know we couldn't really say how things were in our letters. We knew of too many people who disappeared. They had written truthfully about the Japanese and their letters were probably intercepted."

"I was afraid of that. That is why we never said anything that could be taken as critical in our letters back," Alex said.

"Leave it at we are glad the Japs are gone," One of Donita's brothers said.

"But what about the children learning Japanese. Will that continue?"

"No, already the baranguay officials are moving to shut the Japanese schools down. The teachers will be asked to leave. We will teach our own children

Alex felt more assured the the Philippines would keep its independence. And if America continued its strong trading ties with the new country, a counterbalance to Japan's influence might assure him of that fact.

After a two month visit, Alex and Donita packed to head back to the United States. Saying goodbye was especially hard for Donita as her family meant everything to her. But she had her own family now, eight growing children that were very much Americans. The couple boarded the steamer that would take them to Negros Island as they took the slow tour through the islands.

Stopping on Panay and then Mindoro Island, Alex witnessed the strong influence the Japanese had had there. With over twenty years of control of the two islands, their teaching program had been very successful and he found Japanese seemed the dominate language.

Reaching Luzon Island, they enjoyed a two week tour north of Manila. This had been the stronghold for the revolutionary forces and again Alex wanted to see how the twenty years of American rule had turned out. He discovered English already fading and a number of grade schools had imported Japanese speakers from Mindoro to teach. Students were happily learning the language that they perceived as the new and upward coming language of Asia. America was already quickly fading in the minds of many.

By the time they boarded their steamer for Hong Kong Alex's mood had changed to one of despair. With the Japanese now solely supreme in the north Pacific, that influence would hold say over all within its sphere of influence. The Americans were gone, pulled back all the way to Guam. And the British held supreme in the south only Hong Kong penetrating the Japanese bubble.

The couple again took a break in Hawaii before boarding a steamer bound for San Francisco. A long train ride and they were home in Washington D.C. where Alex resumed his teaching winter term.

Life resumed to normal as Max continued to arrive for Sunday dinner with the family and on occasion Fredrick and Christine Gillett made an appearance. Alex's photography took on a more subdued aspect as he seemed content to do portraits of the rich and famous of Washington. Visiting dignitaries were among Alex's subjects as his reputation around the world made him a sought after photographer.

As 1925 opened, things began to change. First, Fredrick Gillett gave up his Speaker of House position to run for the U.S. Senate. Winning a seat in the Senate he joined President Coolidge who won his second term. He soon found out that being a junior senator did not hold the power compared to what he had given up.

The year's changes turned deadly when in April Admiral Cornelius Dull's plane crashed on an inspection tour of the Gulf Coast naval installations. Alex and his family traveled to Annapolis where Cornelius was eulogized. The mourners then rode the train that took his body for burial to Arlington National Cemetery.

June 1925 arrived with a vengeance as Maximilian Dull suffered a stroke and died. When Coolidge had moved up to become president after Warren Harding had died in office, he had chosen a Washington insider as his chief of staff. Max had been reassigned to senior presidential advisor. Alex had realized that his brother wasn't handling the stress level when Coolidge had been vice president and had encouraged his brother to go back to Boston and practice law.

But Max had grown used to the levers of power and felt his role as advisor would reduce his stress level. But in talks at Corny's funeral with Max, Alex learned his brother held himself responsible for Cornelius' death.

Coolidge had demanded a review of all federal facilities in the South. He had lost that region in the 1926 election and with his tight financial policy wanted to reduce Federal expenditures. And as political payback, the South would feel the brunt of any cuts. Max was one of the advisors overseeing the cost cutting and had ordered the Navy Department to make recommendations. Hence Admiral Dull and his staff were in the air flying from base to base when bad weather hit.

Alex and his lone surviving brother Zachariah rode the train back to Worcester after their brother had been eulogized by President Coolidge in the National Cathedral. Max was interned in Hope Cemetery beneath the shadow of Holy Cross College. Their 83 year old mother, which was unable to travel for

Cornelius' service, stood over the grave as her oldest son was lowered into the ground.

* * *

The ensuing six years found the Dull family growing ever more despondent at the fate of their family in the Philippines. While letters slowly arrived and money transfers could be made, the news in the letters was not good. Left with no Japan based teachers in which to influence the islanders and unable to support local schools to indoctrinate the young, Japan went a different direction.

A scholarship program for advanced study in Japan produced the desired effect. With free college education being offered along with free room and board in Japan, schools switched readily to teaching Japanese, especially for those good students wishing a professional career. Soon doctors, lawyers, nurses, and engineers were returning to the Philippines to take up positions of influence in the young republic.

By 1931, the influence of Japan on Philippine life was all consuming. The small amount of American and other nations' trade were dwarfed by the Japanese influence. Alex read the latest letter before he began his class room preparation work for fall classes. Now aged 66, his thought of retiring from teaching flooded his mind. The world was pushing toward more and more authoritarian rulers and he felt that his life of pursuing freedom had been wasted.

In late September, his fears were confirmed when Japan invaded Manchuria. As reports came in it was described as a small explosion in Mukden as the pretext for a full blown invasion by the Imperial Japanese Army. The short five months it took for Japan to bring China to terms stunned the world. Hostilities ended in February, 1932 as Japan soon set up the puppet government of Manchukuo.

At Sunday dinner for Senator Gillett and Christine Alex learned the extent of the Japanese invasion. The Senator had seen the reports that the war was actually started by rogue colonels in the Kwangtung Army stationed in leased territory of China.

"How can two colonels start a war Fred?" Alex asked as the two sat in the parlous.

"The reports say it was actually a lieutenant that took it upon himself to detonate a bomb on the rails. The colonels pushed their commander to respond."

"And we know this because the Tokyo government let it out."

"Yes, the national government wanted to expose the action of their officers and withdraw the troops. But under their government structure, the army and the navy hold cabinet positions. If either quits the government over a dispute, the government collapses."

"Unbelievable," Alex offered. "I knew there were hot heads in Japan, but to start a war. And then to get away with it."

"I'm not sure how much they will get away with. The League of Nations is talking. Our Major

General Frank McCoy sat on the Lytton Commission and traveled through Manchuria, Japan and China fact finding. Their report found that the Japanese had acted aggressively and that Manchuria should be returned to China."

"How hopeful are you that that will happen?"

"Not very I'm afraid."

Fredrick's opinion held as Japan withdrew formally from the League of Nations rather then to submit to a withdrawal. This action set the world on a collision course with Japan as nations refused to recognize the Manchukuo puppet state. The United States even passed the Stimson Doctrine, named for President Hoover's Secretary of State, Henry Stimson. It set the policy of the United States to not recognize any territory gained by aggression.

Frustrated, Alex had made his move toward retirement. With the death of his two brothers, his aging mother had liquidated most of her inheritance from her father and divided the proceeds among her children and grandchildren.

Alex's second son Felipe had finished engineering school, married and had started a family when he got a job in Hawaii. Visiting their son, Alex and Donita made the decision that the Hawaiian climate appealed to them. It was closer to the Philippines if they needed to quickly visit and it certainly had less stress then the nation's capital.

That stress level had been enhanced with the stock market collapse in 1929 and although President Hoover seemed to be bringing the nation back by the time of the election, the voters choose a new direction. Franklin Roosevelt soon had the country tied up as he attempted to socialize the economy.

The election of Adolf Hitler in Germany in 1933 was the final insult to Alex. They sold their Georgetown home, crated up their household goods and headed to Hawaii. At 69, Alex looked forward to a life in their beach front home in Kailua.

A chance meeting after their arrival with the Dean of the School of Journalism soon had him posted as Professor Emeritus at the University of Hawaii. As Dr. Dull unpacked his collection of photographs, he organized a new course on photojournalism.

His quiet retirement in the islands was broken by the arrival of National Geographic editor Gilbert Grosvenor. Alex was asked to do one more trip and photo shoot in Germany. Hitler had been in power for two years and everyone was interested in the German miracle. The showcase event of the new Germany would be the 1936 Olympics in Berlin.

Alex resisted. "I'm sure you have a younger photographer who could get the job done."

"I do, but he's in Spain covering the Spanish Civil War."

"And there's no one else?"

"There are too many things going on around the world. Its all hands on deck. I'll make your retirement a lot easier."

Alex wasn't concerned with the money issue. His inherence from his mother had arrived at an opportune time. Selling out at the top of the market, his mother had moved the returns to cash. With the collapse of the economy, Alex had been able to purchase beach front property at depressed prices and put the remaining funds into the bank. "Cash is king' in a depression had been driven into his brain over the years and he luckily had heeded the advice.

But something else moved him to one more trip. A need to see his German relatives one last time and experience what they were going through in the New Germany. He reluctantly accepted.

Leaving Donita in Hawaii with their son's family nearby, Alex boarded a steamer now armed with the latest in 35 mm camera from Leica. Designed with three interchangeable lenses, the high quality of the optics made the small format cameras suitable for enlargements. Alex loved the freedom at his age of not lugging his old glass format camera with him.

Traveling first to Baden-Wurttemberg and his relatives, Alex observed life as he went. All across Germany the Nazi banners announced the New Germany. Greeting his relatives, he was anxious to find the real truth.

"Alex, lets take a walk," his cousin said after he had dropped his bag in the foyer.

"What is it?" he asked.

"Alex, you need to understand what the new Germany us all about." His cousin directed their walk along a lonely tree lined street to a local park. He made sure no one was nearby as he talked. "There are ears everywhere now. All listening for dissenters to the new regime. The Nazis stand no dissent."

"I've heard some of these stories. So they are true?"

"Worse that that. The truly criminal acts aren't well known."

"Such as the purge?" Alex asked.

"The Night of the Long Knives we call it. Killing off political rivals. Oh sure, excuses were made about treasonous acts. But it was pure murder."

"Jesus. And no one says anything?"

"If they do, there is the concentration camps. Places to go to get reeducated. Learn the Nazi way of life or die resisting."

"However did they award the Olympics to these killers then?"

"Good question. The decision was made in 1931 before the Nazi took power. There was talk of moving the site but someone convinced somebody to let Berlin continue to host the games. The Nazis are all sweetness and light right now. The world is watching and they intend to show the world how wonderful it is here."

A week of visiting the relatives and Alex headed to Berlin and the opening ceremonies for the Olympics. The city was dressed out to impress, if one was impressed by Nazi banners everywhere. The feeling in the city had a festive feeling in spite of the overbearing Nazis. The locals all celebrated the new Germany that seemed to be upon them and the recognition of that fact by the entire world watching the sports events.

Alex went about photographing the entire event: the sports, the athletes, the locals and the city itself. As he prepared his camera and equipment for another day at the sports park, a knock on his hotel door startled him. He had seen on occasion people he knew, but no one had dropped by to see him. Opening the door, he was confronted by three uniformed men standing looking at him. His heart rose to his throat as his blood pressure immediately rose. He noticed the death head lapel pins on each of their uniforms.

"Good morning Mr. Dull," one of them said.

"Yes, good morning," Alex said trying to hid the quiver in his voice from the stress.

"I do hope you are enjoying our wonderful Olympic games. Do you have a minute?"

Alex hesitated, trying to decide if the man wanted to enter his hotel room or not. From his talks with his cousin he knew he couldn't antagonize such men even if he was a famous American.

"No, please. Come in."

"Thank you," the man said as all three men stepped inside and turned to Alex. Alex shut the door not sure what was about to happen.

"We have been directed by Reichsfuhrer Himmler to ask if you would be interested in a personal tour and opportunity to photograph."

Alex waited a bit to see what was being offered to photograph but none came. He knew of Heinrich Himmler and the SS. Originally a battalion of 295 men, by 1936 Himmler had grown the organization into a force in Germany. Everyone knew of the black uniformed troops and that no good ends came from a close encounter.

Alex tried to equivocate on any potential meeting. "I am on assignment here and have my duties to perform so my free time for other activities is very limited. As much as I'd like to photograph other things I wouldn't want to miss anything at the Olympics."

The man gave him a long stare as one who did not get denied much in his life. The pause in the conversation filled the room to a suffocating level.

The man smiled and his compatriots smiled with him. "Of course, we understand such duties. But if you could examine the Olympic schedule and find a date and time you might be available, the Reichsfuhrer would be appreciative."

Sensing he could not get out of a meeting with Himmler, Alex stepped to his official guide and opened it to the sports times. As the three men waited, he ran his finger down the list of events, noting ones he really had to cover. America was doing well at these Olympics and he knew National Geographic would want photos of Americans competing. He found a time where no U.S. athletes would be on display offering a three hour window.

"Here is an opening," Alex said and showed the man the date and time slot. "Would that be acceptable? I'm sorry if there is a conflict. I can look for a different time but it is very tight."

The man took a small notebook from his breast pocket and wrote down the information. Placing the notebook back in the pocket, he pulled and snapped the pocket flap shut. The motion made Alex jump slightly.

"Thank you Mr. Dull. I will check with the Reichsfuhrer and get back to you so please keep that time open for now."

Alex stepped quickly to his hotel door to open it as all three men marched out. He shut the door and relaxed slightly but felt his heart pounding against his chest.

The next day a note sat waiting at the hotel lobby and the concierge handed it to him as he walked in the front door. Alex opened it and it held a hand written note by Himmler stating he looked forward to their meeting. And that Alex should be sure to bring his camera. A car would be provided at the agreed time.

Alex slept fitfully that night, not sure what he had gotten into. He rose and went through the morning paces of photographing athletes in action. The entire time his mind was on the impending meeting. After lunch in the hotel dining room, Alex stepped to the curb with his camera bag to find a black Mercedes sedan with Nazi flags mounted on the front fenders.

The three men that had come to his room stood ready and one opened the rear door while another stepped around to the driver;s side. Once in the back seat, Alex moved over as one man climbed in the back next to him while the other rode up front next to the driver.

No conversation was initiated as Alex watched the street as the Mercedes pulled out into traffic. The other cars moved away, fearfully it appeared to Alex. The Nazi flags on the front noted the car as an important party member and all Germany knew to give it a wide berth. A short drive and they pulled into an enclosed courtyard passing SS guards at the entrance. all of them brought their rifles to attention in front of their faces as the car passed.

The man in front climbed out and opened the rear door. Alex climbed out with the other man as he led him into the building. Not knowing where he was except he assumed it might be headquarters, Alex followed the lone man, the other two staying with the car,

They walked by a security desk at the base of a set of stairs without stopping and climbed to the second floor. A large double doored room loomed up at the end of a long corridor off the top of the stairs and the man led Alex to the room and opened one door.

Across a large high ceiling room an ornate French provincial desk sat, a lone man sitting bent over. Alex glanced around the room at the sparse furnishings except for large portraits hanging on the wall. He didn't have time to recognize who the subjects might be as the man stood and extended his hand.

"Mr. Dull, so nice of you to accept my invitation."

Having only seen pictures of Himmler, Alex recognized the Reichsfuhrer immediately. He walked to the desk and shook the man's hand.

"Reichsfuhrer, this is an honor. Thank you for inviting me."

Himmler waved the other man out of the office and Alex heard the large door clank upon his leaving.

He took a second to glance again at the room but Himmler caught him looking.

"So, you are probably wondering why I invited you."

"Yes Reichsfuhrer."

"Did you eat? I can have something brought up."

"No thank you. I ate before your men picked me up but thank you for your consideration."

"Good. The reason I asked you here . . ."

Before Himmler could finish, a knock at the door stopped him. Himmler looked in the direction of the noise with a look of annoyance. Alex realized no one disturbed the Reichsfuhrer.

But the door opened and the black uniformed man Alex had been dealing with offered profuse apologies for the interruption. As he spoke a large man in uniform stepped into the office and Himmler stood up. Alex stood, turned and recognized Hermann Goring.

Goring bellowed out, "What is this, Himmler? As Reichsstatthalter of Prussia I should have been told of this meeting."

"It is nothing, I can assure you," Himmler said.

Alex, in his talks with his cousin, had learned a bit of Nazi politics. Goring, holding the most powerful position after Hitler in the Nazi Party, had been named Minister President of Prussia. As the Prussian State was dominate of all the German States, this position was supreme in Germany.

With that power, Goring had named Himmler head of the Gestapo, or secret police. From that position Himmler had created the SS to enforce control over all other aspects of Germany. Now, Himmler was maneuvering for more and more power as Goring maneuvered to maintain control. Somehow Alex found himself in a power struggle within the Nazi hierarchy.

"Then why are you scheduled to meet with the Fuhrer in thirty minutes?" Goring asked.

Meet with Hitler Alex thought. He had no idea that this involved the Fuhrer himself. He felt beads of sweat forming.

"Reichsstatthalter, let me introduce you to Alexander Dull, the famous photographer from America."

Goring strode across the room and shook Alex's hand. He smiled broadly as he looked him in the face.

"Yes, I know. You photographed our advance into France in 1914. My airbase was actually quite close when you were outside Paris. Wonderful pictures."

"Thank you," was all Alex could blurt out. He knew he was in between two very dangerous people but tried to maintain his composure. "Can I ask then if this meeting concerns the Fuhrer himself?"

Himmler spoke first. 'Yes Mr. Dull. I thought you might like a chance to meet him and take some photographs for your magazine."

Alex noticed Goring's demeanor sour as Himmler spoke.

"That would be an honor sir. I'm sure my editor would be very excited to get some exclusive photos."

"Reichsstatthalter, I imagine you would like to join us?"

Goring offered no response to the obvious question. Alex imagined that time with the Chancellor of Germany was a guarded prize that the underlings fought over. He just stood and waited.

The door opened and the man offered that the car was ready. As the three men exited the room, Goring turned to Alex and said, "Mr. Dull, why don't; you ride with me."

Hesitating to answer to not offend Himmler, Alex searched for a polite way to respond. Himmler helped him out.

"That would be fine of course. I'll follow in my car."

Knowing now that Goring held the dominate position on their relationship, Himmler naturally gave way. Reaching the courtyard, the guards at the door snapped to attention. Next to Himmler's sedan sat an even larger Mercedes convertible, the top down. Goring directed Alex to the door held opened by a uniformed Luftwaffe officer.

The two stepped in and sat down, the officer closing the door. He climbed in front as the driver pulled out. As they swung around the courtyard to the exit, Alex noticed Himmler in his black sedan following closely.

Turning out on the street, Alex saw the crowds on the sidewalk all recognize Goring and begin waving. Goring raised his arm and waved back as they motored the short distance to another courtyard. Alex assumed the building held the Chancellor's office but was too overcome by his position to really notice. Guards quickly opened the door even before they had stopped as the Luftwaffe officer jumped out to attention.

Himmler arrived and the three men walked up the steps and into the building. Everywhere guards snapped to attention as they climbed the stairs to the second floor. A long corridor with guards the entire way led to another office. The high ceilings echoed at their foot steps before the three men stopped to inform the manned desk. Goring asked if the Fuhrer was available, knowing the meeting was already scheduled.

The desk sergeant stood and escorted them to the the door, opening it. Walking in, Alex noticed a smaller man by the window, staring out. The man turned and Alex recognized Adolf Hitler at once.

Goring spoke first. "Mein Fuhrer. I am excited to bring the famous American photographer to meet you. Mr. Alexander Dull has agreed to photograph you for his magazine."

Hitler strove across the room and greeted Alex warmly. "Mr. Dull, of course. I am familiar with your work. Who isn't."

"Thank you Chancellor. It is an honor to meet you."

"I so enjoyed your photos of your valiant march into France. And your work with the Japanese during their struggle with Russia. Wonderful."

Alex was a taken aback to have his work described in such glowing terms. He considered his work stark war shots that held the gruesome nature of conflict. This man seemed to relish in the death of war and the images taken of it.

"Thank you, Chancellor. You are very kind," Alex said.

Goring interrupted the talk when he asked, 'Mein Fuhrer, as you know, Mr. Dull has been covering out games and found the time to have this meeting. Perhaps we can . . ."

Hitler cut him off, "Of course, he is a busy man. We need to let him get to work. Where would you like me?"

Alex placed his camera bag down and pulled out his Leica camera. He noticed all three Germans perked up that he used a fine German camera for his work. Looking around the room for the best lighting, he directed the Fuhrer to the window he'd been standing in.

"Now Chancellor, lets start with that gaze you had when we just came in the room."

Hitler took on a stern look staring out the window as Alex crouched down and snapped photos. More shots followed as alex adjusted his subject pose. Changing lenses, Alex directed the Fuhrer to a seated position for shots of him as he worked at his desk. Different angles gave way to another change in lenses.

Finally Alex said, 'I think I've captured you, Chancellor. Perhaps a couple with the Reichsstatthalter and the Reichsfuhrer."

Alex motioned Himmler and Goring into the shot and had them looking over Hitler's shoulder while standing behind the desk. Alex noticed Goring's demeanor take on one of distaste at sharing Hitler with Himmler. Similarly, Himmler had a facial expression of gratitude to be getting his picture taken and hopefully published in a world famous magazine. For Alex, he smiled inside knowing he was contributing slightly to the jealousies of the Nazi Party.

Finally finished and as he put his camera away, Alex heard Hitler ask, "Wonderful Mr. Dull. Do you know what issue they might be published in?"

"No Chancellor. I'm not privy to the magazine's schedule. But I'm sure they will want to get the Olympic photos out very soon."

"Of course. I'll look forward to them then."

"Again think you for this opportunity Chancellor."

"Yes," then Hitler switched gears instantly. "Goring, I need to talk to you."

Himmler escorted Alex from the room as the Reichsstatthalter stood waiting for them to eave. Now back in the black sedan, they drove back to the courtyard and deposited Himmler. Saying his goodbyes, Himmler left Alex with his three SS troops who soon drove him back to his hotel.

As the Mercedes drove off, Alex stood on the sidewalk frozen. He couldn't move after the experience he had just had. The hotel doorman broke his inaction.

"Can I get you something Mr. Dull?" the attendant asked. "A drink perhaps?"

Alex turned to the man as he opened the front entrance door. He seemed to sense that a stiff drink after what he had just gone through was appropriate and Alex suddenly agreed. While not a heavy drinker, he made the quick decision that his afternoon sports events could be missed as he stepped into the hotel bar and ordered a glass of wine. He would need more then one as he sat and drank alone.

Chapter 23

Kailua, Hawaii
October, 1936

Knowing that the Olympics ended on August 18th, Alex had suggested not teaching Fall Term since he wasn't sure he'd be back in Hawaii in time. The dean offered that he could start late as the popularity of his classes would allow his tardiness.

Arriving by steamship the first of October, Alex dove into teaching. He had stopped in Washington D.C. and delivered his film to the National Geographic magazine. Learning of Alex's photo shoot with the Fuhrer, the editor offered to set him up with an appointment with Mussolini or Stalin. Alex declined the assignment stating that he had spent enough time with evil and someone else could take the job.

As each day came and went, Alex knew that his international travel days for the magazine were over. Now 71 years old, he longed for his simple life of teaching and sitting by the beach at home. The second Sunday after his return brought a surprise. He and Donita had continued then Sunday dinner tradition and anyone available was invited to dinner.

Alex was enjoying walking his two Golden Retriever dogs on Kailua Beach which he did every day. The five mile long beach offered him exercise to keep his body moving and although some days he felt it more then others, he kept at it.

He looked up upon approaching home and saw a lone figure walking toward him, Recognizing who it was immediately, he smiled as his fourth son strode up to him. He handed one of the leashes to Max after he gave him a hug.

"What brings you out so early?" Alex asked.

Max Dull had been named after Alex's oldest bother. When a string of boys kept coming, by the fourth son he and Donita had decided to start naming them after their brothers. The fifth son would have been named for Donita's oldest brother but nature had other ideas when the first of four girls arrived.

Now a U.S. Navy Commander stationed at Pearl Harbor, Max had gradated from Annapolis. Having a political connection in Washington helped with his appointment. That his grandfather held the Medal of Honor assured acceptance.

"I thought we might chat a bit before the others arrive."

"Sure, should we do another lap on the beach?"

Max nodded that more beach walking sounded good and the two men each with a dog continued walking south toward Lanikai Beach. The early morning sun and the trade winds fought for which would dominate. But once again, it was a glorious day in the tropics.

Max said, "So dad, rumor is that you met Hitler."

"Not only Herr Hitler, I met Goring and Himmler."

Max looked at his dad blankly. Alex recognized a confused look.

"You may not know Heinrich Himmler. A decidedly creepy fellow. Goring made him head of the secret police. Himmler is the one commanding those troops you might have seen in black with the death head on their uniform."

"Oh, the SS. I have heard of them. So, how was it?"

"To be standing in a room and feel evil all around you. Not a good place."

"That bad eh. I thought Hitler was getting Germany moving again. Seems that the carcass the Weimar Republic left needed some saving."

"He has brought the country back. But at what cost? And these Nazis. Pure ideologues. No good comes out of a industrialized country run by true believers."

"And you don't think Roosevelt isn't an ideologue?" Max said.

Alex looked around for any nearby listeners. For a U.S. Naval officer to be berating his commander in chief would not be good for his career. Seeing no one near by Alex said, "I hope you keep such thoughts to yourself son."

"I do. But there are mary in my unit that think his socialism will ruin the country. Look at the unemployment roles. You know Hoover had us coming back but the voters didn't agree."

"I know. It has been bad. And now this farce at London. That naval treaty they tried to inflate will never last," Alex said.

The Second London Naval Conference had agreed to terms and been signed in March of 1936. Missing were three of the main players in the world. Hitler had withdrawn Germany from the League of Nations in 1933. Italy refused to participate in the conference as it was under sanctions by the League of Nations and Japan walked out on the conference.

The conference had been a continuation of the original Washington Naval Conference with other disarmament conferences in the ensuing years. In 1927 the nations met for the Geneva Naval Conference but not much could be agreed upon. In 1930 the First London Naval Conference saw success when submarines, destroyers and cruiser had seen limitations placed on them.

Another attempt was made at the 2nd Geneva Naval Conference in 1932 but failed to reach any great agreement. Alex had followed the events from his original interest at the Washington Naval Conference. But he realized that as the great powers continually met in an attempt to limit war, more and more wars broke out. The 1930's continued to raise the threat of war as Germany, Japan and Italy made moves to build their forces.

Meanwhile, the democratic countries believed disarmament would stop war. Britain passed numerous laws limiting the private ownership of guns as the mood of peace prevailed. France, shocked at the losses suffered in the European War, continued its war weary attitude long into the 1930's with the commiserate public disdain for all things military.

"Dad, I wanted to ask you about your time with the Japanese. How was it when they attacked the Russians?"

Alex turned to face his son, "However do you mean? What are you getting at?"

"Well, you were in Japan before they attacked, right. You didn't know when you went over there they were going to war?"

"No, came as a complete surprise. But I'm still not following."

Alex knew his son had made the rank of full Commander and assignment to Hawaii. Alex knew his son had not been assigned a ship but worked a staff job for the admiral. Max had not been more forthcoming as to what his new job entailed. And now he was asking about Japan.

"I was just wondering if you got any hints that the Japanese were about to attack. Their surprise strike on the ships in Port Arthur had to have planned out ahead of time. Troops would have been in training and moving to ports. Any whispers that things were about to happen?"

"No, not for me. I was just minding my own business photographing Japanese life. National Geographic wanted a informative photo spread on day to day life in Japan. I was taking shots of civilians going about their life. Along with the images of the famous shrines and public buildings. I wasn't near any naval or army bases. Wasn't what I was there for."

"I understand. But when the attack happened, did things suddenly became more evident. Things that were just there but when war happened, were obvious."

"You mean an 'ah ha' moment? No, never had one. Just started making contacts to switch to covering the war. Was lucky to get imbedded in a Japanese army unit that was sent to the fighting. Spent the time taking pictures and staying alive."

"Oh, OK," Max said.

"Why the sudden interest in Japan?" Alex asked.

"I just thought I'd see if the Japs had any specific things to pick up on before they went to war."

"Are you expecting them to attack sometime soon?"

"Oh no. Just speculating."

"Max, we have family in harms way if there is a war in east Asia. You remember that don't you?"

"Yes Dad. I am aware of the family. And if I knew anything that would help them I would say so."

"OK. Let's head back. Your mother will be wondering if we got lost."

They were soon back at the house as the other children arrived with the full gaggle of grandchildren. Donita was in her element as she worked hard in the kitchen with help from the wives and daughters. Alex sat and watched the horde from his easy chair by the big windows overlooking the beach.

He knew Max knew more but could not divulge any national secrets. Alex was pretty sure he worked in Naval Intelligence at Pearl Harbor. Max never offered what his specific duties were but Alex knew that with his son's aptitude and ability to reason that he had always possessed that the Navy would naturally put him to good use. He had finished at the top of his class at Worcester Academy and finished second in his class at Annapolis. Alex knew his fourth son's ability so was confident he would be in the center of any information.

* * *

Alex didn't have long to wait to confirm his son's knowledge of impending Japanese action. In July of 1937 Japan used continuous confrontations between its forces and the forces of the Republic of China as justification to begin a full scale invasion. Ever since the Boxer Rebellion and the subsequent agreements between the foreign powers and China, Japan had been using the agreement to increase its forces inside China.

With its invasion and occupation of Manchuria in 1931, the puppet sate of Manchukuo had been receiving Japanese settlers as they squeezed the locals out. Now a major conflict had broken out as Japan moved to absorb more of China into its empire.

In Europe the war drums had began to pound louder. As Alex continued his class work at the university three days each week, his walks on the beach left him time to contemplate the turn of events in the world.

In 1936 Germany had reoccupied the Rhineland which had been demilitarized under the Versailles Treaty. In 1938 Hitler absorbed Austria in the Anschluss making it part of Greater Germany. Later that year the Sudetenland Germans were brought into the German Reich when Britain and France agreed at Munich to chop off parts of Czechoslovakia. By March of the following year with Poland and Hungry annexing parts of the country and the province of Slovakia seceding, the remaining Czech portion was absorbed by the Third Reich.

As 1939 moved through the summer, tension built in Europe. Hitler had made demands on Lithuania and had received concessions in the Memel land transfer. Poland sat between East Prussia and Greater Germany and Hitler now made demands to the Polish government. As Britain offered guarantees to Poland, France joined the collation against German aggression.

On Sept. 1, 1939 German troops, using a faked attack by Polish forces, invaded Poland. The Blitzkrieg that followed ushered in the new German way of making war. Using combined air and land forces to overwhelm their enemy, the Wehrmacht conquered Poland in six weeks, joining the Soviet Union's invasion to divide the country between the two.

April 1940 saw the forces of Germany conquer Denmark and Norway which set up the invasion of France and the Low Countries in May. By June 14th French forces sought an armistice and Germany held supreme in Western Europe. The Battle of Britain followed beginning in July and did not really end until May of 1941 by which time Great Britain had stopped any threat of invasion.

Hitler turned to his main nemesis, the Soviet Union. After subduing Yugoslavia and Greece in the spring, Germany invaded the Soviet Union on June 22nd. The war went Germany's way as it captured Soviet forces by the hundreds of thousands while occupying the Ukraine and Belorussia. Only winter weather and a counterattack by the Soviets outside Moscow saved the capital from falling into German hands.

As 1941 came to an end, Germany was stunned but holding its line to repeated Russian winter attacks. Alex read his newspaper reports of the war news as he sat on the deck overlooking the beach. The Christmas tree blinked its lights in the living room as Donita busied herself cooking for tomorrow's Sunday dinner. December 7th had been announced as a birthday party for one of the grandchildren. The entire family living on Oahu had committed to attending.

The day broke clear and sunny, a few stray clouds siting over the islands off Lanikai Beach. Alex knew of the observation bunkers siting atop the hill where army troops manned telephones to headquarters. War rumors had been moving through the islands and Alex knew they would be in the mix of things in any attack.

The Hawaiian Island chain held a strategic position on the middle of the Pacific Ocean and any country controlling them held a supreme position. The news of Roosevelt's embargoing potential war material exports to Japan had raised the threat level. It was an action joined by the Dutch with an oil embargo. All an effort to force Japanese forces out of China. Britain had joined the coalition that wanted Japan aggression pushed back.

At noon the crowd began arriving with Alex and Donita welcoming their large family. The grandcildren ran to the beach to play while the adults gathered to watch. The warm winter weather allowed swimming although some of the adults forgo the experience claiming it was too cold. Alex dove in and swan with the kids as he always did.

Three of his sons had joined him as they all played with the kids in the surf. Missing was Alex's youngest son Max but everyone knew Navy business often kept him away. As the group ate and the birthday celebrate opened presents, Alex sat watching the peaceful scene. He suddenly saw a figure enter the house from the front door. Max took off his shoes before stepping into the living room but it was his facial expression that caught Alex's attention.

"Son what is it?"

"Later Dad," Max said as he sat down on the floor and began to play with the presents. Nieces and nephews joined in and soon a wrestling match broke out with Uncle Max, the nieces being knocked down by the roughhouse boys. Soon someone got hurt and Donita stepped in to break things up. The other parents announced it was time to head home and soon Alex and Max were siting alone staring at the ocean.

"Dad, the Japs have attacked. That's why I was late. All hell is breaking loose out in East Asia."

"The Philippines?" Alex asked right way.

"No, not yet. Malaya has been invaded. The British have reported large numbers of transport and troops landing about two hundred miles up the coast from Singapore."

Alex knew that the Japanese had absorbed French Ind-China from the Vichy government. Under the German-French Armistice, a new government had been set up in southern France at Vichy. Japan had moved and although administered by the French, Indochina had become a Japanese puppet colony. Ships could easily interdict British possessions to the south from such a forward position and that was what appeared to be happening.

Alex said, "Not that the British have the forces to stop them with all they are doing in North Africa plus defending their island."

"I don't know Dad. If Japan throws their fleet at them the British down't have anywhere near the forces needed in the Pacific. Singapore could be lost as well as Hong Kong."

"Hong Kong is indefensible. But Singapore? Really? The Gibraltar of the East. Isn't that what they call it?"

"But you need ships and planes or otherwise you starve to death on your rock."

"So what are we doing?"

"Not much. Waiting mostly."

"What are we waiting for?"

"To see if we are attacked," Max said.

"But Roosevelt has been maneuvering for this for years now. He's pushed Japan wherever he could, along with Germany. Sending our old destroyers to Britain."

"Lend lease. More then old ships are handed over to Britain."

"Whatever," Alex said. "Roosevelt has been working as hard as he could to get us involved. So nothing yet?"

"Nothing so far. He moved the Pacific Fleet from San Diego to Pearl last month. The carriers are out delivering war planes to Guam and Wake Islands. We are building up troops and material here on Hawaii."

"So, do you think he'll ask Congress for a declaration of war?"

"Against who? He hasn't asked for Germany over the last two years. And against Japan, do you think the Congress will vote for war to save the British Empire."

Max was right in his assessment. If no Japanese attack came against the interests of the United States there would be no pretext for war. Expecting the United States to act on its own to declare war without a direct attack? Could the isolationism that had gripped the country since the end to the First World War be broken? And for the British?"

"Do you think the Dutch East Indies are next?" Alex asked his son.

Chapter 24

Honolulu, Hawaii
October, 1942

What was now being called the Second World War had just ended. Captain Max Dull sat in his office and read the latest naval reports on the conclusion of the war. He had followed the progress of the Axis Powers as they completed their aggression against their neighbors.

In Europe, after its winter losses during the Soviet winter offensive, the Wehrmacht rebounded with its summer offensive. With Stalin expecting a repeat in a German attempt at capturing Moscow, he was stunned when the Germans struck out for the oil fields of the Caucasus. All summer German forces rolled up Russian territory until they closed with the Caspian Sea, cutting off all oil supplies moving north to the Soviet forces.

Attempting to redeploy his forces, Stalin ran into fuel problems and by September knew he wouldn't be able to check the Germans. Britain continued its loses with a defeat in Egypt and the Germans capturing the Suez canal. Now moving through the Middle East, Rommel's forces were aimed at the Russian province of Georgia and a connection with Army Group South.

After initial peace feelers through the Swiss, Germany and the Soviet Union met in the city of Brest-Litovsk in what would soon become part of Poland and signed an armistice. Russia ceded control over the

Baltic countries and established an independent Ukraine. Poland moved its borders east freeing the old Imperial German lands of East Prussia and Silesia.

The British, now fighting alone, signed a peace treaty soon after giving up any claim to Mesopotamia. With their loses in Asia, Great Britain and Japan reached an agreement where Malaya and Singapore were retuned to the British Empire but Hong Kong became Japanese.

Japan retained the Dutch East Indies and the oil wealth the islands of Sumatra and Borneo held. Britain ceded its portion of Borneo to Japan.

"Its done Captain. We never fired a shot," Max's admiral said. His tone of disgust evident.

"Yes sir," Max said.

"What use is this wonderful fleet Roosevelt built if we don't use it."

"Not easy to unilaterally declare war on someone who doesn't attack you."

"Just a matter of time if you ask me. Japan will now consolidate its position. Move more settlers into China while they move the Chinese aside. You're Filipino aren't you?"

"Yes sir."

"Look what they've done there. Might as well be a province of Japan itself. They all speak Japanese now. They have a good puppet government. The Japs even base ships at our old base at Subic Bay. And we don't do anything."

"Same as Thailand. Another Japanese puppet kingdom."

"You are correct Captain. All of southeast Asia under the boot of those militarists. Add in Europe as a Nazi war machine and we are very alone out here in Hawaii."

Max nodded his agreement. It had suddenly become a very small world indeed. With the United Sates holding hegemony over the Western Hemisphere and Britain holding out with its remaining empire, much of the world had entered a new Dark Ages. A time of subjugation to authoritarian regimes.

"Maybe a new president can change that," Max said.

"Get rid of three term Frank you mean. Well, he said he'd keep us out of the world in his 1940 campaign promise and the American public bought it. Fools all of them. Fight now before those bastards get stronger I say."

"So the Admiral thinks we should have declared war even though we weren't attacked, sir?"

"Too late now. What I thought back then doesn't amount to a fart in a gale. But mark my words, we will be fighting one or both sometime in the near future. And God help us then."

"Yes sir."

Chapter 25

Harvard University, Cambridge, massachusetts
April 22, 1950

It was the Spring Term at Harvard University as students moved across Harvard Yard as they went about the evening. Day classes finished, the evenings were set aside for studying, library research, various club meetings and special lectures by visiting dignitaries. Siting in the north end of Harvard Yard sat the venerable gothic styled Memorial Hall.

Built in 1876, Memorial Hall held two of the iconic venues on campus: Annaberg Hall which besides being the most impressive space, served as the dining hall for the freshman class and Sanders Hall, a one thousand seat traditional auditorium. Tonight Sanders Hall was reserved for a special event, one which had to be moved from the smaller ballroom of Loeb House due to the demand for tickets.

Harvard was celebrating the naming of the George Frisbie Hoar Center for Political Science made possible by a very large donation by Maximilian Dull some years before. Though a successful Boston lawyer Maximilian had never married and before his death in 1930 had bequest his gift with the understanding that his late uncle would be recognized.

As the auditorium filled to capacity, two men walked out onto the stage and took their seats. To their left a lectern sat waiting the opening remarks. At the appointed time and with the seated audience buzzing in anticipation, the younger of the two men stood and walked to the lectern. He adjusted the microphone as the lone newsreel camera swung to take in the scene.

"Good evening ladies and gentlemen. For those who don't know me I am Dr. John Duncan, Department Head of the School of Journalism here at Harvard. It is my great honor to be introducing tonights most special guest. And from the change of venue to accommodate the demand, a very popular guest it would appear."

Dr. Duncan took a breath and he turned and smiled at the older man still seated. The old man smiled back.

He continued. "As part of our week long activities in establishing the George Frisbie Hoar Center for Political Science, tonight we welcome Dr. Alexander Dull. Professor Dull is a local boy who received his undergraduate degree from Holy Cross College. He received his Masters in Visual Arts from the University of Paris and his Doctorate in Journalism form the University of Hawaii. Recognized as one of the founders of photojournalism, Professor Dull is also a linguist extraordinaire. Fluent in over ten languages and conversant in many more, Dr Dull currently holds status at the University of Hawaii as a Professor Emeritus. Please welcome Dr. Dull."

The audience clapped in appreciation of what they were about to hear. Dr. Dull had just recently published a memoir that was creating a fire storm of controversy in the country, especially in Washington, D.C. Dr. Duncan moved across the stage and took up his seat opposite Alex. He adjusted the microphone as the newsreel camera moved to a position to take the two into view.

"Dr. Dull. An honor sir."

Alexander adjusted his microphone before answering, "Thank you for the invitation." He turned to the audience and added, "I hope I can entertain this crowd. I'm an old man now and I'm not sure I have much to offer this young audience."

"Professor, I'm quite sure tonight will be everything everyone hopes for. First, let us start at the beginning. You are a local boy."

"Born and schooled in Worcester, left when I was twenty two years old. Been roaming the planet ever since."

"Yes, your resume is very clear on that fact. Study in Paris. Photographing the West. Then off to the Philippines. Just in time for the Spanish American War. Tell us about that period."

"In Germany I met Dr. Jose Rizal whose writings become the rally call for independence in the Philippines. I would relate Dr. Rizal's writings to our own revolutionary writer, Thomas Paine. Both men inspired others to seek freedom for their people."

"But Paine wasn't executed for his writings."

"Saddest day of my life. I met with Dr. Rizal in prison a few days before his execution by the Spanish. He was at peace. An amazing man who inspired me to take up the torch for Philippine independence."

Dr. Duncan flipped his notes. He asked, "And you met your wife through Dr. Rizal?"

"Yes, she was a nurse in Dr. Rizal's hospital. We've been married over fifty years now and have eight wonderful children. I lost count on the number of grandchildren. Filipinas love large families."

"And I understand they all live in the Hawaiian Islands near you. That must be special to have family all near by."

Alexander grew quiet as he thought for a moment. Dr. Duncan sat and waited as Alex seemed to compose himself, a small quiver in his expression. He pulled himself together and answered. "We do still have my wife's family in the Philippines."

"Yes, a subject I want to get to. But if we could first address your time with National Geographic magazine. You were one of the first photo journalists they hired. Tell us about that."

Alexander's expression widened at the change in subject. "I started with the magazine in 1903. Just before Thanksgiving. I remember because it was the first year I'd been back in the United Stares and my family was looking forward to a Thanksgiving together. Unfortunately I had to get to Japan right away as tensions between Japan and Russia were looking like a war was about to happen."

"Your photos from the war are still classics. Right up there with Matthew Bradley's photos of the American Civil War. How ever did you get started with the magazine?"

"An amazing story actually. In 1896 I had returned from the studying at the Sorbonne and wanted to display my photos of Europe. At an exhibit at Holy Cross College a young man chatted with me, stating how much he loved my work. His name was Gilbert Grosvenor."

"The first editor of the magazine. How ever did he find himself in Worcester?"

"And still editor of the magazine I will add," Alex added. "He was attending Worcester Academy and was about to graduate. We discovered we were both alumni of the academy. And loved tennis. We played a bit before I headed out west. We became good friends."

"And he looked you up at an exhibit of your Philippine photos in Washington D.C you put on I understand."

"Hired me on the spot. Gave me two moths to get to Tokyo. That took all my Japanese language skills to pull off."

Dr. Duncan again flipped his notes and said, "But you pulled it off. You were there when the Port Arthur fell. That issue of the magazine was one of the largest printings up until that time. But before the magazine your work caught some of the most momentous events in Asia. However did you get involved with the Boxer Rebellion."

"I had been translating for the Germans in the area of the Philippines that they controlled at that time. As you remember, the four powers all divided the islands into separate zones. I happened to be living near Cebu City and knew both the local languages and German."

"And they let you travel with them to Peking?"

"I was good friends with most of the naval officers and talked my way onto one of the cruisers heading to support the eight nations alliance. Those were the powers that fought their way through and relieved the delegations trapped in Peking. The Chinese had committed terrible atrocities against westerners"

"Yes, your photos of some of those killings swayed public opinion around the world."

Alex remembered the event and hung his head slightly. He recalled the brutality of it all and the retaliation the allied powers extracted from the Chinese. "And the photos published were the censored ones. I have others that were not allowed to be shown so as to not cause even more hatred toward the Chinese."

"Yes, Professor. I'm sure your catalogue has some heart wrenching images. Your work in the Philippine-American War certainly swayed public opinion."

And that was the crux of the controversy in his memoir. Alex had written truthfully about what his photos had done and how thirty years later, he realized it had all gone terribly wrong. But Dr. Duncan passed on pressing on the issue, at least for now.

"But lets go back to you magazine work. After the Russo-Japanese War you returned to the Philippines."

"I based myself out of my wife's family's compound near Cebu City. I would travel around east

Asia for National Geographic and spend my off time at home."

"Yes, you had to have been home occasionally to have had those eight children. How did your wife take you traveling all the time?"

"It was fine. She had her extended family to live with. We built a house near her family so she was perfectly happy."

"I want to talk to you about the Washington Naval Conference that took place in 1922."

Alexander shifted in his seat. The subject that was causing such consternation in the country had been brought up. Part of him wished he'd never wrote his thoughts down and now he wished he was back in his little world of academics in Honolulu. But this was the reason he was here, besides honoring his late uncle. He knew his thoughts were important and Dr. Rizal would be proud of him for making them known.

Dr. Duncan noticed the shift in attitude, but said, "You were instrumental in convincing the great powers at that time to set the Philippine free. How did that all come about?"

Alex thought back the almost thirty years and it felt like yesterday. The events were seared in his memory. The twists and turns of political maneuvering that brought about an independent Philippine.

"First I certainly wasn't the only one. There were many others who had a hand in moving the Great Powers to relinquish control over the Philippines. And not least among them all was Mark Twain. Although he died in 1910, his writings certainly swayed many."

"And your photos."

"Yes, the two were very instrumental, I would agree."

"Mark Twain breathed life into the anti-imperialists in the country that had been fighting ever since Hawaii had ben annexed. With the war with Spain and the territory that was added to the United States the anti-imperialists fought hard to keep Americas away from European schemes."

"But they did not prevail. President McKinley followed by President Teddy Roosevelt made sure the great American Empire stood resolute. At least until 1922," Dr. Duncan added.

"Give my brother Maximilian a lot of the credit," Alex said. Once again his mind drifted to happy times as a young boy with his older brother. That Max had stayed in Boston after Harvard Law and worked the political machine meant Alex had pull in Washington when he needed it. Max had befriended a young city councilman in 1887. Working closely with Calvin Coolidge, Max had moved up to be Chief of Staff when Coolidge became Massachusetts governor.

When Coolidge became a candidate with Warren Harding for vice president, Max was again involved and become Coolidge's Chief of Staff when he won the election. Max moved to serve President Coolidge when Harding died. Alex had used that connection as well as others to move the Washington establishment toward his goal.

"Yes, we could have almost named our political science center after your brother. It was generous of him to award the money to name it for your uncle."

"Uncle George, as we called him, deserves all that you honor him with. He led the anti-imperialist forces in the U.S. Senate. Of his twenty seven years of service in the senate, those were his finest hours. I just wish he could have lived to see the day where America relinquished at least part of the empire to its freedom."

"But is was your cousins' widow who added to the movement for Philippine independence. Tell us about that."

Alex thought back to his youth and time with his cousin Rockwood Hoar. Son of the U.S. Senator, Rockwood won a seat in the U.S. House of Representatives and died in his first term. At age 51, his career was too short. His widow eventually married Fredrick Gillett ten years later. Gillett spent thirty two years in the House, including six years as Speaker."

"Speaker of the House at the critical time of the Washington Naval Conference. I would add. Quite a family connection. How much did he help in your endeavor for the Philippines."

"Along with my brother in Coolidge's office, the Congressman was instrument in getting our government to propose initially."

"And the other powers eventually went along?'

"Of course the Germans' were out of the picture in the Philippines. Japan took all their possessions and that was why the other powers took so long to reach agreement. Britain and the United Sates didn't want

Japan to hold that much territory in the Philippines. Although Versailles was signed, the final disposition of Philippine German territory was left out of that treaty. Hence its inclusion on the Washington Treaty."

"But the powers met in Washington ostensibly to write an agreement on warship tonnage. A treaty to limit the size of each nation's fleet and avoid an naval arms race. How did it get around to territory discussions?"

"Beside limiting capital ships, article XIX of the treaty went to limiting construction of fortifications and naval bases in the Pacific Ocean. As that issue was being discussed the topic of the Philippines came up. It was the American who initially proposed vacating the islands. Britain agreed in principal and the two powers worked the reluctant Japanese."

"Why do you think the Japanese finally agreed then?"

"You have to understand the Asia mindset. They think in longer terms then we do. They understood that they had been on their islands since 1898, building schools and teaching the locals Japanese, along with other subjects. Taking over the German territory all those schools the Germans had built became Japanese language centers. After four years, the majority of the younger people were fluent in Japanese. They understood with the Americans and British leaving, Japanese would become the second language of the islands, after Filipino."

Dr. Duncan checked his notes and added, "If you could enlighten out audience, Filipino is what?"

"It is a standardized language of Tagalog, the native language of the tribe living around Manila. With so many native languages, the country needed a common language so Filipino was created. But now Japanese is as common as Filipino. The power in Japan knew that language would eventually move the Philippines into their camp, much like Thailand. Technically independent, but both countries would be allied with Tokyo."

"Much like the Quisling regime in Norway. Nazi stooges doing the bidding but looking like a local popular government."

Alex shifted agin in his seat. This is what he had brought to the world. Nazi power in Europe with a victorious Third Reich holding sway over three continents. And a ruthless Japanese Empire running wild across the world's larges ocean. All springing to life from his act of kindness for an old friend. Freeing the Philippines had allowed the forces of evil upon the world.

Many now considered the world had entered into a period as bad as the Dark Ages of medieval Europe, only worse. This affliction encompassed the entire world and not just Europe. All from one small conference in Washington so many years ago. If only he could redo his life, Alex thought. Stay to his photography and let politics play out. Keep the United States engaged in the world and maybe, just maybe have a different result.

Nazi Germany in Europe now held power along with Imperial Japan astride East Asia. Their positions combined with Stalinist Russia continuing its terror regime athwart the Asia mainland left only the United Sates and a beleaguered Britain holding the Western ideals so cherished by many. The forces of evil were on the march while the forces of enlightenment dwelled on the margins.

Dr. Duncan brought Alex back from his thoughts when he said, "We should talk about your book now. You make a very powerful case for American involvement in the world. Maybe a bit too late, but how do you reconcile your new attitude to your view in 1920."

"I'm afraid the world changed, and not for the better. Who knew that in 1920 the five powers that met to hammer out a treaty would fade from the world scene. France succumbed to a delayed defeatism left over from World War I. Italy would revert to Fascism, the United Sates would turn to isolationism and Britain would drift to socialism. All of those five shifted to a weaker position except Japan. Especially weaker in comparison to Japan and Germany."

"Yes, Germany's quick victories in Europe led to a peace treaty with the Soviets in September 1942. Three short years and Germany had moved into it supreme position in Europe. And in its peace treaty with Britain after Churchill had been voted out of office, Germany gained what is turning into the greatest oil find in the Middle East. All in German hands."

Alex added, "Now with Japan controlling the Dutch East Indies and their oilfields along with gains in

Indochina from the Vichy French, it is an intolerable position."

"Luckily the British signed a treaty with the Japanese before Japan invaded Australia, preserving that impotent part of the British Empire."

"And to think it was all set in motion in 1920."

Dr. Duncan asked, "Please, Professor Dull, explain your thinking on how Philippine independence led to our situation today."

Alexander knew this was the critical question. He had raised it in his memoir and the firestorm continued to sweep the country. He noticed most of the audience move forward waiting his answer.

"In freeing the Philippines from all outside powers, the United Sates suddenly moved out of the Western Pacific. Our bases in Guam are far enough away from the East Asia littoral to offer no effect. In Asia, it is these sea lanes north and south that matter. The outer islands of the Philippines, Formosa, Okinawa, and the former Dutch East Indies control the inner sea lanes along the mainland. Control those islands and you control the seas."

"You memoir states that the absence of the United States was critical."

"Exactly. Without our presence in that critical zone, when the Japanese moved south into Malaya and Indochina. We were no longer astride their shipping lanes. We were not a direct threat. And with everyone in the Philippines speaking Japanese, it was easy to co-opt them into being a budding ally. With no American influence there, our forces would have to stage out of

Hawaii if we were to contest the Japanese. Or help the British from its bases in India."

"A very different world picture then if we had stayed in the Philippines. I see your point."

"Lets image that in 1920 I had failed. The ship limitations had gone into effect but America retained forces on Luzon Island. If we had retained our naval base at Subic Bay and our air force had a airfield where the old Clark Airstrip had been. The Japanese would not have moved south leaving a potential enemy astride their shipping lanes."

"You surmise then the Japanese would have attacked us?"

"Probably the same way they did against the Russians at Poet Arthur. A surprise attack and then maneuver for a climatic sea battle as the United Sates sortied out to meet the enemy. Maybe a sea borne air attack against our fleet at Pearl Harbor. The British showed how to do it against the Italian fleet at Toronto in 1940. My God, they damaged three battleships using twenty one biplanes. Biplanes."

Alex continued, "At the time the Japanese probably had the finest naval air force with the best pilots in the world. With their seven fleet carriers, they could have launched hundreds of planes in any attack. In war games in the 1930's we showed how it could be done with simulated air attacks off our carriers against Pearl Harbor"

"Pearl Harbor. Thats' in Hawaii?

"The U.S. Navy's main base in the Pacific. Imagine an early morning Sunday attack catching the fleet at anchor with hundreds of war planes. It would have crippled the American fleet for years before we could have built new ships."

Dr. Duncan said, "But it never happened because we were't in anyones way. We were safe behind our oceans in isolation. President Roosevelt tried to get us involved with his Lend Lease Act. That certainly moved us close to war. But the one spark that would ignite the Americans never came."

"Exactly. Germany didn't bite when we sent our old destroyers to Britain. Or sold them war materials. Those acts were ignored as the Wehrmacht rolled over the Russians until Stalin, seeing only a prostrate Britain struggling to survive herself, called for an armistice. His armies had taken huge losses and by 1942 the Germans hadn't lost a battle. Stalin's prospects looked dire so he sought a way out. He knew the Japanese by 1942 had conquered what they wanted and could turn there eyes on Siberia."

"There had been those border skirmishes between the Soviets and the Japanese in 1938 and '39," Dr. Duncan added. "There was a real threat of the Japanese and Germans working in concert to crush Russia totally."

"Exactly. As the British signed an armistice with booth Japan and Germany in 1942, that left India and Australia out of the picture for the Japanese. Only Russia remained nearby for Japan to target."

"I'll leave it with one last question. Professor Dull, we are the last major power standing against darkness. Are you advocating that the United States become engaged then?"

Alex thought about that question as he had thought about it many times. And always he arrived at the same place.

"I am an old man. It's my birthday today and I get to celebrate in Worcester tomorrow my eighty five years on Earth with my beautiful bride. My three brothers are gone, bless their souls. I live in a tropical paradise where its hard to dwell on such world events. So I leave it to the younger people to decide. It will be their blood and treasure that will be expended saving Western Civilization."

Alex closed by saying, "And they will need to decide when to undertake such an endeavor. Not an easy decision to make. At one time the Philippines could have been that catalyst to war, but we set them free. A big mistake. I'm afraid history will decide how big."

The End

Author's Notes

In 1977 I was attended a history course while an undergraduate student at the University of Oregon in Eugene. Taught by Dr. Paul Dull, the course was entitled History of the Far East 1900-1940 if I remember. It covered the rise of Imperial Japan and the class held such a notoriety that students from as far away as Portland would drive the two hours each way to take in the lectures.

Professor Dull was uniquely qualified to teach such a course as after graduating from Harvard University, he had spent the 1930's traveling throughout China, Korea and Japan. Fluent in all three languages, at the start of World War II he announced to the class that he was one of only seven people in the country fluent an all three languages.

I remember one of his lectures he challenged the class as to what would have happened if Japan had never attacked the United States. He felt that the U.S. would never have declared war on Japan without an attack as it would be perceived as acting to save the British Empire.

Roosevelt was a known British Empire hater and would have been loath to agree to war under such circumstances. That Germany declared war on the United Sates right after Pearl Harbor was a moronic decision by Hitler since the U.S was not in the mood to declare war on both Germany and Japan. Japan was perceived to be the enemy after the sneak attack on Pearl Harbor.

Dr. Dull's challenge stuck with me over all these years. When I married into the Philippines and began living in the islands the concept of this book developed. Wanting to showcase the importance of the Philippines to the history of Western Civilization, I put a plot line together in an attempt to offer a compelling story of the Philippines.

If the United Sates had not been siting on the shipping lanes of Japan as they made their move south for resources, would Japan have attacked? I think not. Since American forces were in Subic Bay, Corregidor Island and Clark Air Base, the Japanese took the American position as a threat and attacked to eliminate that threat.

My plot does one thing better then Professor Dull in that I removed American forces from the Philippines and so reduced the threat level to Japan.

As for many of the other subjects of my plot, most are true. The Japanese were interested in the Kingdom of Hawaii before the U.S. backed coup overthrew the Queen. Germany had its Asiatic Squadron in Manila Bay soon after Dewey's victory causing problems. Germany was interested in acquiring more colonies and viewed the Philippines as a potential gain. Prince Henry was commander of the Asiatic Squadron for his older brother Kaiser Wilhelm.

The Japanese did receive two modern British built battle ships at the same time depicted in the storyline. The Germans could have easily had the forces depicted in the story there also.

The Visaya region of the Philippines did not participate in the Philippine Revolution. While the Muslim population later fought a rebellion against the occupying American forces, the southern region of the Philippines had a much different attitude then the Manila area. Thus, Germany and Japan could have easily occupied those islands.

The Washington Naval Conference dealt with land issues as well as ship construction. A limit on defensive construction on occupied islands was agreed upon. In my scenario, if the Germans and Japanese each occupied parts of the Philippines in 1898, Japan would have ended up with the German portions as they did with most of the other German Asian and Pacific colonies. Allied with Britain in World War I, Japan scooped up as much as it could during that conflict.

Would the other powers in 1920 have agreed to Philippine independence and the removal of the Japanese. Maybe. The Harding-Coolidge Administration was fixated on cost cutting at the time so removing a money drain like the Philippines would have appealed to them. If everyone left the islands, then the powers involved could see the advantage to such an agreement.

Lastly, would the United Staes have declared war in 1941 or 42 if they hadn't been attack by either Germany or Japan. Isolationism continued running strong and I think Dr. Dull had his finger on the answer. The United States would not have moved on Japan to save the British Empire if Japan had left America alone.

I gave my fictional characters the Dull name in honor of Dr. Paul Dull and his class. It was the best and only history class I ever took. History has always been too important to me to sit through any hack professor lecturing me.

If you enjoyed this book then you might be interested in the author's other alternative history books:

German Golfers Who Changed the World

and

Task Force Bismarck

The following is an excerpt from German Golfers Who Changed the World .

Chapter 1

Potsdam, Germany   May 8, 1939

Ernst von Mueller sat at an outdoor table overlooking Sans Souci Palace. He turned his head slightly to the right to where he could see Frederick the Great's 'New Palace'. This spot was one of his favorites in all of Germany. He sipped his coffee and waited.

He had arrived early for his golf game with the von Mueller family. The years of Nazi rule in Germany had taken the old customs and thrown them overboard. Ernst sat and pondered the missing formal trappings of what had been Imperial Germany.

The Great War had ended the German Empire. The resulting Versailles Peace Treaty had crushed the German economy. And through all that, the finer parts of German culture had struggled for existence. The thug Hitler and his criminal gang had stolen the legitimate government away and were now attempting to replace the cultured Germany with Nazi propaganda.

He was forced, as Deputy Foreign Minister for North American Affairs, to carry the Nazi baggage. And Ernst had to be a member of the Nazi Party in order to do it. He still wrestled with his conscience over what he had become.

Now war loomed on the horizon. Hitler was again gambling with Germany's future in a vain attempt to aggrandize the Nazi Party. Ernst knew Germany could never survive another Kaiser Wilhelm-type administration of the war.

The Great War had been catastrophic for Germany. *To lose all that Germany had over some ridiculous Austrian affair with Serbia - it was madness,* Ernst thought.

A madman was about to shove Ernst's beloved country into war with Britain and France over a Nazi sham. Hitler had bluffed his way into the Rhineland and then grabbed Austria.

The Sudetenland had fallen in his lap due to the weak-kneed British and French selling out their ally, Czechoslovakia. Now it was Poland's turn. Hitler risked war with the Allies over the Polish Corridor and the City of Danzig. *The 'Austrian Corporal' goes too far,* Ernst thought. But he had to be careful. Such thoughts could get one shot in Germany. And not only his life would be at risk: his entire family was in the balance.

Ernst sipped his coffee and focused on the view of the Sans Souci Palace. He pressed his thoughts toward Frederick the Great and the rise of the Kingdom of Prussia. And he waited.

Today was the von Mueller family golf day. When nice weather finally hit, every Saturday was reserved for golf. Any family members that could make the date would show up.

Ernst saw two brothers walking up the street to join him. They carried their clubs in bags over their shoulders.

His younger brother Fritz spoke first. "Hey, you always beat us here! You must grab the first tram running to get here so early."

"Yes. Fritz and I were convinced that we would beat you here today," Ernst's other brother Francis said.

Francis was third in line and a Captain in a Parachute Division while Fritz was a Major in the Army's War Plans

Office. Both had followed their father into service to the Fatherland.

Ernst's father, Otto von Mueller, was a general in the Wehrmacht. As the two brothers sat down, a black Mercedes sedan pulled up to the curb. The engine was switched off and two men stepped out, one older and one young.

"Father, you took the Mercedes out of the garage. And look who you let drive it," Ernst said.

A tall, lanky nineteen-year-old closed the door gently on the black sedan. He handed the keys to his father.

"What, can't I drive Father's prized possession?" Duke asked.

A man with a white apron appeared next to the table. "General von Mueller. Once again you honor me with your family. Golf time I suppose?" the man asked.

"Sergeant Link. You know full well that every Saturday during nice weather is golf time for the von Mueller family," Otto replied.

"I'll get one more coffee and one hot chocolate, right away," the sergeant said.

"Hot chocolate? Nein. My youngest graduates from Berlin Polytechnic next week. It is time for him to drink a man's drink. Two coffees," Otto said.

The three older brothers all began to laugh.

"So Duke, have you decided yet? The Wehrmacht or the Luftwaffe? And don't tell me the Kriegsmarine, just to be different," Francis said. With one son in the Army and one in the Air Force, Duke was the tie-breaker since Ernst was exempt from military service due to his government work. The German Navy was the third option.

"Father hasn't heard yet, but I've signed up with the Luftwaffe. They said I can go into flight training to be a fighter pilot."

"Well Father, there goes the family name. After all those years of von Muellers in the Prussian Army, now you only have Fritz to carry on the tradition," Francis said.

"Francis, it's quite alright that you and Duke joined the Luftwaffe. All my sons serve the Fatherland equally, as they should. We need all of our men to be ready."

Sergeant Link returned with more coffee. He placed them down and then retrieved some sweetbread from the tray. "I thought you would need extra energy today."

"Sergeant, your thoughtfulness is appreciated. How is your son doing?" Otto asked. He had known the sergeant since their time together in the same regiment during the Great War.

"He's doing fine. He's in basic training right now. His last letter said that he was accepted into radio school."

"Luftwaffe, isn't it, Sergeant?" Francis asked. "Good choice. I'll keep my eye out for him. If he's like his father, he'll be a good man to have in my unit."

"He'd like that. He knows all of you from your years stopping here before your game," Link said.

The five von Muellers finished and paid their tab over Sergeant Link's protest. It was a regular event, the sergeant trying to stop Otto from paying, his argument that he owed his life to Otto waved off each time.

Loading up the golf bags in the Mercedes's trunk, the five squeezed into the sedan. Otto drove the short distance to Potsdam Golf Course.

Once on the links, the brothers took their turns at the tee and headed out after their ball. Ernst caught up with his father and the two walked along talking.

"So Father, do you think Germany will ever shake the 'Bismarck Myth'?" Ernst asked.

"What? That old tale. You believe that?" Otto asked.

The 'Bismarck Myth' was supposedly the curse placed on Germany by the 'Iron Chancellor' upon his dismissal in 1890. Kaiser Wilhelm II had fired Bismarck in a political feud.

The myth stated that Germany would be cursed with unstable and ineffective governments. The resulting disaster in the Great War after Germany's resounding success in the Franco-Prussian War of 1870 seemed to confirm the curse.

"First the Great War disaster under Wilhelm. Now Hitler's pushing us to war with the Allies on one side and Poland on the other. And what about the Soviets? We are surrounded once again. And with only the Italians for partners," Ernst said. "It appears that Bismarck will be correct again."

"Ernst, hold your tongue. You can't be sure who's listening, even out here. You must never bring this up again. Germany will get through this period, like it has so many other times. It's our duty to help it reach the greatness it has been destined for," Otto said.

Ernst left his Father on the fairway to walk over to where his ball lay, while Otto continued on toward his own ball. Ernst stood and waited for his other family members.

As he stood, Ernst reached the conclusion that if it was within his power, he would end the 'Bismarck Myth'. He had a diplomatic trip to England lined up soon. Maybe he could find an answer there. Anything to throw the boot of the Nazis off his country's neck.

Chapter 2

Tempelhof Airport, Berlin, Germany   May 22, 1940

"Is there a Colonel von Mueller present?" the office orderly called to the waiting room.

"Ja. I'm Colonel von Mueller. What is it?" Fritz von Mueller asked. He walked over from his spot by the window overlooking the waiting planes on the tarmac.

"Telephone, Sir. Your headquarters." The orderly handed the phone to Fritz.

"Colonel von Mueller here," Fritz answered. He listened as his commanding general got on the phone. General von Blucher was head of the War Plans Department of the German General Staff of the Wehrmacht. His department was responsible for the future conduct of the war.

With the German Army well on its way to smashing the British and the French armies in Belgium, the War Plans Office Order of Battle was on track to a decisive victory in the opening battles of the Western Campaign. Poland had been quickly eliminated the year before. Then a lightning operation in the spring had been conducted to eliminate Denmark and Norway and secure the iron ore shipments from Sweden. Although the German Navy had suffered at the hands of the British Royal Navy, both countries had been conquered.

For General von Blucher's command, it had been a successful 9 months. Now it was time to take France and Britain out of the war. The gambit continued to work precisely as planned. General von Bock had invaded the Netherlands and quickly pushed on into Belgium. This action had forced the French and British to honor their commitment to help the Belgian Army defend their country.

Once the Allies were committed to fighting deep inside Belgium, General von Rundstedt applied the decisive thrust through the Ardennes Forest and into the rear of the Allies. Armed with the majority of Germany's Panzers, von Rundstedt quickly advanced toward the English Channel to cut off the Allied Armies in Belgium. It was working brilliantly. But there were persistent rumors of changes from the Fuhrer. Changes that could endanger everything that had been accomplished.

"Colonel, I'm glad you made it on time. I wanted to confirm that you received your orders to attend the meeting. You have the briefcase for your report with you?" General von Blucher asked over the phone. Normally, the general would be attending such a high level meeting. But old war injuries suffered during World War I had forced him to enter the hospital. "I picked you for this assignment because you wrote most of the report and you're the most familiar with our recommendations. The Fuhrer is indicating that he doesn't want to humiliate the British by capturing their entire Expeditionary Army."

"General von Blucher, you aren't expecting me to argue with the Fuhrer, are you Sir?" Colonel von Mueller was suddenly suspicious as to the desirability of this assignment. Maybe the general really required a stay in the hospital or maybe he didn't? Fritz knew that if this assignment was headed where he was thinking, he wouldn't need a hospital. A morgue maybe, but no hospital.

"Nein, nein. You are to report on the contingencies we have mapped out and let High Command make their decisions. Take good notes as to the direction they expect the war to take so we can do our job," von Blucher said. Fritz von Mueller was known for his brilliance in anticipating problems and his attention to detail, all of which covered the complications of moving an army in battle. Others often forgot about the logistics of supplying millions of men at war. Colonel von Mueller was an expert at devising a campaign and making sure it had the best chance at success.

"Sir, you can be assured that I'll represent your command as you would. Thank you for the opportunity," Fritz said. There was some apprehension in his voice he hoped the general didn't recognize. Fritz would be willing to die for his general rather than show disgrace in any way.

"Good. I know you can get the job done. Best of luck, Colonel," the general said as he ended the call.

Fritz walked back to the windows of the ready room. Other officers were patiently waiting. Most of the others were much higher ranked than Fritz, and he felt decidedly out of place. He headed to a quiet corner to collect his thoughts. Today would be a very important day in the military career of one Colonel Fritz von Mueller.

"Excuse me, Colonel. I couldn't help but overhear them call your name. Are you related to General von Mueller?" The person asking the questions had the braids of a general on his shoulders.

Fritz quickly came to attention and clicked his heals. He saluted smartly and looked straight ahead at the opposite wall. "Sir, jawohl. General Otto von Mueller is my father."

"At ease, Colonel. Otto and I served in the Great War together. We were both captains in the 4th Regiment of the Bavarian Landwehr. We fought together near Ypres, Belgium. I see he is back in Belgium with von Bock's Army. Chief of Staff, if I recall," the general said.

"Sir, thank you for remembering my father. Yes, he's Chief of Staff under General von Bock." Fritz relaxed just a little. But considering that most of the other waiting staff were now watching this intercourse, Fritz kept things very military. The German Army was a demanding institution and Fritz had a family tradition to uphold.

"Colonel, will you be attending this meeting at Army Group West?" the general asked. He seemed to realize that a colonel was a little out of place standing here with so many generals. Some of the higher ranking generals had colonels along as aids, but there were no other colonels in the room that were unattached.

"Sir, my commanding general is in the hospital with complications suffered during the Great War. I was ordered to take his place," Fritz answered.

"I see. Well, any son of Otto will represent himself well. If anyone starts in after your head at the meeting, you can count on me for support. Some of these fellows can be very nasty at times," the general said.

"Thank you, Sir. I appreciate the support." Fritz hoped he wouldn't need it. The general saluted and returned to his party. Fritz again snapped to attention, clicked his heels and saluted as the general left.

Fritz heard the start of an engine outside and turned to see smoke belching out of the starboard engine on the Junkers Ju 52 nearest him. Soon the second and third Ju 52 in line began turning over their starboard engines. Once running smoothly, each plane turned over their port engine. More smoke as each large radial engine caught. Finally, the third engine in the nose of the plane started.

The Junkers Ju 52 was the standard passenger plane of the Luftwaffe. An older design than the new American DC-3, German aeronautic engineers were too busy designing fighters and bombers to spend much time on transport planes. The Ju 52 got the job done with enough comfort for

Germans. And if the Fuhrer rode in one, who could complain?

An officer came into the waiting room with a clipboard. As ground support at the airport, it was his job to make sure the right people got on the correct plane. There was a definite pecking order in Nazi Germany, and one did not attempt to move up where one wasn't invited.

The officer called out the six names that would be on Fritz's plane. He checked them off and then escorted them out to the third plane in the lineup. Once these first six were aboard, the officer walked over to another waiting room and shortly thereafter six more high ranking officers stepped out. They all headed to the second plane in the lineup.

Finally, the officer walked over to a third door in the airport terminal and waited. Fritz had a window seat in the back of the plane on the right side that faced the terminal. He watched the ground control officer. Suddenly, the door moved and the officer quickly snapped to attention and raised his arm in the Nazi salute. Standing motionless, the staff officer held the door open.

Watching intently to see who would appear, Fritz was taken back as Adolf Hitler stepped out of the door and walked briskly toward the first plane. Hitler was quickly surrounded by Hermann Goring and Heinrich Himmler as they kept pace on each side of the Fuhrer. Right behind came Joseph Goebbels and two officers that Fritz didn't recognize.

Fritz suddenly felt his palms go sweaty and the blood rise in his head. He would be giving his report to the High Command of the Nazi Party. He knew this meeting was important but he hadn't quite realized just how important. He fought back the apprehension he felt. He was a capable German officer from a long line of German officers. His breeding would carry him through and would make sure he didn't embarrass the family. Now he was glad of the one general along that knew him and might speak up on his behalf.

As he sat in the back of the plane, Fritz overhead the generals all talking about who had walked out with the Fuhrer. Goring, as head of the Luftwaffe, was expected. Himmler, as head of the SS, was also expected. Those two stuck to Hitler like glue.

As head of propaganda, it was unusual for Goebbels to attend a high level Army meeting. Fritz then heard talk about the other two officers. One was Martin Bormann, aid to Hitler, and according to one general, all around nasty fellow. The other was Franz Halder, Head of the German General Staff. Fritz should have known that, but Halder had just recently replaced von Brauchitsch in what was described as a Hitler-inspired plot. Rumors had Halder as more amenable to Hitler's demands.

The lead Junker began to taxi off the tarmac. Soon the second and third planes were moving. Fritz looked up at the blue sky over Berlin. Large cumulus clouds hung over the airport. It would be a good day for flying, considering the typical spring weather found in Central Europe. He hoped it would last the entire flight to outside Trier. Army Group A had established its headquarters in the old Roman city on the Moselle River. Trier was close to the Ardennes, the principle line of attack of the Army. It would be about a two hour flight for the three planes.

As the planes lifted off the runway, Fritz looked as four Messerschmitt Bf 109 fighters swept down and formed a fighter escort for the three lumbering transport planes. He watched as the Messerschmitts paced back and forth above the Ju 52s. The Junkers were significantly slower than the Bf

109 and the fighter pilots worked to keep their faster planes on station.

As Fritz watched the fighters fly a pattern over the Junkers, he wondered if one of the pilots was his youngest brother. Duke von Mueller was now a Flight Lieutenant in the Luftwaffe and had been assigned to Bf 109s. The last he had heard he was flying cover for von Bock's Army over Holland. But, you never knew. He might be up there right now. *If he was, Duke would be surprised that his older brother was among the big shots in the planes below,* Fritz thought.

The three radial engines of the Ju 52 droned on as they headed west over Germany. Fritz watched the countryside slide by below. He battled to stay alert as the sun on the plane and the vibration from the engines all conspired to put one to sleep. Looking around the cabin, Fritz noticed quite a few dozing off.

Fritz concentrated on watching the escorting fighters fly their protective pattern. He attempted to time the pattern in his head. Anything to keep his mind sharp so he'd be ready when they landed. He figured out the pattern the faster fighters were flying and started predicting when they would reappear on his side of the airplane.

As this mental exercise continued, Fritz noticed in the distance a large river flowing north and south. This could only be the Rhine River and Fritz started looking for Koblenz where the Moselle River entered the larger Rhine. Trier would be just a short distance up the Moselle.

As Fritz focused on finding Koblenz, the corner of his eye caught movement. His mind computed that this wasn't the Bf 109 fighters as they were still on their pattern to the south. This movement was to the north and higher than the German fighters had been. Fritz turned and focused on the area where he thought he had seen something. The scattered cumulus clouds that had started this trip were now interspersed with stratus clouds. Obviously a front was moving in from the northwest and the cloud cover had increased since Berlin.

Continuing to watch the area where he had seen movement, the clouds parted to let blue sky sneak through. Just on time, the four Messerschimtts came over the Junkers and banked to the west to continue their pattern. That's when Fritz saw black dots high and to the north of their position. He strained to make out the type of plane they were. The fighter pilots hadn't seen them and were turning away to the south to continue their patrol pattern. That maneuver put the unknown dots behind the fighter pilots.

Fritz watched intently as the objects grew bigger. He perceived them change direction. They were suddenly coming down straight at him. As they dove closer Fritz could begin to make out some detail. These were not German planes. These planes had a fork tail with twin motors. *No German plane had a configuration like that*, he thought. *There is only one plane that looked like this.*

Recalling Jane's reference book on world airplanes, he remembered having seen this plane before. It was an American Lockheed P-38 Lightning that was headed straight down on them.

Fritz jumped out of his seat and rushed to the cockpit to warn the pilot. As he stuck his head in, he heard the pilot confirm the sighting. He dropped down and looked out the side window,, bumping a general as he did.

"What's going on, Colonel? Go back to your seat now," the general barked.

"I'm sorry Sir, but we have enemy aircraft off our starboard side and I was trying to warn the pilot."

351

"What? That can't be. The Allies have no planes that can reach this far into Germany," the general said. As he spoke, he also turned and looked out the window.

Fritz ignored the general and concentrated on the looming fighters. He could make out six of them now. As he watched, the four Messerschmitts came streaking over the transport planes and began climbing to meet the challenge. The threat had finally been reported to all the planes.

Just as Fritz focused on the coming air battle, his Ju 52 banked hard left and dropped it's nose toward the ground. Fritz fought the pull of the turn and moved back to the cockpit door. He could see that the other two Junkers were also turning and diving, trying to put distance between the Junkers and the P-38 fighters. It would be futile if the Messerschmitts failed to stop the Lockheed fighters. *The transports are slow cumbersome hulks compared to these 'fork-tailed devils' falling from the sky*, Fritz thought

Obviously, the Americans had sold these P-38's to Britain. *But how did they have such range to be this far into Germany?* Fritz thought. He had remembered talking to his younger brother about airplane development. The 1930s had seen the greatest leap in aircraft performance. Planes were often obsolete before they even went into production. The American's had obviously done something special to give these P-38s such range.

But Fritz and his companions didn't have time to dwell on aircraft performance. They were about to be introduced to aircraft armament. The P-38 Lightning was the latest design, Lockheed had read the battle reports on fighter performance and had made sure their airplane could out-shoot anything it went up against. While the large two-engined American fighter could be outmaneuvered by the smaller single engine Bf 109, this wasn't going to be a dogfight.

The P-38s were in a dive from above. The Messerschmitts struggled to climb to meet the dropping Lightnings. Every pilot knew altitude was life in an air battle. The higher plane always had the advantage and the pilots in the P-38s homed in for the kill. Four Lightnings were pairing off with the four Bf 109s. That left two P-38s to take on the escaping transports. The Germans were outnumbered and outgunned.

While the Messerschmitt carried six .30 caliber machine guns capable of firing 2000 rounds per minute, the Lightning carried .50 caliber machine guns and 20 mm cannons for a combined rate of 4000 rounds per minute. A Lightning opening fire created a stream of bullets that acted like a buzz saw on a target. In addition, conventional planes had their guns outboard in each wing. The Lightning concentrated all its guns in the nose. Such concentrated fire devastated any other plane.

The final advantage of the Lightning soon became very evident. As Fritz strained to watch the developing fight from his diving transport, he saw the four P-38 open up on the four Bf 109. He hoped that his brother wasn't one of them as the Messerschmitts seemed to stop in midair from the weight of the volley. With the 20 mm cannon on board, a Lightning could open fire from 1000 yards, out-distancing the .30 caliber round that needed to close to 250 yards to be effective.

The German pilots knew what was at stake and pressed on to close the range in spite of the withering fire they were receiving. Only poor shooting by the British saved the German pilots from certain instant death. Fritz watched and guessed that the British had just received these planes and had little experience in them. One bit of luck for the Germans.

But that was the only luck the Germans would receive this day. Smoke showed from most of the engaged planes as they crippled each other in their fury. One Bf 109 pilot jumped from his stricken plane just before it exploded. Two other pilots, realizing the gravity of the situation, rammed their stricken planes into two Lightnings. The fourth Bf 109 swung around for another go in spite of oily smoke streaming from the engine nacelle.

That left two crippled Lightnings with smoke pouring from at least one engine still diving on the transports. The two Lightnings that had not joined battle were circling around to attack the transports from the west. Fritz looked down toward Koblenz and saw German fighters climbing up to join the battle. Hopefully they would arrive in time to make a difference.

The two unscathed P-38s now were within range of the first two transports. They opened up with no mercy. They seemed to sense the importance of these three lumbering planes and were determined to deal death this day.

Fritz continued to brace himself in the cockpit door to watch the two other transport planes try to reach any safety on the ground. The Lightnings would have none of it and the first Junker was slammed by the first burst. The .50 caliber bullets punched holes in the thin Ju 52 fuselage, but the 20 mm cannon tore chunks out of the plane. No plane could withstand such punishment. The Junker carrying the Fuhrer and his party broke apart about 2,000' above the ground. The fuel exploded and a giant fireball engulfed the plane. Pieces of plane flew through the air.

The second transport carrying the German General Staff was similarly eviscerated quickly by the second unscathed Lightning. Another explosion and fireball with more debris falling out of the sky. From the time Fritz had seen the dots in the sky until the entire High Command of Germany was vaporized had been less than two minutes.

Fritz's plane was the lone survivor. He knew he wouldn't be a survivor long. The pilot continued his dive for the ground even though he knew it was useless. Fritz yelled that fighters were climbing up from Koblenz and the pilot yanked hard on the controls to dive the Junker to the north. If help was on the way, the pilot knew he wanted to head towards it. The hard right bank saved their lives as the wounded P-38 fired where the Ju 52 would have been. He paid for it with his life as the remaining Bf 109 had turned and caught up to the Lightning. The Lightning blew up.

The smoking Bf 109 kept diving past Fritz's Junker to attack the two remaining, undamaged P-38s. The two Lightnings were struggling to pull up and turn back toward the remaining transport. Now the British pilots were at a disadvantage. The big two-engine Lightning was slow to turn and the nimble Messerschmitt moved in for revenge. In spite of damage from the initial attack, the pilot handily kept the plane in control. The German dove on one of the turning Lightnings. He could turn faster than the big plane and came in on top and to the side for a clean shot. The Lightning's left engine immediately caught fire and the pilot banked away. The canopy flew off and the pilot bailed out of his doomed plane.

But his sacrifice allowed the remaining Lightning to complete his turn and line up on the Junker. Fritz looked in horror as he saw the smoke of the guns. Instantly the interior of the Ju 52 became a screaming hell. Bullets ripped through the cabin, tearing bodies apart. The 20 mm cannon shells were the worst. While .50 caliber bullets made big holes in people, 20 mm shells vaporized humans. As the Lightning guided his aim down the length of the Junker, bodies exploded into red mist. Fritz ducked as body parts flew through the cabin.

The burst flew by Fritz and a sharp pain in his leg knocked him flat against the cabin wall. He was right next to the co-pilot as he was hit by a 20 mm round. The copilot instantly ceased to exist, replaced by vaporized blood. Fritz was coated in sticky blood while pieces of human body hit him.

The pilot jerked the plane and screamed as a .50 caliber round tore his lower leg off. The plane started into a death dive and the pilot fought unconsciousness to keep his plane under control. Fritz realized that in spite of the bleeding from his own leg, the pilot needed immediate attention if they were going to make it to the ground.

Grabbing his belt, Fritz leaned down and put the belt around the pilot's leg. He pulled tight on the belt to form a tourniquet. The pilot's bleeding slowed. How he intended to land with only one foot didn't cross Fritz's mind. The Lightning was still out there and another pass would send his Ju 52 up in a ball of fire like the other two Junkers. Luckily for Fritz, the British pilot had aimed for the cabin and thus saved the engines and fuel from certain destruction.

Fritz tried to look for the one remaining P-38 but couldn't find it. Fritz had a hard time tracking anything since his plane barely maintained control. The pilot couldn't work both foot controls and was trying to work one at a time. He finally grabbed Fritz and told him to get beside him and put one foot on the right peddle. Together, they worked out a system that allowed the transport to settle down and head for an open field to land.

Quietly praying as the Ju 52 dropped down for a landing, Fritz braced himself. *With a fixed undercarriage, at least we don't have to worry about lowering the wheels*, he thought. But there were plenty of other things to dwell upon. The pilot slowed the transport as much as he could while yelling at Fritz to push in or let out his peddle. Fritz felt the first bump as they touched the field and then another. The Junker settled down onto the ground as if it was a routine grass field landing. The Ju 52 seemed to have a survival instinct all its own as it rolled to a stop.

Fritz thanked God for getting him down safely and stood up. Now that he could focus on the gore in the plane, he vomited all over himself and what was left of the co-pilot. Groans were coming from the back of the plane but Fritz wanted to help the pilot out of the plane first. He had fought hard to get them down and he deserved to be taken off right away.

Just as Fritz unbuckled the pilot, he was accosted by a badly injured general.

"You. I need help now." The general bled badly from a stomach wound, his intestines hanging out. Fritz reached down and pushed the intestines back into his abdomen. Then he took off his military coat and shoved it into the wound. Pulling off the general's belt, he placed it over the coat and cinched it up tight.

"I'm sorry, General, but that's all I can do for now. Let me check the others and see if the plane has a first aid kit," Fritz knew the general needed more than any first aid kit could offer. But he wanted to move on to the others.

"Don't leave me here," the general pleaded.

"Please, General, I'm checking the others and I'll be right back. I won't leave you."

As Fritz moved into the cabin, his stomach tried to vomit again. Of the six men who had been riding back here with him, he could only identify three bodies. There was the general he just treated, an obviously dead colonel that had been cut in half by a shell and the general that had fought with his father. He had been on the same side of the plane as Fritz and had not been subjected to the murderous fire the others had.

He bent down to check the general and saw that his right arm had been shot off. He also bled slowly from the leg. Fritz pulled up the general's pant leg and saw that he had been grazed by a bullet. He had been lucky, too. Pulling off the general's belt, Fritz placed a tourniquet on the general's upper arm. There was no one else to help. The other three officers were just assorted body parts and blood.

Hearing voices outside the plane, Fritz could see movement when he looked out the holes in the fuselage. Two civilians were running to the plane. The door opened and a man stuck his face into the nightmare.

"Ach du lieber! Mein Gott!. There are still people alive in here. Help me get up into the cabin." The first farmer struggled to climb up into the Junker. The second farmer pushed his friend from behind.

"Hans, there is gasoline leaking. I can smell it now. We need to get away before it catches fire," the second farmer said. He started to move away from the plane.

"Karl, there are people alive in here. They need our help. Don't leave."

"Hurry then. We don't have much time," the nervous farmer said as he waited outside the door.

"Come, let's get you out of here," the farmer spoke to Fritz. Fritz nodded and pointed to the general missing the arm. He was closest to the door and Fritz motioned to the farmer to help. Fritz then headed through the bloody cabin to get the pilot out.

"Come on, Captain. There is gas leaking and I need to get you to safety," Fritz said. The pilot had drifted into semi-conscious and only mumbled back to Fritz. "This may hurt but we can't wait here."

Fritz carefully lifted the upper body of the pilot but he was too heavy to carry. He turned to see if the farmer was behind him. The general, with a little help, had managed to move to the door where the nervous farmer waited, who quickly led the general away from the plane.

The first farmer grabbed the pilot's one remaining leg trying not to touch the bloody stump where his foot had been. The pilot groaned in pain and the farmer stopped.

"Come on. We have to get him off the plane." Fritz moved backwards with the farmer in tow. They stepped over the general with the stomach wound.

"You're not leaving me are you? My God, get me out of this death trap before it blows up," the general yelled at Fritz.

"We'll be right back. We won't leave you."

The three men struggled to get out of the plane and move away toward the two others. The first farmer waved at the nervous farmer to come help but he was content to stay put and console his wounded general.

"Look, I told you it was going to blow," the nervous farmer yelled.

Fritz turned to see a small flame catch on the wing. Leaking gas mixed with hot metal had suddenly ignited into flame. Small right now, it was rapidly spreading.

"Come on. We need to get the other general," Fritz said. No one else moved. Fritz didn't wait for help. He ran back to the plane and climbed up into the cabin. The left wing fuel tank burst in a ball of flame. It knocked the plane hard enough that Fritz slipped on the blood in the cabin and fell against the fuselage. Flames were licking through the multiple holes in the plane as Fritz scrambled to his feet and headed into the cabin.

"Don't let me burn. Get me out of here!" the general implored.

Fritz bent down and with all his strength, rolled the general onto his shoulder and grabbed his legs. The general screamed in agony as his wound pushed down on Fritz's shoulder. Fritz turned and fought his way to the door, trying not to fall on the gore as he stepped. The flames were coming into the cabin now. Hopefully the right fuel tank would hold long enough to get away.

As he lowered the general down so he could climb out of the cabin, the first farmer grabbed the general. Fritz looked up into the man's eyes and tried to show as much gratitude as he could for the help he received.

"Come on. I think we better get out of here," the farmer said.

Together, they carried the general to the others and laid him down on the grass. Just as Fritz collapsed on the ground the plane's right wing caught fire. The fireball engulfed the entire plane, as both fires converged into one.

"You're bleeding," the nervous farmer spoke to Fritz. Fritz looked down at his leg and finally recognized that he had been injured. With all the blood that had been splattered on him, he was surprised the farmer could tell the difference. Fritz pulled up his pant leg and saw the raw wound on the side of his calf. The .50 caliber bullet had grazed his leg. It stung more than anything. Compared to the rest of the people involved in this fight today, Fritz thanked God that he was alive.

You may see all of W.B. Martin's books at:

wbmartinauthor.com

Acknowledgements

First I would thank Timothy Johns, my tireless editor. Though he works hard that my writing is presentable, place no blame on him for the final product. That all rests with me.

My proofreaders offer valuable feedback at different phases as my draft is put together. Dick Martin, Marsha Wiles, Larry Stoddard, Barbara Foster, and John Briggs have all kept me from straying too far off on tangents.

John Ewing was an early supporter who didn't get to see the final product. His wife Bertha Ewing was invaluable as a listener as I read out loud to her on one of my many edit jobs.

Finding Morwenna Rakestraw to do the cover layout was a relief and I appreciate her sticking with me.

Mitch Press of World Book has offered his wisdom from his family's years in the book business. While not all encouraging, his guidance as publishing transforms in the digital age has been invaluable.

Finally, I need to thank my wife Agnes for her support of my writing. She is everything in what I do.

Dear Reader,

Thank you for your selection of reading material. I hope this book measured up to your expectations. The most critical part for a new author is getting the word out to other readers.

I would appreciate your help in spreading the word. There are three important things you can do. You need to understand the importance of the first one to my becoming a successful writer. Amazon.com is huge in the new book publishing era. So please:

1.   Go to Amazon.com and leave a review
2.   Tell a friend about this book
3.   Tell your social network about this book.

The more positive reviews that are made in various places will help readers find me.

Again, thanks for your support.

W.B. Martin

And check out my website at wbmartinauthor.com